I Want You Back

JOANNE TRACEY

First published in Australia in 2020

by Joanne Tracey

https://joannetracey.com

Copyright © Joanne Tracey 2020

Print ISBN 978-0-6484533-4-5

Kindle ISBN 978-0-9943134-9-2

Epub ISBN 978-0-9943134-8-5

Cover design by Lana Pecherczyk of Book Coverology

A catalogue record for this book is available from the National Library of Australia

For Grant and Sarah...

Always

CHAPTER ONE

There was no denying that Andy Campbell was the cutest guy in the office. Everyone knew it – Andy especially. I didn't think there was a woman in the company who hadn't fancied herself crushing on him at least once during her employment – and I wasn't an exception. I'd decided some weeks ago that Andy Campbell was going to be the man who helped me get over my ex-boyfriend, Jamie. Until now, however, it had been all wide eyes and soulful looks from me, and nothing but friendly banter from Andy. It wasn't so much that he didn't know I existed; rather that until he needed me for something or other, there was always someone else on his radar. Given I was the company's human resources manager, and his team had the highest turnover in the call centre, he needed me more often than he probably would have liked.

'Hey, Jones,' he said, grinning the sort of grin that only a man who knows he can get away with slacking off on a Friday afternoon just because he's Andy Campbell can grin. 'I'm not interrupting you, am I?' His tone carried all the confidence of knowing I'd pause for him even if I were in the middle of something extremely important.

'No, not at all,' I said.

'Just thought I'd let you know that the new operator hasn't worked out. I need you to performance-manage her out.'

'Which one?'

'Krystal. She really impressed in the interviews and in training, but I just don't think she's the right fit.' He shrugged to indicate he'd done all that any reasonable manager could be expected to do.

If I remembered correctly I'd cautioned him against choosing Krystal. She was more the build a relationship and find a solution to the problem sort of girl, rather than the answer the call, shut them up and move them on type of person that Andy's team was all about. There had been candidates far better qualified for that approach – but less attractive – that Andy could have chosen.

'I'll need more than that to go on,' I told him. 'Get me the data on where she's dropping behind and we can talk to her. I assume it's a call-handling time issue?'

'Come on, Jones, can't you just take my word for it?'

'You know I can't, Andy. It's a little something to do with legislation and unfair workplaces and me having nothing to wear to industrial court if we end up there.'

'Not even this once?' He grinned as I shook my head in warning. 'Okay, I'll deal with that next week.' He turned to go, then looked at me again. 'Before I forget – do you want to join me for a drink after work?'

He asked so casually that at first I didn't think I'd heard him correctly. 'Sorry?'

'A drink. After work. With me. What do you say?'

A little tingle of excitement rushed through me. Andy Campbell, the cutest guy in the office, was asking me, Calliope Jones, out for a drink. In my head there were winged cupids flying around and playing trumpets, but I kept my face – and my tone – expressionless. 'Tonight?'

His smile told me he knew I was faking my disinterest. 'I'll come by at four thirty – Roger's usually buggered off by then.'

Roger was my boss, the human resources director, and well known for his vanishing act on a Friday afternoon.

'We'll go to the Mitre,' Andy said.

Some of my excitement turned to disappointment. As one of the busiest pubs at the financial end of Collins Street, the Mitre wasn't exactly where I'd suggest for a drinks date. A laneway bar would have been more . . . intimate. Not that it mattered. Andy Campbell had asked me out!

'Sounds good,' I said.

'Great. I'll be by for you at four thirty. Don't be late.' And then he was gone.

A date with Andy Campbell meant just one thing: an emergency conference with the girls.

Alice Delaney and Tiffany Samuels had been my best friends since our first day at primary school in Brisbane. We were inseparable growing up, had drifted away to different cities for university and work, and had somehow all ended up here in Melbourne. I was the first to arrive – dropping out of university to follow a man. The man lasted a month, but I stayed. Tiff transferred here a few years ago with her job; and Alice – and her dog, Stella – turned up on Tiff's doorstep suddenly last September when a redundancy and a broken engagement drove her out of Sydney. We'd all settled in different parts of town and were also in completely different industries – Tiff was flying high in banking, I'd somehow ended up in HR, and Alice had set herself up in business as an astrologer – yet we'd never lost that connection we had when we were young.

I tapped out a text: *OMG Andy Campbell asked me out for a drink tonight!!!*

Alice was the first to respond. *OMG!!! Andy Campbell!!!*

Tiff's reply came through before I could respond to Alice. *This needs a con call – I'll dial you both in.*

Once all three of us were on the line, Alice didn't bother with the usual pleasantries. 'Wow, Cal, Andy Campbell! You've had your eye on him for weeks now with no result. What's changed?'

'I have no idea. It just happened.'

'Has anyone remembered that we're supposed to be meeting up tonight?' Tiff sounded disgruntled. 'Are you throwing us over for him?'

I'd forgotten our plans in the excitement. 'I'm so sorry, Tiff – that completely slipped my mind.'

'It's okay, Cal,' Alice said. 'This is your first date since Jamie. I think you're entitled to bail on us just this once. Isn't she, Tiff?'

I could hear the smile in her voice, but mine slipped at her reference to Jamie.

'When you put it like that, I guess so,' said Tiff.

'Where are you going?' Alice asked me.

'The Mitre.'

'Really? On a Friday night?' Tiff wasn't impressed. 'That's not very romantic. The place will be full of suits – you won't hear yourself think, let alone talk. Although,' she mused, 'he's supposed to be your rebound man, so talking isn't a priority. The Mitre could be perfect.'

'Yes, well –'

'What are you wearing?' Alice asked.

'I don't have time to go home to change, so just what I wore to work.'

'Which is?'

'My brown tweed skirt, those brown boots that do up really easily, a pink jumper, my striped scarf and a denim jacket. I feel quite short and frumpy, but don't have much choice.'

'Not at this stage of the afternoon,' Tiff agreed. 'At least pink always looks good on you – it brings a bit of colour to your cheeks. Why didn't you go with jeans?'

'Because when I tried them on this morning, I could only do them up if I sacrificed my internal organs.'

Alice giggled. 'Have you still got the seam marks from the last time you wore them?'

'I sure do. I think they must have shrunk while I had them on. Anyway, I can't change clothes, so advice, please.'

'Okay, make sure you touch up your make-up and fluff your hair,' Tiff said. 'And don't act too desperate – try and play it at least a little bit cool. Alice?'

'Remember the three-date rule.'

Alice had vowed that after her last big mistake – the one that had her running to Melbourne – she would stick to a strict set of rules. The problem was, most of her rules were flexible and evolving. The exception was her three-date rule: you couldn't sleep with a man until after the second date, and preferably not until the third. Central to this rule was the inclusion of one daylight date – just in case you'd had wine goggles on when you met him. Alice argued that men were always on their best behaviour on the first date, allowed more of their true self come through on the second, and were feeling confident of success on the third, which was when the cracks in their act began to show.

'Actually,' she added, 'given that you work with Andy Campbell and have seen him in daylight, I think you could be exempt from the three-date rule. Plus, you've been out together for work functions, which is almost like a date.' I could hear the wheels of her brain turning, and pictured her nose screwing up as she mulled over the complexities. 'In fact, forget the three-date rule on this occasion – feel free to sleep with him if you want to. It'll be good to get the first one since Jamie over and done with.'

'I agree,' said Tiff. 'Jamie's been gone for over three months now – more than enough time to get over him.'

Rather than argue, I thanked them for their wisdom and, after promising to text later with progress, hung up. Yes, Jamie had been gone for over three months, and yes, that should have been enough time for me to have gotten over him, but I hadn't. I no longer consumed my weight in wine and ice cream every time I allowed myself to feel the empty space inside me that he'd left, but that didn't mean it wasn't still there. My hope was that Andy Campbell would help with that.

A couple of hours later, I contemplated myself in the bathroom mirror. Long blonde hair that hadn't seen a hairdresser's touch in far too long hung in shaggy layers around a face that needed to get out in the sun. My mascara had smudged during the day, making the shadows under my blue eyes darker. I rubbed at it with my pinky finger, but just succeeded in making the skin red. I rummaged in my bag for my compact powder and some lipgloss.

At the basin beside me, one of the newer call centre consultants was getting her face ready for Friday night. She pencilled a thick black line around her already heavily kohled eyes and smudged the edges, and followed that with a layer of red lipstick and another of shiny lacquer. She stuck her index finger in her mouth and pulled it out so it made a popping sound.

'To get the lipstick off my teeth,' she said. 'You know how it is.'

I nodded vaguely, but my gaze was caught by her outfit – midriff-baring black T-shirt with spaghetti straps, a silver-sequinned miniskirt, black fishnet tights, and come-fuck-me black stilettos with studs. In what language was any of that appropriate wear for casual Friday? I opened my mouth to say something, but closed it when another operator sauntered in wearing tracksuit pants and purple fluffy boots. Someone really needed to do something about the acceptable attire policy in this place – oh wait, that would be me.

My title might have been human resources manager, but I didn't get to do a lot of human resourcing. My job was more about the tasks that Roger didn't want to do. Things like arranging interviews, phone screenings, telling people they hadn't got the job he'd all but promised them in the interview, and manning what I called the departure lounge – redundancies, resignations and dismissals. Dealing with acceptable attire probably fitted on that list too. I sighed heavily and left them to it.

Andy was waiting for me at the lifts. 'Thought you must have decided to stand me up,' he said, in a voice that implied no girl in her right mind would ever consider standing him up.

I beamed back at him. 'Not a chance.'

'Great. Let's go then.' He casually threw an arm around my shoulders and ushered me into the lift.

Ten minutes later, I was puffing my way up the Collins Street hill behind him. Somewhere between leaving work and now, the elastic in my tights had given way. I tried to hold them up through the fabric of my skirt, but could feel the other side slipping dangerously below the curve of my hip.

'Come on, short-arse, keep up,' he urged.

'Your legs are so much longer than mine,' I complained.

He stopped and waited for me to catch up. I hoped he'd put his arm around me again, but he didn't.

'Okay, let's walk at your pace, but don't blame me if there aren't any tables left – you know how busy the Mitre gets on a Friday night.' He steered me down a laneway already full of drinkers nursing glasses of something designed to cure the stresses of the week, and headed straight for the bar. 'What can I get you?'

'Oh, whatever you're having is fine,' I replied. 'I'll just duck into the bathroom.'

'Sure, see you outside.' He was already casting his eyes around the crowd.

By the time I'd dealt with the wayward tights, Andy was at the centre of a group from work – a group that included a skinny blonde cow called Felicity ('call me Flick – everyone does') who'd had her eye on him since she'd started last month. I smiled and took the drink he offered me, but his attention was already back on Flick. I might as well have been invisible.

I pushed my disappointment down where it belonged, plastered a smile on my face and wandered into the group. So much for a date; it seemed that all the team leaders, and a good number of operators, were here, leaving me wondering who was actually monitoring the calls until the lines closed at six. Maybe that's why they'd invited me, so I wouldn't be able to ask any awkward questions later. No, that was unfair.

'Callie, over here,' called Kerry, one of the staff trainers. I smiled and pushed my way through the crowd to her. 'I'm so glad you could make it,' she said. 'Andy said he'd get you here – it's been months since you came out with us.'

Although I used to enjoy these Friday evening sessions, in the weeks and then months after Jamie left I'd welcomed any excuse not to join in. The last thing I'd wanted was to have to explain to my colleagues what had gone wrong with my relationship.

'I normally have problems getting away on a Friday afternoon,' I explained. Roger had a habit of throwing things over the fence on his way out.

'Yes, I noticed that. But you're here now.' Her gaze shifted to where Andy had somehow isolated Felicity from the rest of the group. 'Look at him in action,' she said wistfully. 'You're so lucky you've never fallen under his spell.'

'Not like the rest of us,' said Lucy, another colleague. 'How have you managed to stay so immune?'

'Just lucky, I guess,' I murmured. If only they knew the plans I'd had for Andy Campbell.

'As for the woman he turns his charm on – well, she doesn't stand a chance,' said Lucy.

'Of keeping his attention or her job,' agreed Kerry. 'Why do you think the turnover in his team is so high?'

I turned to watch Andy with Felicity. The way he was looking at her, the way he'd turned his body to lean in as if concentrating on everything she said – it was as if she was the only woman in the world at that moment. I took another sip of my drink. It reminded me of how Jamie used to be with me.

When I left an hour or so later, I loitered briefly in the lane just in case Andy noticed and came running after me. He didn't, so I trudged back to Collins Street to wait for a tram, hoping that Hen, my horrible flatmate, wouldn't be at home. I didn't think I could deal with her, or her equally horrible friends with their horrible manners and their horrible taste in music.

After their antics last Friday night, old Mrs Gianello from downstairs had cornered me at the mailbox on Saturday. 'I don't mean to complain, dear, but that girl with the big black boots was playing music very loudly last night. They were all stomping so heavily I was worried about the floor caving in around my ears.'

The entire house had at one time been the Gianello family home. At some point over the years they'd converted it into two – an upstairs flat where Hen and I lived, and a downstairs flat where Mrs G and her cats lived. We shared a common front door into the entry hall, from where Mrs G could access her unit, and stairs led up to ours.

'I'm sorry, Mrs G,' I'd said. 'I'll have a word with her.' Again.

I'd mentioned it to Hen when she came home briefly that afternoon, and she'd been predictably aggressive.

'So now some old lady's telling me what music I can and can't play in my own house?'

'It's not like that. It's just that you do play it very loudly, and way past the time you should. Maybe if you just turn it down a bit and take your boots off to dance? And while I've got your attention, I noticed this week's rent isn't in the account yet?'

'Whatever.' She'd flicked her hair and stomped off.

Perhaps I'd get lucky tonight and Hen and her friends would have already gone out. Although the way the evening had turned out so far, I didn't hold out much hope.

I hadn't got far up Collins Street when I heard a text come through. I stopped and rummaged in my bag for my phone. Alice.

Hey, how's the date going?

I grimaced before replying. *It's not. It was a whole group thing. I've just left.*

Her reply came flying back. *Come and meet us. We're in the basement bar in Little Bourke. We're waiting for a table upstairs and if you hurry I won't have eaten all the bar snacks.*

I hesitated for a few seconds. I could go home and feel sorry for myself with a takeaway Chinese meal and a bottle of wine in my room – doing my best to avoid Hen. Or I could meet the girls and find a way to laugh about this.

There was no contest really.

On my way.

CHAPTER TWO

After squeezing my way into the bar, I peered through the dimness to find my friends. For someone who had flown through the night, Tiff looked as she always did: fabulous – from the top of her sleek up-do to the tips of her perfect pedicure. Alice, with her wild red hair, was her usual boho self. She had a talent for throwing on random pieces of clothing and making them look as though they'd been chosen deliberately. Tonight she was in a patchwork-style skirt topped with a red velvet jacket that should have clashed but somehow seemed the perfect outfit for a Melbourne Friday night. In comparison, I felt even frumpier than I had earlier. My skirt felt tighter, and my pink jumper became something that someone much older than me wouldn't be seen dead in.

Alice spotted me and waved. Tiff seemed to be in the middle of a story about her delayed overnight flight. She paused briefly to kiss me.

'If the time on the ticket is 9.30 pm, that's the time they should be putting that plane into reverse and getting the show on the road. You know what I mean?'

Alice and I grinned and nodded.

'I'd been wearing the same clothes all day – and that's never a good idea in Hong Kong in June.' She wrinkled her nose so we were in no doubt what she was talking about. 'And sitting up all night unable to sleep didn't help matters.'

'I thought you usually rode up front,' I said.

'Yes, normally, but Ainsley – you know, that new boss of mine? I'm convinced she's the one who spread the gossip about Alice and Luke when she was still working there.'

Alice and Tiff had joined the same bank straight out of university – Alice based in Sydney, and Tiff transferring down to Melbourne. Alice had been steadily climbing the corporate ladder when she became involved with one of her colleagues, Luke, and broke off her engagement to be with him. Their story should have had a happy ending, but Luke changed his mind and instead reconciled with – and then very quickly married – his ex-girlfriend. Alice was devastated. To make an already bad situation worse, somehow word had spread to management, with the result that Alice lost her job and Luke was promoted. Alice saw it as a sign and packed up everything to start again down here – with a whole new set of rules designed to stop anything like it ever happening again.

Alice grimaced. 'I still can't believe she's been

parachuted in above you.'

'You and me both,' Tiff said. 'Anyway, she's decided to exert her authority and save some money by insisting that, regardless the length of the flight, we have to fly economy. I told her that if she expects us to fly overnight and land at sparrow's fart ready to do business she's got another think coming. So she kindly offered to let me work from home today. Bitch. It's why I had to fly out on Saturday afternoon last week, because even with the extra night's accommodation it's marginally cheaper.'

Alice sighed. 'Still, plenty of people would have been thrilled to have an all-expenses-paid weekend in Hong Kong. That's why I booked you on that tour – so you could see more of the city than the bars my brother takes you to.'

My ears pricked up at the mention of Matt Delaney. Alice's brother had been posted in Hong Kong for the last five or six years. Like Tiff, he was in banking – one of the slicker investment-style ones. Other than Alice complaining that he never came home to see the family, most of whom were now living on the Sunshine Coast of Queensland, I hadn't heard much about Matt in years. I certainly hadn't seen him since the summer I was eighteen. It might have been fourteen years ago, but if I closed my eyes I could still conjure up an image of him – tall and tanned, his boardshorts riding low on his narrow hips, the surfboard that was his constant companion that summer upright in the sand beside him as he evaluated the waves. In my mind his eyes reflected the light that sparkled on the blue water, the sun bouncing off the natural highlights in his tawny hair, his smile wide and confident.

I blinked twice and brought my focus back to the present where Alice was asking Tiff about the tour. 'How was it? You didn't say.'

Tiff shrugged. 'It was okay. A bridge, a village, a beach, a buddha and a cable car. Not much more to say. Anyway, let's not talk about that now – I want to find out what happened tonight with Cal.'

'Oh god,' I groaned. 'Pour me a drink and I'll tell you the whole sorry story.'

Tiff waited until I'd taken a mouthful before she pressed me. 'Well? What happened?'

'It ended up being a big group from the office. I have no idea why I thought he meant it to be just him and me. The giveaway should have been when he said we were going to the Mitre. And then the elastic on my tights gave way.' I giggled. 'It wasn't funny at the time, but you should have seen me in the toilet cubicle trying to work out whether I should take them off, which would have involved taking off everything else first and then wriggling back into it all in a confined space – or whether I should put my undies on over the top of them, which would have meant much the same.'

'Not a picture I needed,' said Tiff, grinning. 'What

did you do?'

'Pulled them up as high as I could and tucked them into the top of my knickers. They're still like that. Want to see?'

Alice choked on her wine. 'Now that would have been interesting to explain away if the evening had ended the way you wanted it to.'

'Wouldn't it just? I've often wondered how it works with those chicken fillets women wear in their bras – how would you get them out of your bra without him noticing?' I pondered the problem. 'Think about it – his hand would have to be in or around that area for you to get the hint he's interested in the whole getting naked thing, so what would you do? Take the fillets out earlier and hope he doesn't notice a sudden deflation and change his mind before the action gets started? Or finely tune the removal somewhere between the first hand-up-top movement and the first squeeze of breast?'

Alice giggled. 'What came first – the fillet or the hand?'

Tiff was straight-faced. 'That actually happened to me once. Don't look at me like that – it was before I discovered the power of a good uplifting bra. I remember his hand went in and came out with the fillet.'

'Oh. My. God.' I brought my hand to my mouth to hold the laughter in. 'What did he do?'

'He threw it on the floor and it lay there quivering like something vaguely biological. It looked like one of those blobby fish without eyes from the bottom of the ocean.'

'What did you do?' Alice was fascinated.

'What could I do? I reached in and pulled out the other one and got on with it.' She shrugged. 'Boob's what he wanted, so boob was what he got. After a minute or so he wasn't thinking about anything else – I made sure of that.'

I laughed, but wished I had Tiff's confidence. Her tights wouldn't have been brave enough to lose their elastic.

The food arrived – an assortment of Asian-style bar snacks. Alice's sigh of relief was audible.

Tiff grinned and shook her head. 'You can't possibly be hungry.'

'And yet I am.' Alice dipped a spring roll into sauce, and held her hand under it to avoid drips as she guided it to her mouth.

'You do know there's a fine line between hungry and horny. Why else do people put on weight when they're not having sex?' Tiff didn't wait for us to answer. 'Because we mistake being horny with being hungry – that's why.'

Alice screwed her nose up. 'Can't it just mean that I'm hungry?'

'Perhaps, but you're hungry an awful lot.' Alice grinned wickedly and Tiff frowned at her. 'How long has it been?'

Alice deliberately misunderstood her. 'Since I last ate?'

'Since you got laid.'

'I hate that expression,' I protested. 'It sounds so male – like it's an itch you've got to scratch.'

Tiff raised her eyebrows. 'It is an itch, and you can't rely on toys forever to scratch it.'

I covered my ears. 'I don't want to hear this. No wonder we don't have relationships if we can make do with *toys*.'

'Trust me, sweetie, only when the real thing isn't available. So, Ally, how long?'

'Nearly a year, I suppose. How good do those satay sticks look?' She signalled to a waiter, pointing to the dish on the table next to us.

'Seriously?' Tiff seemed surprised. 'Not since you came running down here with your tail between your legs after the Luke thing?'

'Well, she was in love with him, and he did break her heart,' I said. 'It's not every day you leave your fiancé for your lover only to find out that your lover's proposed to someone else and didn't tell you about it.'

Tiff turned to me. 'And you?'

'Not since Jamie.' I felt the familiar rush of emotion to the back of my throat and sipped my wine to swallow it back down.

'How long has it been for you?' Alice asked, seeming anxious to take the focus away from me. 'Or are you still having random sex with my brother every time you're in Hong Kong?'

I lifted my head. Tiff and Matt Delaney? Since when? And surely Alice had a rule about sleeping with a best friend's brother?

'You know about that?' Tiff said.

'Of course I do. I know what my brother's like, and I know what you're like, and I know that when you're in town you often catch up for drinks. You don't need to be Einstein to figure out what comes next.'

'Fair enough.' Tiff seemed unconcerned. 'But no, not this time – Matt was in Singapore. This was some guy I met on that tour you booked me on. We sat together, and then I fell asleep on his shoulder. He missed his drop-off because he didn't want to wake me, so when he asked me for a drink I couldn't very well say no. Anyway,' she shrugged, 'one thing led to another. You know how it is.'

Alice said that she didn't know how it was.

I pretended to. 'Oh, that's romantic. Are you going to see him again?'

Tiff smiled at me. 'I shouldn't think so. It was a one-night stand that we doubled up – okay, tripled up – on, but he's not my type. A travel writer for god's sake, but a lovely distraction.'

'What's his name?' Alice was addicted to the travel pages. She was always dreaming about where she'd go if she decided to be irresponsible again.

'Jake Stewart.'

'I know his stuff. He writes for the weekend lift-outs. I follow him on Instagram too. Hang on, I saw some shots he posted last week from Hong Kong. Maybe from when you met him?' Alice flicked through her phone, then passed it over to us. 'Here.'

The photo was of a casually stubbled man posed in front of a bridge.

'Yeah, that's him,' Tiff said. 'I took this photo – and he hasn't even given me credit.' She studied it more closely. 'I've perfectly exposed that bridge. After all these years, I haven't lost my touch.'

Tiff had been quite the amateur photographer back in high school but, as far as I knew, hadn't picked up a camera in years.

'He's cute,' Alice said.

'Absolutely,' I agreed. 'In that thrown-together look that writers, surfers and artists do so well.'

I took a closer look. He was grinning in a way that seemed as though he was looking past the lens and into the eyes of the photographer. I glanced at Tiff whose eyes kept darting back to the photo when she thought no one was looking.

'How old is he?' asked Alice.

'Probably our age, maybe a little older. Mid to late thirties? I wasn't really interested in finding out.' Tiff's attention was still on the photo. I didn't think she was studying the composition.

'So not your type,' Alice said.

'And absolutely so her type,' I added.

Tiff handed the phone back. 'I think I know better than you two what my type is – and it isn't Jake Stewart.'

Alice and I grinned and raised our eyebrows at each other, just as the waiter arrived.

'Oh good, here are our satay sticks,' Alice said. 'Talking about sex is hungry work.'

'Save some room for dinner,' Tiff warned. 'If they ever have a table ready for us, that is. Anyway, that tour helped me realise that we're going about this man thing all wrong.'

'Who says we even need a man?' Alice asked. 'I'm fine without one. A little itchy perhaps, and very often hungry, but fine.'

I didn't think I needed a man either – not unless that man was Jamie. After tonight's effort, everything else just seemed too hard.

'We've been thinking too much with our hearts and our –'

'Don't say it,' I interrupted. 'I hate that word.'

'Okay,' Tiff smiled at me, 'we haven't been thinking logically about it. We need to tackle the problem the same way we'd look at any other project. Decide on the outcome, set the scope, and determine our CTQs.'

'CTQs?' I asked.

'Critical to quality requirements,' Alice explained. At my questioning look she shrugged her shoulders.

'What can I say? I haven't been out of corporate for that long. Besides, no matter how hard you try there are some things you can't forget.'

'We're talking about those requirements that are absolute deal-breakers,' Tiff continued. 'Anything else falls into the nice-to-have category.'

'It all sounds too hard and unemotional,' I complained. I couldn't tell them that the only man who met all my criteria was Jamie.

'Perhaps,' said Tiff, 'but I know exactly what I want in a man. I don't believe you two do.'

I opened my mouth to interrupt, but Alice stopped me with a warning glance.

'What about you, Ally?' Tiff said. 'You've allowed yourself to stay frozen since Luke. Don't you think it's time?'

'Maybe,' she conceded. 'It's just that no one interesting has asked me out.'

'What about Mac?' I said. 'You talk about him a lot.'

Alice had met Mac soon after she moved to Melbourne; they'd bonded over their dogs, and had been coffee and walking buddies ever since. Alice insisted – perhaps too often – that they were just friends.

She wiped the last of the satay sauce off the plate with her finger, grinning cheekily when Tiff frowned at her. 'No, he's a friend so that's a no-go area. Besides, Mac is not what I want. He's trouble – and trouble is the last thing I'm looking for. After Luke,

I'm staying away from colleagues, friends and bosses – and especially colleagues who are friends who tell you they're single when they're obviously not. My next man will be someone completely unconnected to me and absolutely not trouble.' She looked wistfully at the empty plate. 'I'm not leaving anything up to chance any more. Haven't you noticed how people like to portray Fate, Destiny and Serendipity as these kindly figures that will guide you through tough times. Don't believe any of it! "Leave it to Fate" basically means, in my humble opinion, do nothing and maybe something might happen, or it might not. But whatever does or doesn't happen will be the decision of those trouble-making siblings Fate and Destiny. And as for Serendipity – all I'm saying is that gal's not as sweet and innocent as she's made out to be. She's just there to give you an excuse when you need it.'

I stifled my giggle into my wine glass, but Alice hadn't finished.

'It's almost like a school yard. Reason, Control and Discipline – the anti-fun cops – hang out in the library, and then there's me on the main quadrangle with the cool kids, Temptation and Impulse. Everyone knows those guys are going to be a bad influence and get you into trouble – and that's exactly what happened.'

'Which one am I?' asked Tiff with a completely straight face. 'Temptation or Impulse?'

'You're definitely Temptation.'

This time I couldn't stop the giggle. 'Which makes me Impulse. I think I rather like being Impulse.'

'You might laugh, girls, but I've learnt my lesson. I would have been perfectly happy with Hayden if that bitch Temptation hadn't whispered in my ear and told me to go for it with Luke. "It's serendipitous," she said. And look how well that turned out.' Alice looked at us with her eyes wide and nodded. 'Exactly. That's why I'm going along with whatever it is that Tiff's come up with. It can't possibly be any worse than leaving me to my own devices.'

'I'm glad you feel that way,' Tiff said, 'because I've decided that from now until the end of winter you girls are going to say yes. We're all going to say yes.'

'Yes to what?' I asked.

'Yes to everything. To every invitation that comes your way. None of this staying at home because you don't know anyone, or because it's cold outside. If you're invited, you say yes. It's that easy. By the end of winter, you'll know what you want. I guarantee it.'

'But what has that got to do with a bus tour in Hong Kong?' Alice was looking puzzled.

'It was something I wouldn't normally do – I only agreed to shut you up. But look at what came out of it – a couple of nights of great sex and the realisation that we all need to push our boundaries a little and see what happens.'

Alice smiled. 'That sounds like something I'd say.'

I was still stuck on the idea of saying yes to every invitation. 'But I can't fit into any of my clothes. Remember I lost all that weight in the break-up diet? Well, I've put it all back on, and because we cleaned my wardrobe out after Jamie left, I've got nothing to wear. Maybe we can start in September – it'll give me a couple of months to lose weight.'

Tiff smiled gently at me. 'We think you're gorgeous, Cal. You're the only one who doesn't.' I dropped my eyes to the table. 'I'm serious – you look beautiful. Doesn't she, Ally?' Alice nodded. 'But if you're really serious about dropping a few kilos, just do it. Otherwise buy a bigger size – you'll still look beautiful and might feel more comfortable.'

It was alright for Tiff – she was tall and never still. She ate when she was hungry, and had even been known to forget to eat when she was busy. Who did that? Also, the weight had further to be distributed with her and a little bit extra wouldn't be noticed until it was a lot extra. Alice always seemed to carry a little more than was fashionable, but was genuinely comfortable with her curves. I was shorter, so the weight sort of clumped – mostly around my bum.

'It's never going to be the perfect time,' Tiff said, 'it can only be the right time. I figure the first challenge this week is general maintenance – tidy up the split ends, buy clothes that fit, and deal with any hair where it shouldn't be. Alice, that means deforestation. Don't think I don't know how long it's been since you shaved your legs, and as for your eyebrows . . .' Alice waggled them and grinned. 'Instead of sitting on our expanding arses waiting for something to happen, or someone to come rescue us, we're going to work out what it is we really want and do something about going after it. No distractions, no excuses.'

Alice and I looked at each other. Tiff waited. She knew that if Alice was in, she had me too.

Alice nodded slowly. 'Sure, why not? What have we got to lose?'

'Cal?'

I squirmed in my seat, before finally declaring, 'I guess I'm in too.'

Tiff topped up the glasses, before raising hers in a toast. 'In that case, Project Yes starts now. Here's to us getting what we want.' We clinked our glasses together. 'And no, Alice, that doesn't start with pork sliders.'

CHAPTER THREE

A text message woke me on Saturday morning. I reached for my phone and saw it was from my younger sister, Clio. Clio and her husband, Owen, lived in Brisbane, not too far from the family home where we grew up and where Mum and Dad still lived. Our younger brother, Angus, was off the coast of Scotland somewhere researching puffins or gulls – I was never sure which. A marine biologist, he'd started looking at whale migration patterns from Hervey Bay and ended up in Shetland tracking birds instead. As you do.

Hey Cal – just checking in to make sure you're ok. It's been weeks since we spoke.

I groaned and rolled onto my stomach and tried to go back to sleep. After last night's disaster I wasn't up to pretending to my sister that everything was rosy. She was so happy with Owen and hated to think I mightn't be experiencing the same level of bliss in my life. It was lovely that she cared, but it was getting harder and harder for me to pretend that everything was fine.

I owed Mum and Dad a call too. My parents were

both busy people so didn't exactly wait around to hear from me, but even so, it had been a few weeks since we last spoke. It wasn't so much that I was avoiding them, but rather that I knew Mum's conversation would be full of Clio and Owen and what they'd been doing. Then her tone would lower and she'd ask gently, 'And how are you doing, Calliope?' I'd make some breezy comment about how things were good and work was keeping me busy, but mothers are never fooled.

'Have you heard anything from Jamie?' she'd inevitably ask. I'd say no and try to change the subject, but she'd still say something like, 'Oh well, I'm sure you're better off without him.'

I'd agree that she was right, while all the time knowing she was wrong – so wrong. There was nothing good about being without Jamie.

I punched at my pillow and screwed my eyes shut, but sleep was slipping further away. I reached for my phone again and tapped out a reply to Clio.

Hey yourself. All good here, just soooooooo busy. Out and about at breakfast with the girls – will call later.

That should keep her happy for a week or so.

It was 9.20 am so I figured I might as well get up. The apartment was quiet – Hen must have stayed over at her friend Izzy's place last night. Pulling a cardigan on over the T-shirt I'd slept in, I scrambled through the clothes piled messily on the floor for some pyjama pants and my ugg boots. I'd definitely clean in here today, and keep it clean. Maybe even hang my clothes up when I got home each night. I used to be organised, and neat – even though we never officially lived together, Jamie used to spend a lot of time here and liked the apartment to be tidy. My standards had slipped since he'd left. Lots of things had slipped since he'd left.

I'd started putting on weight in those last couple of months we were together. I'd thought things would get better after he'd confessed to the affair, but instead they got worse. He'd sworn she was a one-off who meant nothing, but I hadn't been able to let go of my suspicions – even though I knew I was driving him away with my paranoia. Chocolate and comfort food helped me feel better, temporarily – but Jamie pointed out on more than a few occasions that I was putting on weight. When we broke up I lost those kilos quickly, but in the months since then I'd fallen back into the comfort-food trap and the kilos had come back – and brought a few friends. Alice would tell me that I'd been swallowing my feelings – 'Some Cancers tend to do that,' she'd say – and she'd be right. But not any more. From now on I would treat my body like a temple that Jamie would want to worship in.

I pulled the cardigan more tightly around me and padded through to the kitchen, ignoring the chaos Hen had left in the sitting room, turned on the heating, flicked the switch on the kettle, and opened the fridge to search for breakfast inspiration. Something healthy.

Then I saw Thursday night's leftover pasta – that would do the trick. I'd start my diet on Monday. No carbs, more veggies, and definitely no chocolate biscuits.

As I was waiting for the microwave to do its thing, I decided to throw out everything that didn't fit into my new eating plan. Except the fridge was virtually empty anyway. I'd obviously been living on a diet of takeaway for longer than I'd thought. Rather than emptying the fridge, I actually needed to stock it. Some yoghurts that I could eat for breakfast – rather than the muffins I grabbed on my way into the office – would be a good start. Except the last time I bought yoghurts, Hen ate them all. In fact, Hen generally helped herself to whatever I brought into the house.

For about the twentieth time that week – and the week before, and the week before that – I wondered why I put up with her. It wasn't as if we were friends; we barely spoke to each other. The only thing we'd ever had in common was Jamie. He'd introduced her to me when I was looking for someone to share the rent with. She'd just broken up with a friend of his and was down on her luck, he said. So I agreed – and had been regretting it ever since.

I mightn't be able to start my diet today, but I could at least get this apartment back into some sort of shape – starting with the kitchen. Hen hadn't washed the dishes from whatever meal she and Izzy had shared last night – and several nights before that from the look of it – before they'd trashed the sitting room.

I'd just finished putting the last plate back in the cupboard when I heard a knock on the front door. Looking through the peephole I saw it was Tiff.

'How'd you get in downstairs?' I asked as I let her in.

'Mrs G was out watering her plants and recognised me.' She looked around the sitting room and grimaced. 'Hen?'

I nodded and retrieved several beer bottles and stacked them on the kitchen counter.

'And you're still cleaning up after her?'

'It's either that or live in a pig sty.'

'There's a third option – boot her out. You know you need to.'

'I guess.' I piled the pizza boxes on the counter next to the bottles. 'What brings you here?'

'You. I've made an appointment for you with Athena.' At my questioning look, she added, 'My hairdresser. She has a bit of a thing for Barry Gibb, but she knows her way around hair.'

'But –' I didn't get to finish.

'No buts. Get dressed, grab your handbag and let's go. She's managed to fit you in as a favour to me, so we'd better not be late.'

Once I was strapped in the chair and robed up, Tiff and Athena talked over me as if I didn't exist.

'Look at her ends,' moaned Athena, lifting my hair and frowning. 'And these layers – oh dear, it's a tragedy.'

I struggled to hold back my giggles.

Athena smiled, dimples showing in both cheeks. 'Tiff told you about my Barry Gibb thing, didn't she?'

I nodded and let the laugh escape, unable to stop myself raising my hands to either side of my face in the 'Tragedy' dance move.

The stylist next to us laughed too. 'Don't get her started on Barry.'

'Hey, Helena,' chided Athena, 'don't knock Barry.'

'No, at his age that could result in broken bones.'

'Okay, enough about Barry,' Tiff said. 'We're here to deal with Callie's hair. Her ends might be dreadful, but her hair's long enough that we can cut a good few inches off and give her some shape. Also, her natural colour is good, and I'm thinking if you weave some warmth into it, it'll really brighten her face. Don't you think?'

Athena, back in serious stylist mode, nodded as she walked around behind me, flicking the ends of my hair and tut-tutting over its condition.

Helena came over for a look. 'Why don't you just redo the layers, maybe style it with some loose waves and even a little seventies flick around the face?'

Athena clapped her hands together. 'I haven't done that for ages, but you're perfectly right – it's almost an updated Farrah! She has the perfect face shape for that. Helena, if we're doing an updated Farrah, I think we need some retro pop to get the mood going.'

'Absolutely. Connie, are you okay with that?'

Helena checked in with her client.

'Sounds good to me.'

'Does no one care what I think?' complained Tiff.

'You're not in charge today,' I said, my grin wide. 'If Athena thinks she needs to be inspired, who are we to argue?'

When Athena was finished, Tiff stood back, nodded slowly, and declared it was 'a huge improvement'. I had to agree. The face smiling back at me in the mirror was warm and vital. My eyes seemed bluer, my hair brighter, and my cheekbones higher. All that from a decent haircut to a disco beat?

'It's fabulous,' I told a beaming Athena. 'I love it so much. Thank you.'

'You're very welcome – it was fun.'

Tiff wasn't finished with me. 'Now we're going to replace some of those clothes we threw out when Jamie left,' she announced as we were leaving the salon.

By the time I let myself back into the apartment – still, thankfully, Hen-free – I had what Tiff referred to as 'the perfect winter capsule wardrobe' and instructions how to mix and match all the pieces.

'I'll let you take care of your own accessories,' she'd agreed after I'd refused all the tastefully small and dainty jewellery she was choosing.

I laid out all my new clothes on the bed, and reached into the wardrobe for the box of belts and scarves I'd managed to save from the wardrobe purge.

To the patterned kimono top and new jeans I added a denim-plaited belt that tied at the front with leather fringing, and a skinny cream scarf. My Navaho-inspired earrings with the turquoise centres and new long brown boots would work perfectly with that outfit too.

I could pair the long-sleeved tee with the rust midiskirt and thin tan belt, along with gold earrings, a striped scarf and a denim jacket to complete the look.

I repeated the exercise for each of the separates we'd purchased until I was satisfied I could wear them multiple ways. Then I hung my new clothes in the wardrobe, spacing the coat hangers out to fill the space I'd always kept free for when Jamie left clothes here, and firmly closed the door. Jamie was never coming back.

Before I could think more about it, I bundled the few clothes he'd left behind – I'd hidden them from Tiff and Alice during the wardrobe purge – into the bin. And while I was on a roll, I put the framed photo of Jamie and me that sat on my bedside table into a drawer, and deleted his messages from my phone.

I flipped through my photos to the album titled 'Jamie' and selected all the pictures. My finger hovered over the bin icon. I'd spent too many nights staring into his eyes, crying into his jumper, and replaying his messages. It stopped now. I clicked on the bin to delete them all. Was I sure? Yes. I listened to the little swoosh as the photographic memories of Jamie and me were consigned to the trash.

That was it, he was gone. Now there was room in my wardrobe and my phone for someone else to take his place.

At work on Monday, a few people did a double-take at my new hairstyle and wardrobe. As self-conscious as I felt, I had to admit I also felt a little taller and a whole lot better. Tiff had been right: just buying the right-fitting clothes took kilos off me and added their equivalent in confidence. When Andy Campbell looked twice at me, I smiled briefly and turned my attention to my work.

The morning was taken up with telephone screening and shortlisting candidates for the next intake of operators. Like many call centres, we had a large turnover of staff and were constantly recruiting. I'd put together a plan a few weeks ago that proposed some ways we might begin to improve staff engagement and perhaps keep our recruitment costs down, but Roger wasn't having any of it.

'Each of these initiatives costs money, Callie,' he'd said. 'And spending money – in case you weren't aware – reduces our profit margin.' He waggled his finger at me as if he were lecturing a ten year old. 'I don't expect you to understand that – but I do expect you to go through this latest lot of resumés.'

'But if we can reduce turnover, we can save on our recruitment costs,' I explained. 'Plus, if we're not constantly training new recruits, we'll be able to better maintain productivity – and perhaps even exceed what the client wants. I could work on engagement strategies and a proper benefits and remuneration scheme rather than just completing exit reporting requirements. The initiatives would more than pay for themselves. See, I've worked through the numbers here.'

I went to turn the page to the slide I'd prepared, but Roger shoved the paper back at me.

'If you've got time to waste on exercises like this, you've got time to do the one-on-ones for Andy's team – he's too busy again this month.' And with that he'd dismissed me.

Now I pulled the document out from under a mountain of resumés to see if there was another way I could present it to make it more appealing to senior management. Maybe I could go directly to the CEO, or another member of the executive team. They were always saying how they welcomed any idea that resulted in cost savings. As quickly as the thought occurred to me, I pushed it away. If Roger found out I'd gone over his head he'd make my work life even more unbearable. Besides, none of this was getting these candidates shortlisted. I slid the proposal back under the pile.

A few hours later Kerry dropped by my desk. 'Have you eaten yet?'

'No.' I sighed, stretching my arms high and rolling my shoulders. 'What time is it?'

'Time I dragged you away for some lunch.'

The day was grey and cold, casting an almost gothic light on the stone buildings at the financial end of Collins Street. We ducked down a laneway and into a pop-up that was selling bahn mi – Vietnamese pork and salad rolls. Wrapping our coats and scarves more tightly around us, we huddled on stools outside the shop, ate our lunch and gossiped about colleagues.

'Did you hear Krystal is thinking of resigning?' Kerry said, brushing baguette crumbs from her wool pants.

'No, that hasn't come over my desk yet. What's the story?'

'Apparently the usual – she fell hard for Andy Campbell. They went out a few times and then he switched his attention to Flick.' She shook her head. 'I reckon we could solve half of our turnover problems by either implementing a no-fraternisation policy, or allowing Andy to only employ straight males.'

I grinned. 'I think you could be right. But he'd probably turn them too.'

She laughed. 'Yep, he certainly has a gift. Hey, this is off topic, but you live in Fitzroy, don't you?'

I nodded. 'Uh-huh. Why?'

Kerry looked at her feet and brushed a few more crumbs off her legs. 'You're probably not interested, but a friend of mine is teaching beginner belly dance classes above a bar in Brunswick Street on Tuesday nights and I was wondering if you'd like to come with me. It's something I've always wanted to have a go at, and even though Tessa, my friend, is teaching, I'd feel more comfortable making an idiot of myself if there was someone else in the room I could laugh at myself with.' She smiled shyly at me. 'What do you say?'

Belly dancing? Didn't you have to be tall and willowy with flowing hair and undulating hips for that? Just as I was about to decline, Tiff's face came into view. Project Yes. I couldn't say no to Kerry and still be able to look Tiff squarely in the eye. And Kerry said it was something she'd always wanted to try . . . so why not?

'Okay, sure. Do I need a costume or something?'

Kerry's face broke into a wide smile. 'That's fabulous! Who knows, this could be really fun. Tessa says it helps you get in touch with your sensual self — and god knows I need that! Just wear normal workout tights and a comfortable T-shirt. Tess said some people wear long cotton skirts or have their own coin belts, but we don't need to bother with that. She said we can tie a scarf around our hips to start with.'

'Trainers?'

'No. It's a barefoot type of thing. I know,' her face was alight with excitement, 'maybe you can bring a friend too?'

I knew Tiff was away for work this week, but maybe Alice would be interested. After all, she couldn't say no either.

'Maybe I will.'

CHAPTER FOUR

'Tell me again why I'm here?' grumbled Alice as we gathered in the empty room above the Tradesman's Arms on Tuesday night.

I grinned. 'Because you couldn't say no. Plus, we're about to discover the sensual side of ourselves through the ancient and noble art of belly dancing.' I pulled my hair back into a loose bun at the nape of my neck. 'And because I couldn't say no to Kerry. Speaking of which, here she is now.'

Kerry hurried into the room, dropped her bag in the corner and came across to kiss me on the cheek. 'I'm so glad you came. I was worried it was just going to be me.'

'I've been looking forward to it,' I lied. 'Kerry, this is my friend Alice. As soon as I told her about it, she couldn't say no either!'

An hour later the three of us collapsed giggling onto the chairs that lined the room.

'Oh. My. God. That was so much fun,' I laughed. 'How was I to know my boobs have a life of their own?' I shimmied my shoulders.

'What about when Tessa was trying to teach us that camel movement and told us to pretend we were painting the wall with our headlights?'

Alice attempted an elaborate movement with her breasts that should have resembled a camel walking across a desert, but simply made Kerry and me exclaim together, 'Headlights!' and giggle childishly.

'And when Kerry asked if Tessa wanted us to paint in a straight line or just scribble around a bit?' I could barely talk for giggling.

'You girls are lucky. At least you've got boobs and hips to move. I just have little bumps. See?' Kerry poked her chest out and attempted to move it about, frowning as she concentrated. Which set us off again.

Alice took her hair out of its ponytail and shook it around until her curls had settled into their usual unruly pattern. 'I don't know about you two, but I vote we head downstairs for a drink. What do you think?'

'Sounds good to me,' I said. 'Kerry?'

'I'm in.'

As we gathered our things together and pulled on boots and jackets, Tessa joined us. A slight, pale woman with long grey hair hanging in a single plait down her back, she looked nothing like I'd thought a belly dancing teacher would look. Yet when she danced, she had a grace and lushness that was most unexpected.

She hugged Kerry, 'I'm so glad you came,' and

turned to Alice and me. 'What did you think?'

'It was fabulous,' I gushed. 'Surprisingly so.'

'So much fun,' echoed Alice. 'I had no idea what Callie was getting me into, but I'm glad I came.'

'We're heading downstairs for a drink,' I told Tessa. 'Did you want to join us?'

'That sounds great. Just let me pack up and I'll see you down there.'

'How did you get into belly dancing?' Alice asked Tessa, once we'd all settled onto high stools in the bar with our drinks.

Tessa raised her eyes to the ceiling as if organising the thoughts in her head. 'The easy answer is that I'd become stuck and needed to try some new things. I hadn't long separated from my husband – he'd been gone for around six months – and in that time I really hadn't ventured out of the house. It was a surprise, you see, him going – not what I'd expected at nearly fifty when we should have been coasting through to retirement. Anyway, a friend of mine – Kerry's mother, who, incidentally, I'm not nearly as old as.' She paused for our laughter. 'She told me I shouldn't be sitting around wishing for him to come back, but rather go out and start creating my own life. She dragged me along to a class and I was hooked. That was six years ago and I have to say, it was the best thing I could have done.'

'How so?' I asked. Although Tessa must have been nearly twenty years older than me, part of her story sounded like mine – sitting around waiting for a man to come back.

Tessa smiled, and when she did, her face came to life – much like her body did when she was dancing. 'It was the first thing I'd said yes to, and it pushed me out of the habit of always saying no. I'd always had this vision of myself as uncoordinated and clumsy – maybe from years of being married to a man who thought my only value was in my housekeeping. But the dance brought me in touch with my body and my sensuality – and, let me tell you, my current partner is very pleased about that!' Her grin was wicked. 'Through becoming more conscious of my body, how I can move it and what it's capable of, I became less self-conscious about how I appear to others, and more comfortable in my own skin – if that makes any sort of sense. It wasn't until I started stepping outside of myself that I was able to figure out what I wanted. When Gary, my husband, begged me to take him back, I was grateful at first that he was giving us a second chance – and then I realised I'd moved on and didn't love him any more.' She let out a short laugh. 'The poor bastard was so sure I'd pathetically welcome him back with open arms when the newer model he'd left me for woke up to herself, that it came as quite a shock to him when I didn't. So when Kerry here told me about how she felt she was stuck in a cycle –'

'Of unrequited lust for Andy Campbell,' Kerry added.

'I suggested she try something new that she could do just for her.'

'And here we are,' said Kerry. She smiled fondly at Tessa.

'We're here for much the same reason,' said Alice. 'A friend of ours thinks we're so stuck in our respective ruts that we can't see what it is we really want, let alone focus on going after it. So she's challenged us to say yes to anything that comes along.'

'It's why I said yes when you asked me,' I told Kerry.

'And why I had to say yes when Callie asked me,' added Alice.

'Your friend sounds as smart and as good a friend to you as Kerry's mother was to me when I needed a push in the right direction rather than tea and sympathy,' Tessa said.

'She is, but sometimes we think she needs to take some of her own advice – don't we, Cal?' Alice smiled ruefully.

I nodded. Tiff certainly was great at dishing out the advice.

Tessa laughed. 'People like that tend to fall harder when life hits them, so it's great she has you two on her side.'

'She's a Scorpio too,' mused Alice, 'so can be a tad

on the stubborn side, and she doesn't use her words as much as she should – but we love her anyway.'

'We do.' I finished the last of my wine. 'Well, I don't know about you girls, but it's a school night so I'm for home.'

'Yes, me too,' said Alice. 'I'd love to stay for another, but I'm driving. Cal, do you need a lift?'

'No, thanks, Ally, the walk will do me good. Kerry, I'll see you tomorrow, and Tessa – it's been so lovely to meet you.'

'And you too. Will I see you next week?'

'Yes, count me in,' said Kerry.

Alice hesitated for just a few seconds. 'You know what? I really enjoyed tonight, but I'm not sure if it's something I want to keep on with. But I'd better do another couple of classes just to be sure.'

'Absolutely,' I said without hesitation. 'I really enjoyed tonight.'

CHAPTER FIVE

At home, Hen was spread out on the sofa watching reality TV, her booted feet hanging over the edge, the remnants of her takeaway meal and some empty vodka pre-mixed bottles lying on the coffee table. She grunted in response to my 'hi' but didn't look up.

I'd called in at the convenience store on the corner to stock up on unsweetened yoghurts and frozen meals. Hen rarely looked in the freezer so I figured they'd be safe. I packed them away and looked around the kitchen. The sink was again piled high with dirty dishes, cups and empty plastic containers. Automatically I went to turn on the tap, then stopped myself. No, this had to end.

I marched into the sitting room. 'Are you intending to clean up the kitchen – or any of the mess in here?'

She raised her head briefly. 'Who are you, my mother?'

I sighed. 'No, just the person who has to live with you and who's been cleaning up your shit.' Maybe that did make me her mother – I certainly felt old enough at times.

'Some of it's yours,' she shot back.

'Actually no, it isn't. I've been washing up after myself.'

She shrugged. 'If you're already washing up, it makes sense to do mine as well then, doesn't it?'

I shook my head. 'If you don't clean up after yourself, you'll be left with nothing to eat off.'

'Whatever.'

I stared at her some more, but she didn't turn her head or acknowledge me in any way. 'Lazy cow,' I muttered under my breath and turned to leave the room.

'No wonder Jamie left — he couldn't take the nagging any more.' She said it quietly, but loud enough for me to hear.

I debated demanding to know what she meant. But the fear of how her response would make me feel was enough for me to pretend I hadn't heard her.

I went into my room and sat on the bed, remembering as if it was yesterday the night Jamie left.

When I got home from work that night, the apartment had a burnt smell. I wrinkled my nose and followed it into the kitchen, where Hen had clearly been attempting to cook. A saucepan sat on the stovetop with a blackened blob of something inside that might once have been chocolate. She'd tried to melt it directly on the hob and in the process burned the chocolate and ruined the pan. I didn't cook, but even I knew chocolate had to be melted over indirect heat.

I poked at the black mass, but it was stuck solid. I was considering whether to soak the saucepan in the sink or just throw it away when I saw Jamie leaning against the doorframe. Jamie liked to lean against things – it displayed him at his best.

'I didn't know you were here,' I said. 'I wasn't expecting to see you until later.' My eyes caught the duffel bag at the front door and my heart skipped a beat. I smiled and moved closer to him. 'Where are we going?'

It wasn't like Jamie to be spontaneous. Well, not lately anyway. When we were first together he'd surprise me with treats or mini-breaks away, but that was back then.

He took a step away from me. 'We're not going anywhere. It's not working, Cal. You and me. I'm done.'

I fought for breath. 'No. Don't say that. You know you don't mean it.'

I grasped at his hand, but he shook me off. 'It hasn't been the same since I confessed about that one stupid night with Kylie. You said you understood that it didn't mean anything, but you don't trust me.' He shook his head slowly. 'I can't deal with that any more.'

'I do trust you,' I said. 'I truly do. It's just that sometimes –'

'Cal,' he said softly, 'you don't. You mightn't say it, but I see the question in your eyes every time I'm five minutes late meeting you. I hear it in your voice whenever I get so busy that I forget to call as often as you need me to call. You should see your face every time a text comes through for me. Sure, I messed up, but you promised me you'd give us another go. I can't be with someone who's always wondering what I've been up to, and waiting for me to fuck up again. I can't do that to us, Cal.'

He reached for me then and pulled me towards him. 'This isn't fair to you either. You're not happy – you're tormenting yourself wondering where I am and who I'm with. I'm doing this for you – to give you the chance to find someone you can trust. I can't be that man – not if you won't let me.'

I started to cry. 'But I can learn to trust you again.'

I felt him shake his head. He put one finger under my chin and lifted it until my eyes met his. He wiped at my cheeks but the tears wouldn't stop flowing.

'Here,' he said, offering me a tissue from his pocket. 'It's clean.'

He watched as I blew my nose and wiped my eyes on the sleeve of my jacket.

'I know that it hurts now, and I hate to cause you this much pain – my heart is breaking too – but it's for the best. I can't sit by and watch the jealousy eat you up.' His smile was tender.

'Is there someone else?' Even as the question escaped, I knew I should have kept it caged.

'See, that's exactly what I'm talking about.' He

picked up the duffel bag. 'It hurts now, but someday I hope you'll understand. Maybe then we can be friends again.' He moved back to me and bent to kiss my cheek. 'Goodbye, Cal.'

Through blurry eyes I watched him leave, taking my heart with him.

For the next two weeks I kept everything exactly the same – as if by freezing time I could pretend that night hadn't happened and Jamie hadn't gone. I even left the burnt chocolate in the saucepan on the stove. After all, there was no danger of Hen cleaning it up.

I eventually threw away the saucepan, but I was still putting up with Hen – because she was one of the last remaining links to Jamie. As illogical as I knew it was, and as much as I disliked her, while she was still here so was a little piece of Jamie.

Hen and I didn't even exchange words when our paths crossed the next morning. I made a point of washing and drying the cup I'd had my tea in, and the spoon I'd eaten my yoghurt with, and left her looking in the cupboard – in vain – for a clean plate.

She was on her way out when I walked back into the apartment after work that evening. She was wheeling a suitcase and for a brief, thrilling second I thought she might be moving out.

'Don't get excited,' she said. 'I'm just going to Bali with Izzy for a couple of weeks.'

'That's sudden.'

'Not really. I've known for a while but keep forgetting to tell you. And after your rant last night, I couldn't be bothered.' She opened the front door. 'That'll give you two weeks to clean this place up a bit.'

'And for you to find somewhere else to live,' I muttered as the door closed behind her.

I let out the breath I'd been holding and turned to confront the kitchen. Two weeks without Hen sounded like bliss. And as soon as she was back, I'd tell her to move out. I knew it would be much tighter financially, but I could manage the rent on my own if I had to. I'd done exactly that on those occasions when Hen hadn't paid her share. Maybe it was time to move – to buy something for myself?

As I washed the dishes I did the numbers in my head. The mortgage payments surely wouldn't be much more than rent – and I did have some funds put aside for a deposit. I'd been saving for a wedding and the babies I was sure would soon follow, but with both those things off the cards, buying an apartment could be an option. No more worrying about rental bonds, inspections or messy flatmates.

But if you move, Jamie won't know where to find you, whispered the same voice that had been telling me to tolerate Hen. I smiled ruefully into the sink. That would only be a problem if he was looking for me – and that, I knew, was unlikely.

I was drying the last of the dishes when I heard my mobile ringing. I managed to answer it just before it stopped. It was Clio. Obviously my text on Saturday morning had only bought me a few days of respite.

'You sound out of breath,' she said. 'I didn't interrupt anything, did I?'

'Hardly,' I laughed. 'No, just up to my elbows in dishwater and the phone was on the other side of the room.'

'Fair enough.'

'How are Mum and Dad?'

'Yeah, they're good. Dad's on this health kick again – he's back into running and worrying about what he's eating. Mum's just letting him get on with it. She says she's nearly finished writing the family history.'

'Until she traces some other long-lost relative she needs to include,' I said.

Clio laughed with me. Mum had been nearly finished writing the family history for at least the last ten years, but always found another branch she needed to follow. History was Mum's passion. She'd been studying ancient history when she and Dad met – hence our names. Calliope and Clio were two of the nine Muses from Greek mythology; the daughters of Zeus, they were each responsible for one of the classical arts. Calliope was in charge of epic poetry – whatever that was – and Clio was supposed to be about history. Thankfully Mum had moved away from the gods and into family history by the time our brother Angus was born. He was named after someone from the Scottish side of the family – something he'd taken literally by moving over there a few years ago.

'And all's okay with you and Owen?' I asked.

After a whirlwind romance, Clio and Owen had been married just a couple of months. The wedding was three weeks after Jamie and I broke up, and I had to walk down the aisle pretending to be happy for Clio when my heart and dreams had been broken into a million little pieces. On the upside, the break-up diet meant I'd had no problems fitting into my bridesmaid's dress.

'Well . . .' she paused, 'you're going to be an aunty. Owen and I are pregnant!'

Pregnant. A spear of pain had me clutching at my belly.

'That's fabulous news!' I tried to inject some excitement into my voice. 'I didn't know you guys had decided to try for a baby so quickly.'

'We weren't,' said Clio. 'It was a complete accident. I missed a pill one night and bam, I'm pregnant with a honeymoon baby! Of course it's early days, and I haven't even told Mum and Dad yet – I'll drop around over the weekend. I wanted you to be the first to know.'

'I'm glad . . . I'm so happy for you both.'

'See, Owen,' I heard her saying, 'I told you Callie would be over the moon for us. Owen says hi by the way.' She giggled.

'Say hi back – and tell him I hope he's looking after you. Have you been sick at all?'

'I've never felt better! My skin is fabulous, and I know everyone complains about feeling tired, but I'm absolutely not. And you should see my boobs – they're magnificent, aren't they, Owen?'

'They certainly are,' he called in the background. 'I don't think I've ever seen a finer pair. In fact, get off the phone so I can look at them again.'

I laughed and again said how thrilled I was for them, and hung up. I was happy for them, truly I was. It was just that all the things I wanted and worked so hard towards seemed to drop into Clio's lap. She wasn't looking to get married – she'd been happy playing the field – but then one Friday night she got talking to Owen in a queue outside a food truck, and six months later they were married. She'd always said she didn't care one way or the other whether she had children, but here she was accidentally pregnant – and, of course, glowing happily through it. I, on the other hand, had spent five years planning a future and a family with Jamie, and then, just as it was within my grasp, it was torn away. It didn't seem fair – but then, I knew life wasn't fair. If it was, it would have been me walking down that aisle with the man I loved and celebrating the baby I'd always wanted. I could have hated my sister if I didn't love her so much.

Forcing the subject of Clio's good fortune from my brain, I tried to regain the optimism I'd felt when Hen told me she was going away. Two weeks without her. I might even get some real food in. With her not around, I didn't need to eat from a plastic tray with a plastic fork.

Opening the freezer to take out yet another microwave meal, I noticed the clear plastic bag full of slips of paper. I let out a little laugh. It seemed I couldn't get away from Jamie. There he was in the freezer bag – or what was left of him.

CHAPTER SIX

There were times when I'd felt lonely before Jamie and I split up – when I'd been waiting for him to come home, and worrying about who he was with. But it was nothing compared to the loneliness I felt after he'd gone. The first Friday night, after way too much to drink, I called him. He was gentle and kind, but also sounded exasperated.

'Cal, this isn't doing either of us any good. Why don't you call Tiff or Alice if you're feeling lonely? I can't be that person any more.'

But I couldn't call them, because I hadn't told them. I'd been hoping Jamie would come back before I needed to tell anyone.

It wasn't until the following week, two weeks after he'd left, that I finally came clean to the girls. Tiff had just flown in from somewhere or other, and Alice was celebrating because she'd just landed this radio gig she'd been hustling for. The way she'd described it, it was a cross between a horoscope session and an agony aunt column.

'I'm on every Thursday morning after the 7 am news and before the latest song by the latest boy band. They all sound the same to me.'

I'd tried to be happy for her, truly I had, but then I realised that for those few seconds I'd forgotten about Jamie and I felt my eyes fill.

'What's wrong, Cal?' Even in her big moment, Alice was quick with sympathy.

Tiff looked at my face, then ran her eyes down my body, before shaking her head. 'The bastard's done it again, hasn't he? Who is it this time?'

'How did you know?' I asked between sniffles.

'Oh, sweetie, it's there on your face,' she said. 'And the break-up diet's already taking effect.'

Alice reached across to hug me. 'Poor Callie. When did it happen?'

'Two weeks ago. I didn't tell you because . . .' I faltered.

'Because telling us would make it real?' guessed Tiff.

I nodded miserably. 'And I knew what you'd say. You told me he'd do it again, that it's never just the once – so it's okay if you say you told me so. But this time it's all my fault. He said he feels I haven't trusted him ever since. I've tried, but it just hurt so much when I found out about that night with Kylie, and I haven't been able to forget it. So he's right – I didn't trust him. And now my jealousy's driven him away.'

'Of course you couldn't trust him,' soothed Alice.

'Hmmmm, I'm not sure I buy that,' said Tiff. 'It sounds too convenient to blame you, and you know I never believed it was just one night with Kylie –' She stopped when she saw my face about to crumple again. 'But if that's how he feels, even though it doesn't seem like it now, you're probably better off without him.'

'It'll free you to find someone you can trust,' rushed in Alice, with a frown for Tiff.

Tiff called the waiter over for another round of drinks.

'You know what you need?' Alice said while we waited for them to arrive. 'A banishing ritual to get him out of your life once and for all.'

Tiff raised her eyebrows at the word 'ritual'.

'Don't look at me like that, Tiffany Samuels. I'm not going all new age and navel-gazing on you. One of my clients told me she did this when her husband left and it worked an absolute treat. It's a power-of-suggestion thing, and the least we can do is try it for Callie.'

Tiff nodded. 'Okay, as long as we're just cleaning out her wardrobe, I'm in. I'll bring the bubbles and Alice can deal with the candles.'

So the following day, that's what we did: set about banishing Jamie from my life – even though I wasn't sure I really wanted him banished. Part of me was still holding out hope that he'd change his mind and come back. But I smiled and drank champagne as Tiff and Alice went through my wardrobe, throwing out everything that no longer fitted me now I'd lost a few kilos.

'What if I put on weight again?' I asked. 'I won't have anything to wear.'

'Callie,' said Tiff firmly, 'we're old enough and mature enough that we no longer hold onto a range of clothes for all sizes. We only have clothes that fit us and suit us. Right, Alice?'

Alice nodded, but winked at me when Tiff's back was turned.

'I saw that, Alice.'

'You'll make a fabulous mother one day,' Alice told her. 'Eyes in the back of your head.'

'Not going to happen, my dear. Babies and boardrooms don't mix. Nor do babies and bubbly.' She threw my favourite suede coat into the pile for the vintage store.

'I love that,' I protested.

'Perhaps, but it doesn't love you any more.' She reached the end of the hanger space and turned to look at me. 'Seriously, Cal – this isn't just about whether or not you'll ever fit into anything again. It's about creating room for a new life, and new clothes to fit that new life.' She glanced at Alice for support. 'Isn't it?'

Alice topped up my glass. 'That's exactly what it's about. And now that Tiff's finished banishing your Jamie wardrobe, we're going to banish Jamie.'

'How do we do that?' I asked with some trepidation.

The champagne bubbles were coursing through my veins, but I still wasn't sure I wanted to send Jamie out of my life for good – just in case he changed his mind and came back.

'Okay, let's see if I remember what she told me.' Alice bunched her unruly red curls into a high bun. 'What you need to do is write his name on a sheet of paper – as many times as you want – and as you write you say something like, "Jamie Aldridge, I wish you no harm, but I wish you out of my life." Then you take the scissors and cut the page into pieces while saying the words again.'

'What if she does wish him harm though?' asked Tiff, popping the top on the second bottle. 'I certainly do.'

'I don't,' I protested, although I was ashamed to say that a part of me absolutely agreed with Tiff.

'Well, you should,' Tiff said. 'Especially after the pain he's caused you.'

'Do I have to say it out loud, or can I just think it?' I asked Alice.

She threw a pillow onto the floor and sat cross-legged on it. 'Can you pass me my glass, please? I should have thought of that before I got down here. I think you have to say it out loud, otherwise how is the universe going to know you really mean it?'

'Can't I just whisper it?'

The way I figured it, if the universe didn't hear me

properly, maybe Jamie would only be banished for a little while – until he'd realised that no one would love him the way I loved him.

Alice unfolded herself from her position on the floor. 'I tell you what, Tiff and I will go and source some snacks – banishing a man is hungry work – and you do the writing and talking to the universe and cutting up thing without us as an audience.'

'What happens after I cut him up?'

The absurdity of what I'd said hit Tiff first, causing her to choke on her champagne.

'You put the pieces of him in a plastic bag and put him in the freezer, of course,' Alice said, trying and failing to keep a straight face.

I started to laugh myself. 'I hope no one's listening to this conversation!'

'I'll say,' giggled Alice. 'Cut him into pieces, put him in plastic and freeze him.'

'I say we burn the bastard,' offered Tiff, raising her glass to the ceiling.

'What if I decide I want to unbanish him?' I asked, not entirely joking.

'I asked my friend that, and she'd already asked the friend who told her about it. Apparently you can reverse the process by thawing him out, sticking the pieces back together and saying something like, "Jamie Aldridge, I wish you no harm, but I want you back in my life." You'd need to be pretty sure about it though as these things come back threefold.'

'You just made that up, didn't you?' said Tiff.

'Yeah,' admitted Alice. 'I have no idea how you can reverse it, but I also can't think of any good reason why you'd want to.'

'True,' I replied meekly, as if the thought hadn't really crossed my mind.

'Once he's out of your life, forget him, I say.'

'Like you've forgotten Luke?' Tiff asked.

'Good point,' Alice conceded. 'Maybe I needed to banish him back when it happened and then he wouldn't find his way back into my mind every so often.'

'I know,' announced Tiff with a cheeky smile. 'Why don't we make this a new rule? Whenever we break up with someone, we banish them.'

'Good idea,' agreed Alice. 'I'll add it to my list. Now, let's leave Cal with her murderous intentions while we find something to eat.'

'You can't possibly be hungry,' said Tiff.

'But I am.'

I heard their banter as they disappeared into the kitchen, leaving me with my chanting and my pieces of Jamie.

Tiff appeared a few seconds later holding the saucepan with its used-to-be-chocolate blob. 'And what is this?'

'Hen was trying to melt chocolate and it burned.' I didn't tell her how long the pan had been sitting there on the stovetop.

'So she just left it there?'

I shrugged.

Tiff shook her head. 'This saucepan's ruined. I'll let you get on with your chanting, or whatever it is Alice has you doing, but as well as a new boyfriend, you need a new flatmate. Kick her out, Cal – you know you need to.'

Now, all these months later, I opened the little bag of paper pieces. I hadn't seen or heard from Jamie since that day. I'd visited places I knew he frequented, but he was never there. I'd fallen out of touch with the few mutual friends we'd had, so hadn't even heard him spoken of by anyone but the three of us – and even then his name was only mentioned when it couldn't be avoided. It was as if he'd disappeared. The ritual, or whatever it was called, had worked.

I'd cut the pieces of paper larger than I probably should have and could still read his name in some places. I pulled out a handful of strips and moved them around on the kitchen bench with my finger. It wouldn't take much effort to stick them back together – if I wanted to.

I stared at them for a few seconds more, then resolutely placed them back in the bag, and put the bag back into the freezer where it, and he, belonged.

CHAPTER SEVEN

Krystal asked to meet with me as soon as I got into the office. 'In a room, please,' she choked. Her face appeared paler than usual with two red spots high on her cheeks. There were shadows under her eyes and a slight quiver in her bottom lip.

Once in the meeting room, she handed me a folded sheet of paper. 'It's my resignation. I know I'm about to be performance-managed out, so I figured it would be easier on us all if I got in first.' She took a deep breath and continued, as if she'd spent the previous evening rehearsing her words. 'I'd like to thank you for the opportunity you've given me, and wish the company every prosperity in the future, but I don't feel I'm the right fit any more.'

I scanned the couple of sentences she'd typed, and refolded the letter. 'What if I don't choose to accept this?'

'But,' she sputtered, 'you have to.'

'Krystal, you shone in the assessment centre and blitzed your training. Your colleagues speak highly of you, and I still think you've got the potential that I saw in you at that first interview. Would you feel differently about your decision if you were transferred to a different team? I'm thinking your skills would be more useful in the customer retention area where it doesn't matter how long your calls take – it's resolution of problems we're interested in there. And, if I'm not mistaken, that's something you said to me in your interview – how you love speaking to people and ensuring they have a good customer experience.'

'Well, yes, I said that, but –'

'Don't you believe it any more?'

'Of course I do. It's just that –'

'So what do you say? Do you want me to talk to Ida in the retention team? It would save me recruiting someone for that team who we'd then need to train up. This way I only need to fill the vacancy left in Andy's team, so it's a win-win for me.' I'd deliberately kept my gaze on my notepad as I spoke, wanting to give her the space to consider what I was saying, but now I looked up and met her eyes. 'Don't throw away the opportunity you've got here, Krystal. Not when you don't need to.'

She nodded her head slowly. 'You're right, Callie. Thank you. The retention team sounds right up my alley.'

I smiled. 'Great. That's sorted then. Leave me to talk to Andy and Ida, and I'll get a letter drawn up for you to confirm the move.'

When I spoke to Andy, he wasn't quite so happy about it. 'You can't just transfer my problem to someone else,' he said.

'I'm yet to think there is a problem. She's meeting her objectives, and you haven't been able to give me any data to performance-manage her against.'

'Can't we just put it down to behaviour? What if I said I didn't like her attitude.'

'I'd need examples. No one else has an issue with Krystal – they all speak highly of her. And Ida said she wanted her in the first place, but you insisted on bringing her into your team.'

I held his gaze and his eyes dropped first.

'Yes, well, I suppose Ida is welcome to her then.' He grinned and raised his eyes back to mine. 'Hey, Jones, I was thinking how you and I didn't really get to talk on Friday night, and wondering whether we might want to try again?'

'What? Talking? We're doing that now, aren't we?'

He smiled as if he knew I was deliberately misunderstanding. 'No, I mean how about you and me going for a drink sometime – just us.' He tilted his head to the side. 'What do you say?'

It was situations like this that showed the flaws in Tiff's Project Yes plan. If I said yes to Andy, I was risking my friendship with Kerry – after all, she was the one with the huge crush on him. On the other hand, if I said no, I was going against the conditions of the project. And up until last Friday night, I would have leaped at the chance to say yes to Andy Campbell. But did I really want to be another notch on his belt? That would make me no different to Flick or Krystal.

'Thanks, Andy, but I don't think that would be a good idea.' I smiled to take any sting out of my rejection. 'It would send the wrong message.'

He raised his eyebrows in surprise. 'Really? It's only a drink.'

'I know, but the way rumours travel in this place it wouldn't be just a drink for very long – if you know what I mean.'

He nodded. 'Okay, so you're worried about gossip? You shouldn't believe everything you've heard, you know.'

'I know but . . .' I shrugged my shoulders. 'Sometimes it's hard not to.'

He focused his gaze on me and leaned in closer – the way I'd seen him do with Flick on Friday night.

Just then Kerry came into my office. 'Oh, I'm sorry – am I interrupting?'

'Not at all,' I said. 'Are you ready for lunch?'

She nodded, her eyes still on Andy who was now leaning against the side of my desk.

'We'll continue this . . . discussion later,' he said to me, grinning.

'What was that about?' asked Kerry when we were walking up Collins Street.

'I think Andy Campbell just asked me out.'

'What did you say?'

I looked across at her. 'No, of course.'

'Really? No one says no to Andy Campbell.'

'And that was my problem about saying yes. That and the fact that you're the one who's interested in him. I think he only wants me because he thinks I'm not.'

'Don't sell yourself short, sweetie,' she said, linking her arm in mine. 'You should go – you're different to Flick and Krystal. For a start, you're closer to his age.' I laughed at that. 'Seriously though, what about your Yes Project? It's not like you have to fall in love with him, but you never know – it could be fun. And if he's never going to be with me, I'd like him to at least be with someone I can get the juicy details from.'

A picture of Krystal's face from this morning came into my mind. 'No, I'm not going there. There's nothing about Andy Campbell that's a good idea. Besides, he didn't issue a direct invitation so it doesn't qualify under the Yes Project.' Behind my back my fingers were crossed. 'Anyway, this isn't getting a decision made for lunch – I'm craving noodles. You?'

Just as I was about to leave for the day, Roger stepped into my office. He had his coat over his arm so was obviously on his way out.

'I'm not sure if you've forgotten, but the staff turnover figures are due to the CEO tonight for inclusion in the board papers. Can I assume you're on top of it?'

Seriously? Since when? My surprise must have registered on my face.

'I'm sure I told you about it,' he said. 'Copy me in when you send them through.'

Gritting my teeth I nodded, and opened my laptop back up.

An hour or so later I was waiting for the lift when Andy Campbell appeared beside me. I tried not to let my surprise show – Andy wasn't known for working late.

'What a day.' He sighed heavily and looked at his watch to emphasise the point. 'I think we must be the only people left.'

'You could be right.' I pressed the down button again.

'Do you really think it'll make the lift arrive sooner?' he asked. 'Pressing the button repeatedly,' he explained when I cast a blank look at him. 'Like at traffic lights when you press the button for the walk sign after it's already been pressed. You know it means nothing, but you do it anyway.'

I laughed. 'I think you're right.'

He was smiling that smile at me and, despite myself, I felt my heart beat a little faster. He was very cute – and he reminded me of Jamie. It was the way he was looking at me, as though I was the only girl in the world. I shook the thought out of my head.

'Hey,' he said, as if he'd had a sudden brainwave. 'How about we go for that drink now? Do you have anywhere you need to be?'

'Well, no –'

'Great. There's no one else here to see that we've left together, so no one to spread any gossip. That means,' he said, as the lift doors opened, 'you're left with no excuses.'

'That would seem to be the case.'

'Good. That's settled then. Put your coat and scarf on and follow me.'

He led the way back up Collins Street, turning left up Swanston Street, and eventually onto Little Bourke Street and into Chinatown. Despite the cold, the narrow streets were full of people and he gripped my elbow to keep me close to his side as we walked. My arm was warm where he held it.

'Where on earth are you taking me?' I asked.

'We're nearly there,' he said, leading me up a narrow laneway before turning into what I'd thought was a mesh fence surrounding a car park. Inside was a shipping container turned into a bar, with upturned pallets and barrels and kegs reimagined into tables and seats. There were also, mercifully, heaters. 'Sit here,' he said. 'I'll go grab us a drink. Is beer okay?'

I nodded.

He was soon back with two beers. 'I took a chance on you being hungry so ordered us some sliders as well.'

Beer and dude food – it was perfect. In fact, the hours that followed were surprisingly enjoyable. We drank, we ate, we chatted lightly about anything and everything. As we talked, Andy focused all his attention on me in the same way I'd seen him do with so many other girls over the time we'd worked together. I forced those thoughts back into my brain and locked them away. This was just one night and there was no chance of me falling for him – no matter how much he resembled Jamie right now.

'Hey,' he said softly, 'what's going through that pretty head?' He laughed at himself. 'Oh man, I just realised how bad that sounds. Seriously though, what are you thinking about?'

I looked up from the empty plate of sliders, the beer glasses on the table and into his face, which was now very close to mine. My eyes flicked to his and then down to his smiling mouth. I wondered how those lips would feel against mine, whether they'd be hard or soft, whether he'd kiss me like Jamie used to kiss me – if it would feel the same.

'Do you want to know what I'm thinking?' he murmured.

I nodded, his words hanging in the breath between us.

'I was thinking I'd like to kiss you.'

I felt my lips open slightly as my eyes moved back to his. One little kiss wouldn't hurt. Everyone kissed

Andy Campbell – no one could possibly blame me for wanting to as well. It had been so long since I was kissed, and oh, how I missed it. This was just recreational, nothing could come from it – it was just a kiss.

'I'd like that too,' I said softly, closing my eyes as his mouth lowered to mine.

Right at that moment someone bumped against our table, sending what was left of my beer flying into my lap. It did what my willpower hadn't been able to do – brought me to my senses. There was no denying that Andy Campbell was attractive, but getting involved with him – in any way – wouldn't be smart. Although Kerry had said she didn't mind, I suspected she would if she knew about tonight. Likewise, although no one had seen us leave work together, liaisons involving Andy had a habit of becoming public – and I absolutely didn't want to be seen as yet another notch on his bedpost.

He sat back as I attempted to clean myself up. 'I'm guessing our moment has passed?'

I laughed ruefully. 'I'm so sorry, but yes. I've had a lovely evening, and now I think I'd better go home. I smell like a brewery.'

'I've had a good night too. Maybe we can try this again some other time?'

I smiled but avoided answering his question. 'You stay, but I'm off. Thanks again and I'm sorry.'

'Yeah, so am I.'

•

The smell of beer seemed to intensify on the tram. I was sure I saw people wrinkling their noses and trying not to look at me.

I pictured myself closing my eyes as Andy's mouth moved towards mine, my lips parted, waiting. What had I been thinking? Andy reminded me of Jamie, but he absolutely wasn't Jamie. My only excuse was that it had been a while since anyone had wanted to kiss me – and there was no denying Andy was attractive.

Then there was Kerry – I couldn't tell her about the almost kiss. She might have said she'd be fine if I did go out with Andy, but I knew she wouldn't be, not really. If it wasn't for the beer I was now wearing I might have lost a friend – and all for a kiss.

My phone pinged. I checked the screen – Andy. *Thanks for a fun night. Hopefully next time we won't be interrupted.*

No, Andy, there won't be a next time. I went to put my phone back into my bag without replying, but it pinged again. This time the message was from Clio. It was a photo of her standing in front of a mirror with her trackpants worn low and her T-shirt tucked into her bra. She was smiling and pushing her still flat stomach out by arching her back.

I thought you might get a laugh at the little pot belly I'm getting. Owen says he'll still love me when I'm even fatter than this.

I clutched at my own belly as a fresh stab of pain ran through me. It should have been me sending Clio the photo, with Jamie laughing as I took it. The marriage and babies thing was my dream – not hers.

A short half-sob escaped my mouth before I could force it back. The woman sitting across from me shook her head. I didn't blame her – I smelled like I'd drunk more than I should have and now I was making strange noises as well.

Leaning forward, I pressed the buzzer and alighted at Melbourne Museum. I could walk the rest of the way – the night air would bring me to my senses. It wasn't Clio's fault that Jamie had left; nor was it her fault that she was married and I was very alone.

I turned into my street, let myself in the front door and trudged up the single flight of stairs to my apartment. Without Hen here I didn't have the usual moment of hesitation as I braced myself for the inevitable mess. Instead the flat was quiet, clean and cold.

I hung my coat and scarf behind the door and dumped my handbag on the kitchen counter. Taking my phone out to plug it into the charger I saw Clio's message again. As much as I wanted to, I couldn't avoid it forever.

Sorry, was out on a date. You look amazing. I paused, then erased what I'd just typed. Even hinting at a replacement for Jamie would prompt too many questions. Instead I opted for something light and teasing.

OMG you're HUGE . . . lol. I added a smiley face and a couple of kisses.

If only Jamie hadn't left . . . if only I'd been able to trust him. If only I had another chance with him . . . I'd do whatever it took to make it work this time.

I sniffed the air and realised I was still in my beer-stained clothes. This was what I had come to – sitting around in smelly clothes on my own and wishing for second or third chances.

Before I could change my mind, I retrieved the bag of paper strips from the freezer, found a clean sheet of paper and a roll of sticky tape. Then I emptied the contents of the freezer bag onto the kitchen counter and began the process of sticking him back together.

'Jamie Aldridge, I want you back.'

CHAPTER EIGHT

There was something very weird with Tiff on Friday night. Despite having had, in her words, another bad week in the office, she was as animated as I'd ever seen her. In fact, if I didn't know her better, I would have said that she seemed excited. When I told her about our belly dancing experiment, she was almost effusive in her praise for us – and Tiff didn't do effusive.

'That's fabulous! It's exactly the sort of thing I was hoping would come out of this project,' she gushed.

Alice and I looked at each other with raised brows. Tiff didn't gush either. In fact, Tiff was decidedly not herself tonight.

'What about you, Alice?' she said. 'Aside from dancing have you tried anything different?'

'Well, I asked Mac whether he'd help me scratch my itch, but –'

My wine came out through my nose. 'You what? When? You didn't tell me about this!'

She shrugged and reached for the bar snack menu. 'It was last Sunday. We were out at breakfast with the dogs and I was telling him about the project. It seemed insulting not to ask him, but thankfully he said no. I'm glad he did – I think it would've been a mistake to blur those lines with Mac. He's too good a friend, and if the sex was crap – well, there's no coming back from that, is there? It's why I have the no-sex-with-friends rule.' She paused to contemplate the idea. 'Not that I think the sex would be crap – he seems to have a pretty active social life – but some rules need to be unconditionally kept. Anyway, I've had two dates with the IT guy at the radio station.'

I choked on my wine again. 'You didn't mention that on Tuesday night either.'

'Didn't I? It must have slipped my mind. You know, he's actually quite hot,' she said. 'Plus, our first date was for lunch, so I've already had the daylight date. Then we went for dinner last night.'

'You didn't waste any time,' commented Tiff.

'I couldn't see the point, and Tommy – that's his name – was a sensible choice to say yes to. My fear was that if I hung around I'd need to say yes to a non-sensible but possibly more short-term exciting choice and that would put me right back where I started – in trouble. I'm not about to fall in love with Tommy, but I really like him.'

'I don't believe in falling in love,' said Tiff. 'I think you find someone who ticks the boxes and it grows from there. The falling in love thing is really only about sex – and even then only at the beginning.'

'I still believe in love at first sight – even after Luke – and that should have been enough to turn me off forever,' said Alice. 'That feeling, that rush – it reminds you that you're human. That's how I know Tommy's an in-between option – just someone to get me back on the horse. I'm holding out for love at first sight again.'

'That's the hormones speaking,' Tiff pointed out. 'Like me with Jake the other week. I know logically it was nothing to do with love – just two people who needed to shag each other out of their systems.'

I shook my head. Sometimes I had problems understanding how the three of us could be so close, yet have such different ideas about love and romance. 'What's this sensible and non-sensible choice you're talking about? And how can you say someone's an in-between option? It's all about the heart, isn't it? It's why sometimes, even though our head says we're ready, the heart has other ideas.'

'This is why we need to go to our favourite TV shows for guidance,' Alice said. 'Like in *Sex And The City* – Carrie never made the sensible choices, and that's why she ended up in trouble.'

'She should have chosen Aiden,' Tiff said.

Alice nodded. 'Aiden was always going to be the more sensible choice – he stabilised Carrie. Mr Big was all over the place – he was a disaster waiting to happen. He made her even more erratic. Although if she'd ended up with Aiden, we would have tuned out.' At my questioning look, she added, 'Boring.'

'There was something about Mr Big that reminded me of Jamie.' I sighed.

'Commitment phobia perhaps?' Tiff had never liked Jamie.

I glared at her. So did Alice.

'It doesn't matter what we think,' I said. 'Until she chose him Mr Big was always going to be Unfinished Business.'

'Here she goes,' muttered Tiff.

'It's the ones you almost make it with who are the worst kind of Unfinished,' said Alice. 'Like me and Luke. He'll always be my almost lover.'

'And me and Jamie,' I offered. 'We could have made it. Now we're Unfinished Business too.'

'Yep, there it is,' said Tiff.

'It's true.'

'I know, sweetie,' soothed Alice.

Tiff downed the rest of her wine in one swallow, and poured another. 'You and Jamie had five years together – that's plenty of time to work out that he's a cheating fuckwit who doesn't deserve you mooning about him months after it's over. The thing is – and Alice, you can put this in your rule book – you never end up with the one who got away. That's not how it works. You're not supposed to – that's the whole point. *Sex And The City* was right: the bad boys – the

Mr Bigs – are only there so we can see and appreciate the real thing – the Aidens – when he comes along. That's why you have to have at least one Mr Big before you settle. They cause too much trouble if you fall for them afterwards – or worse,' she looked directly at me, 'if you keep going back to them.'

'But Carrie ended up with Mr Big,' I argued.

'An exception to the rule that has caused way too much angst for women around the world who now think there's a slim possibility their Mr Big could become their Aiden. The *Sex And The City* writers have a lot to answer for with that.'

'What about you, Tiff? What do you want?' Alice asked, before the conversation could get out of hand.

'Ideally, someone exactly like your brother.'

There it was again: Tiff and Matt Delaney. If I closed my eyes and pictured them together, it made sense. The thing was, I'd had a massive crush on Matt for most of my teenage years. You could probably say he was my first love – and they say you never forget your first love. Number two in the Delaney sibling pecking order, behind Laura, Matt was a couple of years older than me so always just out of reach. Until one unforgettable summer night.

'He's as close to my perfect man as it's possible to be,' Tiff was saying. 'Tall, professional, great taste in clothes, and earning good money. Any man I end up with needs to be confident in his own career, and not interfere with me wanting to further my ambitions. I'd prefer it if I didn't meet him through work, but that would be too much to ask, I guess. And someone who doesn't expect me to pop out a heap of kids.'

'Doesn't Matt want children?' I asked. Surely he did – some day.

Tiff shook her head. 'Not interested. He likes Laura's children and all that, but he's like me – career comes first.'

Alice was looking sceptical. 'It sounds to me like you've described a male version of yourself.'

'What's wrong with that?'

Alice shrugged. 'Nothing, I guess – but don't you want someone you can share new experiences with? Someone who can make you laugh? Someone who won't crowd you out, who has his own life and career – so he's not in competition with you, but understands how important it is that you have yours? Someone whose differences will keep you interested.'

I nodded. 'I agree. You need someone to have fun with.'

'That's what I've got you girls for.'

'Similarities are fine, but you need someone to challenge you in order to grow.' Alice pulled a face. 'Man, I'm talking like a new age therapist or life coach. Soon I'll start telling you about closure or journeys, or opening doors and putting one foot in front of the other!'

Tiff laughed, but didn't look convinced. 'I think I know better than you what I want.'

'Okay, so you want someone professional, earning mega dollars and wearing designer suits. You may as well settle for my brother.'

Tiff shrugged. 'What did that woman say in that book they made us read in high school that you and Callie loved but I couldn't see the point of?'

'That would be *Pride and Prejudice*,' I said.

'Yeah, that one. She said something about happiness and marriage and luck being involved.'

' "Happiness in marriage is entirely a matter of chance," ' I quoted. 'Then there was something about how it's better to know as little as possible about the defects of the man you've chosen to spend your life with.'

'Wow, your school fees were well spent,' said Tiff with a laugh. 'She was spot-on.'

'Yes and no,' argued Alice. 'When I talk to a client about relationships –'

'And you're such a good example,' interrupted Tiff with a smile.

Alice acknowledged the smile and continued. 'As I was saying, when I talk to a client about relationships, we concentrate first on what they need, what gets them motivated, and what type of relationship style they prefer.' She stopped for a mouthful of wine. 'Let's face it, ending up with the wrong person is ridiculously easy.

I'm extremely good at it, and I should know better. We all know I've never been good at walking my talk.'

Tiff and I laughed, as we knew we should. We also knew that Alice was right. She had such a habit of falling headfirst into love or lust with Mr So Completely Wrong that it wasn't really funny.

'How does this theory of yours work?' Tiff asked.

'Well, the first step is to know yourself. I already said that, right? In my case, I know I'm a contradiction. I need someone who's relatively stable, yet I want someone who appears not to be. I need someone I can be friends with, but I go after the guy who makes my heart thump but has no follow-through.'

'It's like you just said to Tiff – you're often attracted to male versions of yourself,' I observed with the wisdom that only several rounds of cocktails and a third bottle of wine can bring.

'What you're saying then,' Tiff added, 'is that we need to know what our hang-ups and deal-breakers are?'

'Yep, that's exactly what I'm saying.'

'But how do you know when you've found the right person? The one you can be happy with forever and ever?' Naturally, that was my question.

Tiff and Alice looked at each other and grinned.

'Are you going to say it or will I?' Alice asked.

'I will,' said Tiff. 'Is there really such a thing as happily ever after? Why do you think romance novels end when they do? No one's interested in what comes next because it tends to be pretty disappointing. You think that once you're in a relationship all your problems will miraculously go away, but they don't. Once that first rush of lust dies down you begin to realise that you still have whatever it was that made you stressed and miserable when you were single, but now you have someone to share it with. Plus, you're sharing whatever it was that made him stressed and miserable when he was single. So, when you think about it, being in a relationship is like being single – but with regular sex. Believing it's all going to be rainbows and unicorns is a short cut to heartbreak.'

'That's why one of my deal-breakers is I have to be friends with the guy, so that when the lust dies down there's something to build on,' said Alice. 'But given that one of my rules is I don't date guys I'm already friends with, I'm basically screwed.'

'That's why great sex is one of my deal-breakers. I have you guys for friends,' said Tiff.

'Well, I think that's a depressing thought. Besides, neither of you two have a great track record. I was with Jamie for five years.'

Tiff and Alice looked at each other and grinned again.

'Are you going to say it or will I?' Tiff asked.

'I will,' said Alice. 'Look how that turned out.'

'Oh, ha flipping ha.' I pretended to be offended, but couldn't stop the smile. 'We were happy for a time. I think we could have been again.'

'Except he cheated on you and didn't respect you, and – let's face facts – you didn't trust him.'

'Even towards the end though, the make-up sex was incredible.'

'Except for the fact that it was make-up sex,' Tiff said. 'Which implies there was a problem to start with.'

I shrugged. What could I say?

'Okay,' said Alice, 'if we're being scientific about this, let's talk deal-breakers.'

'And grooming in your case,' added Tiff.

'Okay, and grooming. For me, aside from what I said before, the guy has to be able to deal with my contradictions and hypocrisy, talk about my job without laughing or mentioning his uranus, and able to fix things. It would be extra nice if he could fix my website. Oh, and he has to love dogs. Stella and I come as a package, and I often have Kevin at my place too.'

Kevin was Mac's dog. Mac travelled quite a bit for work and had gotten into the habit of leaving Kevin with Alice and Stella.

'As for grooming,' said Tiff, 'if your eyebrows are joined, I hate to think what's happening down there. I thought you were going to deal with that last week.'

Alice tilted her glass in Tiff's direction and smiled. 'Okay, it's a trip to the waxers for me before tomorrow night's date with Tommy. Cal – your turn.'

'I had a date last night,' I said. 'With Andy Campbell.'

Both Alice and Tiff were silent for a few seconds.

Tiff was the first to recover. 'And we're only just hearing about this now?'

'It was a last-minute thing – both of us were the last to leave the office, so when he suggested we go for a drink I couldn't say no.' I threw the lines out so they didn't seem like a big deal.

'And how was it?' Alice leaned forward in her seat.

'Yeah, it was good.' I shrugged. 'When it came down to it though, I don't think I'm ready to be with anyone else. I know that sounds pathetic, but part of me feels I need to close things off with Jamie.'

'Actually, yes, it does sound pathetic,' said Tiff. 'I love you, sweetie, but you took him back once – that was your opportunity for "closure".' She used her fingers to mime quotation marks.

'That was different,' I protested. 'Yes, he did what he did, but it was my fault he left this time. I'd like the chance to put it right.'

Tiff raised her eyebrows, but Alice nodded slowly. 'Maybe you do need to go back in order to move forward. Until you see the past clearly, you won't be able to move into your future. Hey, that's a great line. I think I'll use it in next week's horoscopes somewhere – it'll be perfect for Cancer.'

'Also,' I took a deep breath, 'Clio called on Wednesday night. She's pregnant.'

'Wow, she didn't waste any time,' commented Tiff.

Alice was quicker to understand what I wasn't saying, and reached out to put her hand over mine. 'Oh, Callie. It's lovely news for her, but I can only imagine how you're feeling.'

I nodded. 'I'm thrilled for her and I feel like such a bitch, but it's like she clicks her fingers and it all falls into place for her. Sometimes it seems as though the minute I'm at my lowest, she's on a high.'

'Isn't there some lake in New Zealand that's empty whenever Lake George in Canberra is full and vice versa? Maybe it's like that?'

Alice glared at Tiff. 'Not helpful.'

'I tried so hard to make it work with Jamie. I kept thinking that if I loved him more he'd need me in the same way that I needed him and I could have my happy ending too. But all that happened was I pushed him away.'

'You can be happy – I'm sure of it. It just might be that Jamie isn't who your happy ending is supposed to be with.' Alice's smile was wide and gentle. 'I know how to make you feel better,' she went on. 'You can make up the numbers for our table at trivia tomorrow night. It's for Tommy's soccer club – it'll be fun. You can come too, Tiff – you can't say no, remember.'

'Yep, a trivia night with a table full of computer geeks. That's bound to make her feel better,' Tiff said, and Alice scowled at her. 'Anyway, I've already got a date tomorrow night.'

'Who with?' Alice said. 'Anyone we know?'

Tiff looked around the room in an attempt to attract someone's attention. 'Do you think our table might be ready yet? I'm getting hungry.'

'That's my line,' Alice said. 'Who's your date with?'

'Jake.'

'The Jake who just a few minutes ago you said you'd shagged out of your system?'

'He called and said he'd be in town and could we catch up.' Tiff shrugged. 'I can't tell you girls to say yes to everything if I'm not prepared to do the same, can I?' Her laugh was weirdly high-pitched and didn't convince us at all.

'Does he make you laugh? Does he make you feel relaxed? Are you able to talk to him?' Alice looked like she had a list of more questions like that.

Tiff stopped her. 'Yes, he does. But that doesn't make him right for me. We had a series of one-nighters that meant nothing – and that's the way it should be. Besides,' she added, 'I'm concentrating on getting to Top Team Masters Conference this year.' Her jaw was firm and her gaze steely. 'I won't be letting any man get in the way of that.'

There was no arguing with Tiff when she was in this frame of mind. No one else's opinions mattered.

While my friends good-naturedly bantered about whether culottes were appropriate corporate wear – Alice said yes, and Tiff was firmly in the no camp – I thought back to the sheet of paper still sitting on my kitchen counter, the one I'd used to stick the pieces of Jamie back together. Perhaps Alice was right – what if Jamie wasn't who my happy ending was meant to be with? If that was the case, what had I done by trying to reverse the banishing ritual?

I was grateful for the darkness to hide the warmth I could feel in my cheeks. It was just a piece of silliness really – and it wasn't as if I believed that sticking pieces of paper back together could make my wish come true. I'd throw the paper out as soon as I got home. The girls didn't need to know anything about it.

CHAPTER NINE

'Someone kill me now,' Alice whispered in my ear.

'Should I remind you that this whole thing was your idea?' I reached for the bottle of wine and topped up our glasses. The men around the table – all Tommy's friends – were drinking beer. 'I'm only here because you asked.'

'Yeah, thanks for the reminder. Somehow I think this,' she gestured towards the wine, 'is the only thing that'll get us through tonight.' She grinned widely. 'And if I have to deal with trivia night for the local football club, then so, my dear, do you.'

'Tommy asked you, so you were the only one who had to say yes.'

'Aaaah, but then I asked you, so you had to too. It's not all bad – there are some cute guys here.'

'None of whom are on our table,' I grumbled, looking around the room. 'Some of Tommy's friends look as though they haven't been outside in centuries. Tommy's the best-looking of them all.'

'He is, isn't he?' Alice smiled. 'And tonight's our third real date, so you know what that means?'

'Does a trivia night with his geeky mates count as a third date?'

Alice grinned. 'If we go for coffee or a drink on the way home and it's just the two of us, all conditions have been met. Besides,' she said with a wink, 'I'm awfully itchy. I'm also awfully hungry – what does a girl have to do to get some snacks around here?'

'Bring your own, I think.' I gestured at the assorted bowls of chips and dips on neighbouring tables.

Alice sighed. 'Hmmm, I didn't get that memo.'

'Does Tommy even play soccer?'

'Careful, sweetie, we call it football around here. And yes, he does. I'm hoping to find some very firm thighs under those slouchy jeans. Now, shhh. We're going into the next round and we need heaps of points.'

The question-caller, or quiz master as he liked to be known, made his way back to the microphone.

'Is it just me, or does this guy think he's channelling that dude from Family Feud?' Alice whispered in my ear. 'Except he's taller.'

'And he speaks in exclamation marks,' I whispered back.

'Okay!' announced the quiz master. 'Our next round is entertainment! Name all original members of One Direction – extra points if you can identify the blond one!'

'Oh, I know this!' I motioned to Tommy who had a pencil poised. 'Louis Tomlinson, Zayn Malik,

Harry Styles, Niall Horan – he was the blond one – and Liam Payne. Yes!' I punched the air in triumph. The others just looked bored, and my face drooped in disappointment. 'But I knew the answer.'

'Yes, but it's probably not something you should be proud of,' Alice pointed out gently.

For the first time I noticed the number of black T-shirts around our table adorned with, I now assumed, the logos of heavy metal bands.

The following five questions were related to movies, most of which I'd heard of but hadn't seen. Alice was able to answer a few – those Jason Statham had been in, or she thought Jason Statham should have been in.

'And the final question in this round! It's a bonus question!' the quiz master announced. 'Name! That! Song! I'm going to play the first few bars of a song, and the first team to call out the title and the name of the artist will score five points! They'll also get the chance to play for another five points in a mystery question! For one lucky team, this could be their way back into the game! Are we ready?'

The first few notes had barely been played before I'd jumped to my feet.

'I think we have someone who knows the answer!' announced the quiz master. 'From Geeks United – and, according to my calculations, if you get this answer right, you guys could be moving right up the leaderboard! So, for five points,' he paused as if waiting for a drumroll, or an ad break, 'give me the song title and artist!' His voice – and his arm – rose in a dramatic flourish.

I didn't hesitate. '"I Want You Back" by Bananarama!'

He looked down at his card, across at me, and back down at his card. 'I'm sorry to say . . . she's absolutely right! Five points to Geeks United! And now, for an additional five points, which Banana married Dave Stewart from the Eurythmics?'

Again, I didn't falter. 'Siobhan Fahey.'

'And just like that, Geeks United rocket into second position with just one round to go – and what a round it is! It's the one you've all been waiting for – sport! In the meantime, we'll leave you with the rest of the song while we take a short break.'

I sat down to applause from the rest of my team.

'How did you know that?' asked Tommy.

'She's a pop music tragic,' Alice answered for me.

'I'm just glad he didn't ask which one married Andrew Ridgeley from Wham.' I raised my eyebrows in relief. 'Or did she actually marry him? I know her name was Keren, not Karen – but I can't remember her last name. And I can never remember the name of the girl Siobhan Fahey formed Shakespears Sister with. Was it Margie, Marcie? I know – Marcella . . . and her last name was a city . . . Detroit, I think.'

I looked around the table but the members of Geeks United had turned back to their beers.

Alice was shaking her head and grinning. 'You're a hopeless case.'

'I know. But I love this song – it reminds me of Jamie.'

'Of course it does.'

'Given I won't be much use for the sports round, I think I'll visit the bathroom,' I tried to keep the tremble from my voice, but Alice wasn't fooled.

'Do you need me to come with you?'

'No, sweetie. You stay here with your man.'

I kept my smile firmly on my face until I was in the bathroom cubicle. What I didn't tell Alice was that the song took me back to the night Jamie left. It could have been written for us.

I smiled ruefully at myself in the mirror as I washed my hands. The truth was, I still believed that despite Jamie's cheating and my jealous thoughts, we'd had – to paraphrase the song's lyrics – a love most people would never know. If Tiff was here, I knew she'd remind me that most people wouldn't want the sort of love that had them wondering all the time where their man was – and she'd be right. It's just that it wasn't like that at the start.

With that thought in mind, I pushed open the bathroom door and walked straight into the man himself – Jamie.

I tripped, and would have fallen into a table full of drinks and snacks if Jamie hadn't reached out to grab me, pulling me hard into his chest and knocking the wind out of me for a second or so. When I recovered my composure enough to look up at his beautiful familiar face, my tongue felt so tangled that no words came out.

'Typical Cal, still as clumsy as ever,' he laughed.

'But how –' I began.

'Did I know you were here? I saw you answer that last question. You've got to be the only person in the room who knew that answer.' He smiled down at me, still not releasing me from his hold. 'Remember how we went to trivia when we were first together and you won the night guessing that Jason Donovan and Kylie Minogue song?'

'I sure do – "Especially For You".' I lowered my eyes and blushed. It was another song I'd had on high rotation after he left.

As lovely as it felt to be close to him, I pushed against his chest to free myself. He dropped his arms, allowing me to step back.

'I wasn't just lurking around the bathrooms,' he said. 'I saw you go in and waited for you. I wanted to talk to you.' His eyes met mine and my breath left my body for a second time. 'It's good to see you, Cal. You're looking good.'

His gaze was doing to my tummy what it always did – making it turn over on itself.

'It's good to see you too,' I managed.

He smiled again, his eyes piercing right into the

part of me that had missed him every day since he left. 'Who are you here with?'

'Alice and her boyfriend, Tommy – I suppose he's her boyfriend – and some of his friends. We're at the table over there – Geeks United.'

Jamie looked at where I was pointing. 'Hmmm, I can see where the name came from.'

I giggled. 'Don't be mean.'

'Come on.' He opened his hands wide in an innocent pose. 'Don't tell me you weren't thinking it?'

'Maybe. But I didn't say it.' I looked across at my table and saw that Alice had noticed who I was talking to. The concern was written all over her face. 'Who are you here with?'

'Just some people from work. I got dragged in at the last minute, and was counting the minutes until I could go home.' He smiled into my eyes, sending my internal organs somersaulting over each other. 'But now I'm glad I came. I was going to call, Cal – I just didn't know how to . . . having left things the way we did.'

I shifted my feet, hoping the movement might force my eyes away from his.

'I'd like to see you,' he said. 'I owe you an explanation.'

'Oh,' I managed.

'What about Tuesday night? Let's have dinner. How about that Italian we used to love in Brunswick Street – you know the one?'

I nodded, then immediately shook my head. 'No, I can't.'

'Come on, Cal – I really do want to talk to you.'

'No, it's not that. It's just that I'm busy on Tuesday night.'

His face clouded over. 'I should have expected that. I'm sorry, I shouldn't have asked.'

He thought I was with someone – and it bothered him. The realisation sent a wave of warmth all the way through me that felt suspiciously like triumph. If I were Tiff, I wouldn't have bothered to explain; I'd have let him continue to think I had someone new in my life. But I wasn't Tiff, and I couldn't help myself. This was Jamie – my Jamie – and he was looking so devastated at the thought of me with someone else that I had to put him out of his misery.

'It's not like that – I'm not seeing anyone. I have a dance class on Tuesday nights, that's all. But, if you're not busy, how about Thursday night?'

I felt myself blush as I suggested the date, and then held my breath as I waited for his answer.

'Thursday sounds great. I'll text you to confirm. Your number hasn't changed, has it?'

Of course it hadn't changed – just in case he ever decided to call.

'That's fine,' I said. 'I mean, yes, thank you.' Oh god, now I couldn't string two words together. 'No, I haven't changed my number.'

His grin grew wider as I tripped over my words. 'I'll look forward to it.'

He leaned forward and lightly held my arm as he kissed my cheek. All the nerves around where his lips touched my skin rushed to savour the moment.

'Yeah, me too,' I said, and watched him make his way back through the bar to his own table. He sat down beside an attractive brunette, and I was pleased when he didn't kiss her or show her any special Jamie treatment.

'Are you okay?' Alice asked when I returned to our table.

'Yes, thanks, I'm fine.'

'What did he say?'

'That I was the only person he knew who would have known the answer to that question.'

'Aside from that. He was looking so intently at you, I could feel it from here.'

'Yeah, I'd forgotten how piercing his eyes can be.'

And how good he smelled, and the way his voice rolled around me. Phone sex with Jamie had never needed much fantasising.

'We're going out on Thursday night. He said he owes me an explanation. He said he would have called before now, but he didn't know how to.'

'Do you believe him?'

I lifted one shoulder in response. 'I can't not believe him.'

'Are you going to go?'

'I have to,' I said simply. 'It's yes month. Besides, I've missed him so much, Ally.'

'I know, sweetie. Just be careful with him, okay?'

I nodded, but where Jamie Aldridge was concerned, I'd never been able to demonstrate any self-control. And he knew it.

CHAPTER TEN

Jamie called me on Sunday to confirm our date, and again on Monday. On Tuesday when he phoned, it was to tell me he had to go to Sydney for the day on Wednesday to rescue a project, but couldn't wait to see me on Thursday. Each call was brief, but let me know that he'd been thinking about our date as much as I had.

I told Kerry about it at lunchtime on Monday. Somehow the news that I'd been for drinks with Andy had gotten out, and she'd heard.

'I can't believe you didn't tell me,' she said. 'Not that you need to, but I still thought you would have.' She smiled but it didn't reach her eyes.

'There was nothing to tell,' I said. 'He was still here when I left on Thursday night, and when he suggested a drink, it was a bit difficult to say no.'

'Because of Project Yes?' she said. I nodded. 'And nothing else happened?'

'Absolutely not, but given there was no one else in the office to see us leaving together, I'm beginning to think that most rumours about Andy Campbell are started by Andy Campbell!'

She laughed. 'I think you could be right. And really nothing happened?'

Her tone had an edge to it, making me suspect that not only were the rumours started by Andy, but also embellished by him.

'No. Some idiot spilled beer on me, so I left at about nine thirty. Anyway,' I added, 'I'm having dinner with my ex on Thursday and that's all I can think about.'

It was an effective way to change the subject, but her obvious relief at my lack of interest in Andy made me doubly glad I hadn't given in to his obvious temptations.

Belly dancing on Tuesday was as much fun as it had been the previous week, although Alice decided to go out with Tommy instead. Evidently Saturday night had gone well.

Even though it was only my second class, I was starting to feel the rhythm in my hips – and felt them roll even wider after Tessa tied a jangle of coins around them. There was something about the tinkly happy sound the coins made that turned the shimmy into a celebration.

Although some of the moves were beginning to come more easily, both Kerry and I were having trouble with the shimmy-walk that Tess made look so effortless.

'Step, hip up, left, right, down,' she chanted, but it all felt wrong.

Kerry and I giggled as we walked forward and

back from the mirrors, our hips going in the wrong direction.

'There's something not normal about walking forward and having your hips slide from side to side before taking the next step,' Kerry said.

'Do you remember your mother doing those exercises where she'd bum-walk across the floor?' Tessa asked us.

'Sure. Didn't everyone's mother do those exercises?'

'Probably. Well, it's that motion we're after for the shimmy-walk.'

Tessa dropped to the floor and demonstrated. We followed, and fell about laughing again.

She shook her head at us. 'I think that's enough shimmy-walking tonight. If you haven't got the hang of it yet, don't worry. It's something that just happens when you stop thinking about what your feet and hips are doing and really start feeling the music. Let's finish with a shimmy!'

I told Tessa and Kerry about Jamie over drinks after class up on the rooftop. The rooftop bar was officially closed, but Tessa knew the manager. The night was clear and cold, but our jackets and beanies kept us warm. Up here, with the lights of the CBD burning just a short way away, and the bustle of Brunswick Street down below, it felt as though I could touch the moon. I actually reached my hand out towards it.

Tessa saw me and giggled. 'I've tried to do that too, on nights where I've felt so full of life and music it's seemed as though anything is possible.'

'It feels weird to be up here when the bar's closed,' said Kerry. 'Usually I'm here on a busy night or a weekend lunch when it's packed.' She wandered across to the remnants of a worn brick wall, rested her hands on the glass safety wall and stared out across the city. 'Should we be making a wish on the moon?'

'Alice would say yes,' I told them.

Tessa smiled gently. 'I would say yes too – at every opportunity.'

'What would you wish for?' I asked her.

'More nights like this – when the music is bubbling inside me and the shimmy is bursting out of me.' She wiggled her shoulders and chest to an imaginary drumbeat. 'What about you?'

Kerry laughed. 'I'm way too predictable. I'd wish for Andy Campbell to notice me – or the willpower to forget all about him.' She shrugged and grinned. 'Or for someone else to come along to help me forget him.'

Tessa threw an arm around her shoulders and hugged her. 'Sometimes, my dear, that happens when you're not expecting it, or looking for it. It's like the shimmy-walk – you'll nail it when you've stopped overthinking it.' She turned to me. 'What would you wish for, Callie?'

'I'm having dinner with my ex-boyfriend on

Thursday night – and I want him back.'

I told Tessa and Kerry about how I'd run into Jamie at the trivia night, and how much I was looking forward to going out with him. As much as I loved Tiff and Alice, their knowledge of the history between Jamie and me – and their urge to protect me further – meant I couldn't share my excitement with them.

Kerry was unrestrained in her enthusiasm. 'That's so romantic – bumping into him like that. Maybe it really is meant to be.'

Tessa was more reserved. 'What did you say went wrong between you two?'

'I found out he'd had a brief fling with someone he'd met through work. It was about this time last year, and we'd been together for just over four years by then. I don't know – maybe things had gotten stale.' I wrinkled my nose as I sorted the events in my head. 'They didn't feel stale to me though. They felt comfortable and safe. It was just us, and no one else mattered – well, not for me anyway. He said he was sorry and it hadn't meant anything, and that he'd felt I'd become distant because I was never around at the same time he was.'

I recalled how angry Tiff had been when I told her that part. She'd said it was typical of Jamie to turn his mistake into being my fault.

'He was wrong about that,' I went on. 'I hadn't lost interest – it was just that I'd started going to this book club and we'd gone from one meeting a month to also going out occasionally on weekends and sometimes during the week.'

'Aaaah,' Tessa said.

I looked across at her to prompt her to say more, but she'd lowered her head and was twisting her drink coaster up and over on the table.

'Jamie and I weren't living together, so I didn't think it mattered if I was out on the nights he wasn't at my place,' I said. It felt good to put it all in words to people who didn't know our history. 'Besides, he often had to work late or travel interstate and I thought he'd be glad I wasn't sitting around waiting for him. Once I found out about the woman he'd slept with, he broke down and said that he knew he'd abused my trust and what he'd done was wrong, but he was afraid he was losing me. He said he knew that was no excuse for what he'd done, but he begged me to forgive him – and I did. He said she was a moment of weakness caused by his fear that I was building a life without him.' I shrugged. 'Maybe he was right – maybe I hadn't been giving as much to our relationship as I had done at the start.

'Anyway, he promised things would be different, but it wasn't until he booked a holiday for us – a week in Phuket – that I realised it wasn't just words. He truly was sorry for what he'd done, and he was serious about taking us back to where we were in the beginning. We had a fabulous time on holiday – it felt just like it used to when we first fell in love. But once we got back, I found I couldn't forget about what he'd done and I couldn't trust him. I wanted to – I tried so hard to – but I kept seeing her and him together in my mind. Every time he was late, or interstate on business, or out with his friends on weekends, I couldn't help wondering if he was with her.'

'And your book club? Did you keep going with that?' Tessa asked, looking up from her coaster.

'No. I was going to, but Jamie found ways of distracting me from what I was supposed to be reading.' I smiled at the memory. 'And then before I knew it, a few months had passed without me going, or even contacting anyone to say why I'd stopped going. They must have thought I'd dropped off the planet.' My laugh was rueful. 'It's a pity, because I really loved the book club – and the women I met through it. I've always loved reading, but it's not something Tiff or Alice are into. You know, I even thought about studying literature at uni. Maybe I should have. That's why book club was something just for me – probably like belly dancing is now.' I grinned and made a snake-like movement with my arms the way Tessa had taught us. 'Not that it mattered. I stopped going out, thinking that if I showed Jamie I loved him more, he'd believe it and want to spend more time with me too. But the more I tried to pretend that I trusted him, the more I felt him pulling away. Of course, that meant that my suspicions grew even more, and eventually he said he'd had enough and left. That was a few months ago and I don't think I've really gotten over him.'

Tessa nodded slowly. 'And you'd take him back again?'

'In a heartbeat. I invested five years in our relationship. I really thought we'd get married and have a family and –'

'Live happily ever after?' Tessa finished.

I was glad the darkness hid the sudden warmth I felt in my cheeks. 'We'd had a couple of really good years – I thought we could build on that past.'

'Even though the present wasn't that good?'

'Perhaps,' I conceded grudgingly. 'But maybe we need to go back in order to move forward?'

'Sometimes. But sometimes it's good to go back so you realise things weren't as rosy as you remember them.' She tilted her head to one side and studied me. 'I used to be just like you – always romanticising the past. Sometime over the last couple of years though, I decided the past was somewhere I still wanted to visit occasionally, but I was selling any real estate I'd left there. And to make that decision, I had to go back and see things as they were at that point in time – not as I remembered them at the best of times.' She paused. 'Sometimes you do need to go back to move forward.'

Her words were the same as mine, but her meaning was very different.

'Are you saying you think I shouldn't go out with

Jamie?' I asked her.

'Absolutely not. I think you should. Go, meet him, pretend it's like the first time – but keep at the back of your mind all that you've learnt about yourself in the months you've been apart. Remember how it was towards the end as well as how it was at the beginning. It's possible for things to go back to their best – but it's more likely they'll end up as they were at the end. But knowing that you've managed alone gives you an advantage. It shouldn't scare you to be alone again.'

I searched her face for more, but her smile was back.

She drained her glass. 'Okay, my darlings, that's quite enough deep and meaningfuls for one evening.' She bent down and gathered her bags and portable speakers. 'You both did really well tonight. You'll nail that shimmy-walk any day soon.'

Kerry grinned and rolled her hips in a figure eight. 'We did do well tonight. Are you going to be okay to walk home?' she asked me.

'Absolutely. I'm only a few minutes away.'

I waved them goodbye, and sat on my own in the darkness on the rooftop for a little longer. I could still hear the drums beating in my chest, and had to stop my shoulders from swaying in time to the music in my head. I thought I saw a shooting star, but it could have just been a Qantas flight to Sydney. I wished on it anyway. I wished for Jamie and me to get another chance.

CHAPTER ELEVEN

Despite Tiff being in Sydney, a last-minute conference call with the girls on Thursday afternoon set the ground rules for my date with Jamie.

Tiff: 'I still don't think you should be going.'

Me: 'You said we had to accept all invitations.'

Tiff: 'I'm sure I didn't have this one in mind when I said that.'

Alice: 'Watch the alcohol – you know that when you have a few drinks your defences completely crumble. Whatever you do, stick to two glasses of wine, no cocktails, and for god's sake, don't look in his eyes. Remember, you are absolutely not sleeping with him tonight – no matter how tempting he is.'

Me: 'Does the three-date rule apply when you've been with someone before?'

Alice: 'Hmmm, I'll need to think through the logistics of that.'

Tiff: 'Sleep with him if you want to, but don't let him know in advance that you want to.'

Alice: 'If she's wearing Spanx, that'll be awkward.'

Me: 'Maybe I shouldn't wear them?'

Tiff: 'No, they're ugly, but they'll give you more confidence to start with – and you'll need that to fake your disinterest. Wear the Spanx.'

Alice: 'I'm not sure I like you telling her to fake anything.'

Tiff: 'It's Cal – she's not going to be able to fake it anyway. Jamie is her kryptonite.'

Alice: 'True. Just try not to sleep with him tonight.'

At the door to the restaurant I paused, took a deep breath and sucked my tummy in. Hair freshly blow-dried? Tick. Legs shaved? Tick. Best Spanx on? Tick. New black jersey dress doing what the saleslady promised it would? Tick. Feet crippled by shoes? Tick. I was looking as good as I had the day I first met Jamie – only more grown-up, and (hopefully) more mature and less easily swayed. Yes, I wanted him back, but there was no reason to appear desperate about it.

Jamie was waiting for me at the bar, leaning against it like he was some sort of romantic hero. When he turned and looked at me, the smile in his eyes set off little whirlpools in the part of my tummy that wasn't constrained.

He met me halfway, kissed my cheek and hugged me. 'I've missed you,' he said into my hair. He felt so good, so familiar.

Over cocktails and starters, he sat back and pushed his fingers through his hair. 'I've fucked up, Cal. I don't know what I was thinking. Hell, I don't think I was thinking. All I know is I've spent most of the last few months missing you.' He leaned forward and covered my hand with his, giving me the full force of those eyes that could still see right into my soul. 'I know I don't deserve you, but I want you back.'

His words were the ones I'd imagined hearing him say those words for so long. My eyes filled with tears, and I thought that I could see some moisture in his too, and melted a little more.

Over our main course, he kept my glass filled as he updated me on what he'd been doing since we parted.

'I've got a new job. I'm working with Josh Booth – do you remember him?' I nodded. 'It's a project director role, so a good move for me. They're a great group of people.'

'What happened at GNA? I thought you'd never leave.'

'Oh, you know how it is – I think I outgrew them.' He reached over to pour more wine. I tried to put my hand over my glass, but he nudged it away. 'You're not eating much. Is everything okay?'

I couldn't tell him there was no room under my Spanx for food, so I smiled and took a bite of the piece of fish I'd been pushing around my plate. He gestured to the waiter for another bottle of wine.

'I have to say, Cal, you're looking pretty hot. Have you been working out, or is it the dance class? You've done something to your hair, right?'

I played it cool, but inside I was beaming. It had only been a couple of weeks, but eating a proper breakfast and replacing takeaway with real food – okay, frozen, portion-controlled dinners – was already starting to make a difference to the number on the scales. I was thrilled he'd noticed.

Over a dessert that I didn't want and more wine that I didn't need, he told me about the half-marathon he was training for, and the romantic getaway Josh had just booked in Daylesford. 'Apparently there are huge four-poster beds you can wallow in, and open fires to make love in front of – you know how we always said we wanted to do that?'

I felt the warmth in my cheeks at his words.

He leaned in closer and reached for my hand. 'As Josh was telling me about it, all I could think of was how much I wanted to be there with you. I was imagining everything I'd do to you in one of those beds.'

As his fingers lightly stroked the back of my hand I was imagining it too.

He looked deeply into my eyes. 'I need you, Cal. Nothing is the same without you.' He smiled in a way I could never resist. 'I really fucked up, didn't I?'

I should have said, 'Yes, you did,' and made him work for what came next. But although I could picture Tiff cringing, I couldn't help myself. I'd missed him so much for so long.

'Nothing's the same without you either,' I admitted.

He leaned over the table to kiss me, and I was lost.

I really hadn't intended sleeping with him. I'd tell Alice that.

I really hadn't intended to be so desperate for him. I'd tell Tiff that.

I'd only invited him in for coffee. Coffee that I had every intention of making, even though I knew he detested the instant stuff and that was all I had. It's just that it was late, we were both a little tipsy, and it seemed unfair and . . . yes, cruel to send him back out into the rain and the cold. Besides, he'd plugged his phone in to charge – and I couldn't send him away with a dead phone.

And I'd wanted him back for so long, and he knew just what to say and do to make me completely mad for him. I knew I was drunk, that my defences were down, but his mouth and hands knew exactly which buttons to press. What else could I do but surrender?

Now, lying in the darkness, listening to him snoring softly, it occurred to me that not once had he asked about me – what I'd been doing, who I'd been seeing.

Not that it mattered. He'd never been overly interested in other people. That's who he was. I knew him so well, and had loved him despite all his faults.

He said that to me when we were making love: 'No one knows me the way you do, Cal.'

I knew Tiff would frown, but Alice would understand.

•

I woke with a beating head and a mouth as dry as
. . . well, something that was really dry. The Simpson
Desert? I knew I shouldn't have drunk that much, and
I'd tried not to – but what with the cocktails and the
sparkles, and the wine with dinner, and whatever that
stuff was called that Jamie had insisted on ordering
to help digest the dessert I didn't want, somehow I'd
ended up drinking way more than I'd intended.

It took a couple of minutes for me to realise that
other parts of me were unusually tender this morning
– and that the pillow beside me was empty.

Jamie was leaning in the doorway to the ensuite,
brushing his teeth, a towel around his waist. How did
he manage to look so fresh when I felt so the opposite?

'Are you leaving?' I asked.

'Yeah, thought I'd get out of here before Hen
wakes up.' He disappeared into the bathroom to rinse
his mouth.

I tried to laugh, but it made my head hurt. 'It's
okay, she's in Bali.'

'I thought it seemed quiet.' He smiled and resumed
his leaning position. Man, he did that leaning thing well.
'None of that clumping around in those ridiculous
boots she insists on wearing.'

'Jamie,' I sat up higher in bed and pulled on a
T-shirt, 'do you think we should talk?'

'What about? Isn't it enough that we're back together?'

'Are we? Back together?'

'Of course we are.'

'It's just that . . . well, has there been anyone else? You know, since you dumped me?'

'I didn't exactly dump you. I didn't want us to break up, but . . .' He shrugged his shoulders. 'Let's not go back through all of that again. I just need to know you can trust me this time.'

'You know I was only like that because you cheated on me.'

'Babe,' he said, moving towards the bed, 'you know it was only sex. You're the one I always wanted to come home to.'

He shed his towel, and I would have swallowed if my mouth didn't feel like the Kimberley.

'Besides,' he said, lifting my T-shirt over my head and pushing me gently back onto the bed, 'none of that matters now.'

He took one nipple in his mouth, circling the tip with his tongue, and rolled the other between his fingers.

'Ohhhh,' I managed, forcing my brain back into my head. 'Don't you want to know if I've been with anyone since you?'

He raised his head, but his hand inched below the sheets. 'Have you?'

I shook my head as his fingers trailed along my

hipbone, leaving a little trail of sensation in their wake.

'I assumed you would have told me anything I needed to know last night.' He smiled as his fingers found their target and I arched my back and moaned. 'But I'm happy to talk about it now if you like.'

'No, not now,' I gasped.

'Good, because I don't want to talk either.'

He pulled away long enough to reach for a condom on the bedside table where he'd left them last night. Holding my eyes, he moved the sheet aside and slid into me, filling me, but maddeningly not moving.

'Do you really care about who I've been with?' he asked.

I wrapped my legs around him to draw him deeper into me, but still he didn't move.

'No,' I moaned, 'I don't care. Please . . .'

'Please what?' He bent his head and sucked again on my nipple.

I twisted underneath him. 'Please just fuck me.'

'Seeing as how you asked so nicely . . .'

That morning there was absolutely nothing that could dampen my mood. My boots zipped up effortlessly over my new jeans, my hair flicked just the way it was supposed to, and the kimono-style top I'd chosen to wear swung in time with my fringed bag. I even tried to whistle as I walked to the tram stop, but decided that was going too far.

The sun was out, and the birds had started to sing again. Jamie was back and I was sure the entire world could see it on my face.

In the office, Andy looked up from his flirtation with Flick as I walked by. I beamed at him and sailed past.

In the meeting about the new dress codes, I stood my ground with Roger on the subject of activewear and ugg boots. Roger didn't see what the problem was, but the CEO agreed with me that the new policy should explicitly forbid both. I'd suffer for that victory later, but still felt like I was winning on all fronts.

Alice phoned mid-morning. 'Well?' Then, as I tried to get my words in order, 'I knew it! You slept with him, didn't you?'

I surrendered any attempt to justify my actions. 'I couldn't help it. He was there, and I was drunk, and he was . . . Oh, Ally, I'd missed him so much. Besides, the three-date rule doesn't apply if you've already been together, does it?'

'I've put some thought into that,' she said, 'and I've decided that when you're considering getting back with someone, the minimum date rule should be extended to at least five dates, so you're absolutely sure you're doing the right thing. Not that I think you've done the wrong thing,' she rushed to add. 'What happens now?'

'Well, we're back together, and he's coming over tonight to cook dinner for me. It's worked and I'm so happy.'

'What's worked?'

I almost blurted out that I'd taken Jamie out of the freezer and put him back together, but even Alice would think that was ludicrous.

'Oh, just me sending the message out to the universe and focusing on it.'

'Yes, well.' She didn't sound convinced. 'I wish I wasn't going out with Tommy tonight, or I'd arrange a debrief.'

'Is Tiff still away?'

'Yes, she has something on in Sydney this weekend.' She paused for a second. 'I have the feeling there's something going on that she's not telling us about.'

'It's probably just work – you know what she's like.' It suited me that something other than my love life was distracting Tiff. As well-intentioned as she was, I didn't want her raining on my parade.

'You're probably right,' Alice said. 'Ainsley really seems to have taken a dislike to her – though I think she's picked the wrong person to target in Tiff. That sort of behaviour just makes her even more determined to win.'

I laughed. 'I wouldn't be surprised if she's already having revenge fantasies about Ainsley.'

'Me neither. But that doesn't change the subject of Jamie,' she warned. 'You know you have to tell her.'

'I know, but next week. In the meantime, how are

things going with you and Tommy?'

'Let's just say that all that tapping away on keyboards has given him skills that are both unexpected and very welcome.'

I could hear the grin in Alice's voice and laughed with her. 'I'm glad. You enjoy, hey?'

'Oh, I am!'

CHAPTER TWELVE

As if the day couldn't possibly get any better, Marion Lynch, an old colleague from a few years back, called for a chat during the afternoon.

'Can you get away for a quick coffee?' she asked. 'There's an opportunity coming up that I think you'd be perfect for.'

I looked through the glass of my office to where Felicity had perched herself on the corner of Andy's desk. They were talking and laughing, even though I could see that a number of calls were waiting in the queue for his team to take.

Although my title was HR manager, it had become obvious over the past year or so that all I was tasked with were administration and departure-lounge duties. I'd stayed partly because nothing I was really interested in had come up, but mostly – and I was ashamed to admit it – because Jamie knew where to find me here. It was the same reason I'd stayed in the apartment, even though Hen drove me mad.

Now that Jamie was back, there was nothing

stopping me looking at other jobs. Although even as I thought it, I could hear Tiff saying that there'd never been anything stopping me. Anyway, it was yes month, so instead of making an excuse about being busy, I agreed to meet Marion.

The first thing I noticed about her was the enormous diamond on her ring finger. 'Oh. My. God. Is this real?' I said, holding her hand up towards the light and watching the stone sparkle.

'It's fabulous, isn't it?' Marion always had been matter-of-fact. 'It's also why I wanted to talk to you.'

'So I can admire your diamond?'

'Ha ha. No, although I still find myself unable to look away from it. I can't quite believe that after all these years Damien has taken the plunge.'

Marion and Damien met soon after Jamie and I did. We double-dated a couple of times in the early days, but the two men didn't really get on, so we all drifted apart.

'No ring from Jamie yet?' she asked, then clapped her hand over her mouth. 'I really should think before I speak. I think I recall hearing somewhere that you two broke up? I can't say I'm really that surprised – not after I heard about him and the operations director at GNA.'

'Actually,' I said in a small voice, 'we're back together again.'

'Sorry,' she said, looking down at her coffee cup, 'I didn't realise. I'm sure the rumours I heard were only rumours.'

It was my inability to trust Jamie that had got me into trouble before, so I resolutely decided to ignore what Marion had said. 'It's okay – it's quite recent. But tell me, what does that spectacular ring have to do with me?'

She appeared grateful for my change of subject. 'Not only are we getting married, but Damien's accepted a role in Kuala Lumpur, so we're moving. That means my role – I'm program coordinator at The Helium Project – will need filling, and that's when I thought of you.'

'The Helium Project? I've never heard of it. What do they do?'

'I suppose the easiest way to describe it is to say we help match skills with small business, but there's more to it than that.' She pushed her red-rimmed glasses back to the top of her nose and smiled at me. 'Of course there's more to it than that. It's probably best that I start at the beginning. Our founder is Alexander McInnes. Have you heard of him?' I shook my head. 'Okay. Have you heard of DotPoint?'

I nodded. 'They're one of those companies that regularly feature in those Top Ten Places To Work lists.'

'They certainly are. Alex created DotPoint and is the company's CEO. He's that rare breed of leader who really is passionate about employee engagement. He believes that if our people are happy, a good customer experience will follow.'

'Plus he saves on recruitment expenses and the hidden costs of turnover if you have people perpetually in training.' I grimaced. 'I rarely have less than a dozen roles on the go at the same time. I've tried to talk to my boss about strategies to keep people around at least long enough for us to recoup our investment in them, but he doesn't want to listen. As a result, I spend my days phone recruiting for roles that I'm going to need to fill again in a few months.'

She pulled a face. 'I've been there. Anyway, soon after Alex established DotPoint, he was asked to mentor a group of entrepreneurs at the local Chamber of Commerce. They'd had a stream of experts in to supposedly teach them about various aspects of running a business, but most had a product to sell that the start-ups couldn't really afford to buy. It was a catch-22 – the start-ups needed access to skills they couldn't afford to purchase, yet without that knowledge the likelihood of them succeeding in business was compromised. Alex hit on the idea of setting up a collective of successful business owners, or people with practical knowledge of, say, digital marketing, social media, banking and finance, who were prepared to spend time advising or mentoring start-ups.'

'What's in it for them?' It sounded like a great idea, but I couldn't understand how it covered its own running costs.

'The start-ups all pay a membership fee. That gives

them access to a certain number of hours per year, with all the hours, regardless of the skills, charged at a level that's pegged to their business results. The higher the gross margin, the higher the membership fee. We do that to ensure that as they become more successful, they also begin to pay closer to market value for the services. It's our way of encouraging them to stand on their own feet. The businesses and individuals involved in the mentoring are essentially donating a certain number of hours per year. It's the membership fees, and donations from other companies, that pay our running costs – we're a not-for-profit. But what do they get out of it? Tax breaks, of course – for the companies anyway – but most of these people just want to give back. It wouldn't work otherwise. We even have a pool of people who were retired too early, but still have a lot to offer and aren't ready to put their brains out to pasture. It's a way for them to volunteer their skills and continue to make a difference.' Marion leaned forward and focused her gaze on me. 'My job is to match the start-ups with the resources. Place the skills where they'll be best used. It's human resources, but not as you know it. It's more of a back-to-basics model – using the resources that are available to be the best you can be.' She smiled. 'Which is why I thought of you.'

'Oh?'

'Remember when we both attended that conference a couple of years back?' I nodded. 'Well, when we were drinking in the hotel bar after everyone else had gone out, you said that when you fell into this game you had all these great ideas about being able to place people where their skills would be of most use. You said it was about helping everyone reach their full potential. If I remember correctly – and I generally do,' I laughed at that, 'you even used the word "nurture". You said you wanted to create a workspace where people felt safe and nurtured and able to grow. This job is exactly that – we're nurturing small business and helping people grow. You'd be doing much more than running a departure lounge.'

Her point made, Marion sat back in her chair and sipped at her coffee, her red lipstick staining the side of the cup. 'What do you think?' she asked.

What she'd described was as far removed from my current job as it was possible to be. After all these years of gap-filling, performance-managing and exit interviews, I'd forgotten the reasons why I'd gotten into HR in the first place. Marion obviously hadn't. This could be my opportunity to do what I'd once dreamed of doing. I felt the hairs at the back of my neck rise as goosebumps of excitement spread across my chest and down my arms. It would mean stepping away from the security of a large corporation and into the uncertainty of something that might not have a future, but I was very tempted to do just that.

'It sounds completely amazing,' I told her.

'Of course you'll need to go through the application and interview process – and the end decision is up to our CEO, Pip Donovan – but I think you'd be in with a chance. We want someone who truly wants to do more than place bums on seats – and you were the first person who came to mind.'

'I'm flattered, but also really excited.'

'I'm glad. We wouldn't be able to offer you a whole lot more money than what you're getting now, and of course there's more risk involved –'

'You're really selling it now, aren't you?' I laughed.

'I know, right? Seriously though, you'd have a lot more autonomy and the satisfaction of knowing that what you're doing is making a real difference to other people. And you can't put a price on that.'

Back in the office I looked at the folder of performance reviews that Roger had left on my desk. He'd obviously gone for the day, after deciding that each review needed to be scanned and electronically filed as a matter of urgency. It was obviously payback from the meeting this morning, but I wasn't about to let Roger ruin my mood. I sat down at my desk and googled The Helium Project.

The website didn't tell me anything different to what Marion had told me, although the pages of testimonials from entrepreneurs made for good reading. And the more I read, the more I was convinced that this job was for me.

'When you think about it, it's a fabulous solution,' I said to Jamie that evening. 'I have so many applicants come across my desk who are in their mid-fifties and have been forced out of their careers way too early. Some can afford to retire but aren't ready to – they want to do something to keep their brain active. How satisfying would it be to harness those skills to help grow someone else's business?'

Jamie kissed the top of my head as he topped up my glass of champagne. He'd arrived at my place with groceries and French champagne to toast, as he'd put it, our fresh start.

'It sounds like a great opportunity,' he said, moving back to the other side of the bench where he was slicing and dicing vegetables for a Thai green curry that he'd promised me would be the best Thai green curry I'd eaten outside of Phuket. I knew he was referring to the special holiday we'd had there.

'Of course I mightn't get it, and it's not going to be advertised for another couple of weeks,' I said, 'but the more I think about it, the more I want it. It really sounds like me, don't you think?'

He paused slightly before answering. 'It does, but you also need security and this job sounds like it won't have much of that.'

'I suppose.'

He raised his head from the chopping board and smiled into my eyes. The bubbles I'd been drinking joined hands and skipped through my veins.

'Anyway, babe, let's not think about that now,' he said. 'You mightn't even get the job. You know what? I think dinner can wait. But I can't wait to kiss you again.'

'You don't have to,' I said, and walked around to take the spoon from his hand.

Much later, with dinner finally cooked and eaten, Jamie poured me another wine while he washed up – something he'd never done before.

'You sit there and talk to me,' he said. 'It'll only take a few minutes. Besides, I made the mess so it's only fair that I clean it up.' His rueful smile indicated that he wasn't just talking about the dishes. 'Have I told you just how sorry I am for hurting you?'

'It's forgotten,' I said. It wasn't, but if he continued as he was tonight, it soon would be. I eased myself off the stool and found a tea towel. When Jamie raised his eyebrows, I said, 'You might have made the mess, but I enjoyed the product of it.'

He nodded and grinned. 'Fair enough. So what did you say this collective was called? Who set it up?'

'It's The Helium Project, and Alexander McInnes, from DotPoint, came up with the idea. I'd heard of DotPoint, but not of him.'

'I've met Alex McInnes,' he said. 'He seemed a bit full of himself, but he must be doing something right – either that or he surrounds himself with the right people. Actually, I think it's probably the latter.'

'How did you meet him?'

'I went for a job at DotPoint – a project director role. I think he was threatened by the suggestions I made to improve the structures of his change-management policy and project office. He might be full of ideas, but he's not so great on execution. As it turned out, I'm glad I didn't get the job – I'm enjoying this one much better. You'd be good over there though – you've got good skills, and you're a woman. McInnes strikes me as being one of those men who doesn't like to have anyone on his staff who'll stand up to him.'

The bubbles that had been dancing in my veins lost some of their effervescence and I felt myself stand a little straighter. 'Are you saying I'd fit in because I'm a yes woman? Besides, I wouldn't be working for him. I'd be working with Pip Donovan. Alex stays away from the day-to-day operations at Helium.'

'Of course that's not what I'm saying. Just that McInnes doesn't like men whose skills are better than his.' He placed his soapy hands on my shoulders, drawing me towards him. 'But that won't be an issue for you.'

Before I could think too much about what that comment might mean, he lowered his lips to mine. By the time he raised his head to smile slowly into my eyes, I'd forgotten what I'd been annoyed about. He gently pushed me back against the counter, pulled my shirt up and over my head, and nuzzled at my breasts through my bra.

'Now,' he murmured, 'what were we talking about?'

'Nothing important,' I moaned.

'That's what I thought.'

CHAPTER THIRTEEN

The next couple of weeks should have been like a dream come true, yet for reasons I couldn't quite put my finger on, things felt a bit flat.

Jamie was as attentive as he had been when we first got together, calling me regularly during the day, and sending me texts that made my toes curl and my heart race in anticipation of him doing what they promised. Although he was often busy with work during the week, and committed each Sunday morning to the running group he'd joined to prepare for the half-marathon, he made sure to see me at least a couple of times a week.

When he got up early to leave one Sunday morning, I did my best to persuade him to come back to bed. 'You've been training during the week. Why don't you miss this morning's run and go this afternoon? I'll make it worth your while.' I pouted in a way that I hoped was seductive rather than ridiculous.

'Don't tempt me,' he said, bending down to tweak my nipple. 'You have no idea how much I want to stay here with you, but Josh is having problems with motivation and I promised I'd help him through it. I can't let him down. You understand, don't you, babe?'

He looked so torn that I felt guilty for asking. 'I'm sorry. If you committed to Josh, of course you should go.'

He surprised me that evening with a bunch of flowers and the ingredients for spaghetti bolognaise.

'What are these for?' I asked, burying my nose in the flowers' perfume to hide the blush in my cheeks.

'For understanding. It means a lot to me that you do.'

At that point Hen stalked out of her room, said, 'Oh, you're back then, are you?' to Jamie, and, without waiting for an answer, slammed out of the apartment. We heard her heavy boots thudding down the stairs. She'd returned from Bali a few days ago and I was already wishing she hadn't.

'I really need to give her her marching orders,' I said.

'Oh, Hen's alright. I think you might be overly critical, babe.' He smiled to take the edge off his words.

'But she –' I didn't get to finish as Jamie pulled me in for a long and very satisfactory kiss.

When I suggested taking it to the bedroom, he said, 'Not yet. Let me cook you a meal, and we'll eat it on our laps watching the television and chat a bit.'

It was as if he'd read my mind. We never just sat and talked – about our future, our dreams, anything.

Dinner was lovely, and it was nice to eat together

so casually, but despite Jamie's intention for us to talk, neither of us had a lot to say. Later, after he'd gone home – citing an early meeting – I wondered why he'd distracted me from talking about Hen. It wasn't the first time he'd changed the subject or avoided an argument with a kiss. As lovely as it was for us not to argue, it felt as though things were left unresolved. But I pushed my concerns away and reminded myself that I had what I'd wanted – Jamie back in my life. And this time he seemed keen for it to work.

Although Tiff was as unhappy about Jamie's reappearance as I thought she'd be, she managed not to be too judgemental.

'I know you're worried about me,' I told her, 'but he's trying so hard to make it work this time. And when you think about it, I was just as much to blame for our break-up last time. It was one drunken indiscretion and I blew it out of all proportion. If I'd believed his apologies back then and trusted him, he wouldn't have left.'

'Hmmmm,' she said. 'That's not how I remember it, but let's not argue about that now. Just promise me you haven't put everything and everybody on hold for him like you did last time.'

'No. I'm still going to belly dancing on Tuesdays.'

'He hasn't even asked you to give it up? Mentioned something about how he wants to spend every second with you?'

I screwed my nose up.

'Ha! He has, hasn't he?'

'Maybe, but I didn't give in,' I said proudly.

It had been the cause of our first almost-argument since getting back together.

'It's just a dance class,' he'd said, punctuating his words with feather-light kisses down the side of my neck. 'Can't you change it to Wednesday night instead? Otherwise, with me having to work late on Monday and train on Wednesday, I'm not going to see you again until Thursday.'

I'd stiffened, all desire immediately forgotten. 'It's not "just a dance class", any more than your training is "just training" or your Sunday morning runs are "just runs". It's something I enjoy.' I'd pushed myself away from him. 'Here's an idea – how about you change your training session to Tuesday nights?'

'Babe,' he'd soothed, reaching for me again, 'I only ask because I miss you when we're apart, and the thought of going from Sunday to Thursday without seeing you drives me insane. I'm mad for you. Don't you feel the same?'

His hand had pushed under my shirt to cup my breast, and his thumb flicked at my nipple, threatening to dissolve my assertiveness.

'Of course I do,' I said. 'But you can always change your training session if you want to see me before Thursday.'

He'd pulled his hand out of my shirt and moved away from me. 'If you're going to take that attitude, I may as well go home.'

He looked expectantly at me, as if he knew I'd change my mind, which annoyed me even more than his expectation that I'd give up something I enjoyed for him. I'd missed having him in my bed for several months; I was sure I could manage another night.

'That's your call,' I said.

He picked up his keys and walked towards the front door, then hesitated – perhaps to give me the opportunity to reconsider. When I stood firm, he turned back and swept me up in his arms, kissing me soundly.

'I can't stay away from you,' he said, leading me towards the bedroom.

'Anyway,' I said to Tiff now, 'I don't want to talk about Jamie any more. I want to hear about what's going on with you. How was your date with Jake? Have you seen him again?'

Tiff turned away to signal to the waiter that we needed more drinks. 'It was okay. I've seen him since, but it's only sex. I've made sure that he understands that.' She paused for a mouthful of wine. 'He's managed to convince me to get my camera gear back out.'

I raised my brows at that. After years of declaring she'd be a world-famous travel photographer, Tiff had put her equipment away in the last year of school and announced that the dream was over and she'd never take another picture in her life. She'd never spoken about her reasons why.

She fiddled with her phone, then handed it to me. 'I took these the other weekend in Sydney.' She looked away as I flicked through the photos.

'Where were they taken?' I asked.

'Cockatoo Island. Jake was doing a story on the islands in the harbour, so I went along with him. It was a miserable day. We both got soaked.'

'Tiff, these are fabulous.'

She'd managed to give the derelict warehouse interiors a lofty sparseness, while infusing the images with texture and light. My favourite was the shipyard reflected in a puddle of water, but it was the portrait of Jake that took my breath away. Somehow she'd managed to get the twinkle in his eyes as he looked beyond the lens to the woman behind it. For all its simplicity, it was a very sexy picture.

I shot a look at Tiff, who was staring wistfully at the photo. 'He looks nice,' I said.

Nice was an understatement. There was a natural warmth about him that came through in the photos.

'He is. In fact, I'd go as far as to say that if he had a decent job and a decent salary and a decent wardrobe, I could fall for him. But as is, he's just a good distraction from what's going on at work.'

'What's going on at work?'

'Ainsley, of course. You know, I had my suspicions when she first came across six months ago. Everyone thought she was so nice, as if butter wouldn't melt in her mouth, but I didn't believe any of it. I'd seen her in action in Sydney, when the Alice and Luke thing blew up and Alice was made redundant. I always suspected she had a hand in it.'

I nodded. 'Yes, I remember you saying you thought she'd spread the rumours. But what does that have to do with you?'

'Ainsley's one of those women who doesn't think there's room for other women at the top, so she sees us all as threats. She gets off on emasculating men and taking their power away, and from grinding her heel into the hand of any woman with a hand on the ladder behind her. I'm that woman and I'm refusing to let go, so she's doing her best to break me. Her biggest problem is that as long as I continue to perform she can't do a thing about me. She actually took me aside the other day and told me straight up that she's loading me up with more project work so I can't achieve my portfolio targets. I told her I'd be seeing her at the Masters conference this year, and she told me not to pack my suitcase just yet. Bitch. I'll show her.'

She reset her shoulders, as if the subject of Ainsley was closed, and smiled. 'Now, fill me in on Alice and Tommy. She seems to be seeing an awful lot of him lately.'

'She is. He's lovely and seems besotted. As for how she feels – I'm not sure. She's certainly enjoying his company, and she doesn't seem nearly as hungry these days.'

Tiff laughed at that. 'Well, that's something, I suppose.'

'I get the feeling though that she's determined to make him fit the picture of who she says she wants – if you know what I mean.'

Tiff was silent for a moment, then said, 'Are you sure you're not doing the same thing with Jamie? Determined to make it work this time?'

'Of course I'm not. Our situation is very different.' Even though I hadn't hesitated in my response, I could hear the lack of conviction in my voice.

'Is it, Cal?'

I lifted my chin and met her eyes. 'Absolutely.'

She smiled and nodded, but I didn't think she believed me.

Although I'd spoken to my parents since Jamie and I'd got back together, I hadn't told them about us. It felt too new for me to share just yet; and, as happy as I was, there was part of me that still felt uncertain about our future.

As it turned out, I didn't need to worry about telling them – Clio did.

She'd phoned one night when Jamie was at my

place. We'd just finished making love and I'd come out to the kitchen to get a glass of water, and when my phone rang I'd answered it automatically. We'd chatted for a couple of minutes about her pregnancy and then Jamie had called to me from the bedroom. I hoped she hadn't heard him, but Clio's hearing was far better than that.

She was silent for a couple of seconds, then said, 'Who was that, Cal?'

'Jamie.' My voice was small, but she had no problems hearing it either.

'Jamie Jamie?'

'Yes.'

'I see.' I didn't think she did. 'How long has it been back on?'

'Not long,' I said. 'I would have told you, but it's still quite new.'

'I see,' she said again. 'Mum will be happy.'

My mother had always liked Jamie. He was the sort of man who was good with mothers. On the few occasions we'd visited them, he'd been completely charming – offering to help with dinner and clear away afterwards, and asking the right questions about whatever it was Mum was researching at the time. I'd never told Mum the whole story about what went wrong between us, but even though she'd said that I was probably better off without him, I was sure she thought I was to blame.

'And you? What do you think about it?' I asked Clio.

'I just want you to be happy.'

'That doesn't sound very convincing. I thought you liked Jamie.'

'I do. He's easy to like. I know how much he hurt you though, and I don't want to see that happen again.'

'It's different this time,' I said. 'He said he needs me, and that leaving was a big mistake.'

'Okay, just be careful. You know where I am if you need to talk.'

Mum phoned me first thing the next morning, and wasted no time expressing her pleasure at the news.

'I don't know what happened between you two, but I'm glad you've both come to your senses. What I don't understand is why you didn't tell us,' she said.

'I think I was scared that it wasn't real,' I confessed. 'I didn't want to say anything in case I got hurt again.'

'I can understand that,' she replied after a brief pause. 'I hope for your sake that it works this time. Your father and I would like to see both our girls settled and happy.'

'What about Angus?'

'Who knows what Angus is up to? We certainly don't. Besides,' she laughed, 'he seems to be having way too much of a good time to think about settling in one place, let alone with one girl.'

Marion called to say her job would be advertised the following week and promised to send me a link when the ad went live. I brushed up my resumé, researched The Helium Project some more, and read whatever I could find online about Pip Donovan and Alexander McInnes. I was as ready as I could be for the interview – if my resumé was good enough to get me through the first round.

I was surprised that Marion hadn't mentioned Jamie being interviewed at DotPoint when she and I first met, so I asked her about it.

'Jamie mentioned he'd had the opportunity to meet your CEO,' I said.

'Really? When was that?'

'Not that long ago. He said he applied for a project director role, but was unsuccessful.'

Her response was some time in coming. 'That's right. I did hear something about that. Apparently he wasn't the right fit – or something.'

It was fortunate Marion couldn't see my raised eyebrows. 'Not the right fit' was HR speak for 'his skills are good but there was something we didn't like'.

'Really?' I said.

'I'm not clear on the details – I wasn't really involved. Jodie Lawrence, the HR manager over there, would know more. I heard he left GNA anyway. Where is he now?'

'SourceData. He's their project director.'

'Good, I'm glad he found something.' And she changed the subject to her wedding and relocation plans.

I felt there was something else going on below the surface, but didn't think I could push Marion any further.

Kerry wandered into my office as we finished our call. I was still contemplating what Marion hadn't told me about Jamie, so when Kerry made a laughing comment about how attentive Andy had been to me at the pub on Friday night, I snapped at her, 'I'm not interested in Andy!'

Confused hurt immediately spread across her face.

Rubbing at my forehead, I softened my tone. 'I'm sorry, Kerry, I didn't mean to snap. It's been a crazy morning.'

I couldn't really blame her for asking. Even I'd noticed the way Andy had switched his attentions from Flick to me. Only a few weeks ago I would have welcomed it, but now I just found it amusing. When I'd told Alice about it, she'd said that all the fabulous sex I was having must be sending off signals. I tended to think Andy was more attracted by the fact that I was no longer interested in him.

'I'm back with Jamie and things are going well,' I told Kerry, for about the fifth time that week. 'I'm absolutely not interested in Andy Campbell. In fact, I'm sure that the only reason he's flirting with me is because he can sense I'm off the market.'

'But –'

I reached over and rested my hand on hers. 'Please

don't, Kerry. I'm not going there – and nor should you. Someone's going to come along who will make your heart sing, and you'll wonder what it was you ever saw in Andy Campbell.'

She sighed heavily. 'Like you with Jamie?'

I paused for a beat. Did Jamie make my heart sing? I couldn't answer truthfully so I avoided the question.

'It'll be like the shimmy-walk,' I said instead. 'It'll happen when you're no longer thinking about it.'

'Do you really believe that?'

I nodded. 'I absolutely do. When the time is right and when we're least expecting it, we'll nail that shimmy-walk.'

Kerry grinned. 'And find the one who makes our heart sing.'

CHAPTER FOURTEEN

'I've had the best idea for your birthday,' Alice said when I answered my phone.

'Sorry?'

'Your birthday – next Saturday, remember? Tommy's not sure he can come, and in case he doesn't, you're coming with me. In fact, even if Tommy does end up coming, you are too. Besides, Mum and Dad would love to see you, and so would Laura and Mick. You won't believe how much the boys have grown. You know she's got five of them now? Unless she's managed to pop out another one that I've forgotten about. You'd think they'd have worked out what causes it by now. I'm sure Mum gave Laura the same talk she gave me.'

'Sorry, Alice, what are you talking about?'

'Mick's fortieth birthday. It's at the surf club next Friday night and I told Laura I was inviting you as well and it's your birthday on Saturday. She said that was a great idea and it's ages since she's seen you. Do you realise you haven't been up there since that summer you spent with us before you went away to uni? Wow, that was a long time ago.'

I remembered that summer very well.

'So,' Alice was saying, 'you're invited. And because it's yes month, you have to come.'

'But what about Jamie?'

I heard her sigh. 'What about him? You have a life away from him – just as he obviously does away from you. Where is he this weekend?'

'He had to go to Sydney for something.'

Actually, he'd been quite vague about his plans. I'd noticed, but hadn't pushed him on it in case he thought I was slipping back into my old suspicious patterns. In any case, he'd distracted me before I could.

'There you go. And next weekend, you have plans – you're coming to the Sunshine Coast with me. Maybe even with Tommy and me. We're flying up on Friday morning so you'll need to put in for an annual leave day. We'll fly home on Sunday. It'll be fun – just like when we were teenagers.'

'Except we're not teenagers, and you'll be smooching with Tommy and I'll be alone.'

'If Tommy comes,' she reminded me. 'And if he doesn't – well, that could be fun too.'

'Alice!'

'Yes, well, I've been sensible for a long time. And I'm sure there's something in the rules that says all responsibility is suspended if you retrace your teenage years.' I could hear the grin in her voice when she added,

'And that, my dear Cal, is exactly what we're going to do.'

A memory filled my mind – soft lips on a dark beach, the waves glinting in the moonlight, the noise of the band from the surf club. No, next weekend would be nothing like that.

Jamie was put out when I told him my plans for the following weekend. 'But I've hardly seen you,' he complained. 'And I'm in Sydney for a few days this week, and there's the work offsite at the end of the week. If you go away it means I won't see you until next week.'

I didn't point out that he was the one who'd been occupied last weekend, and for parts of the one before.

'I'll miss you too,' I said, 'but I'm looking forward to catching up with Alice's family again. I haven't been up there for years – not since I was eighteen.'

'Even so,' he sulked, 'what about me? Aren't you looking forward to seeing me too?'

That's when I realised he'd forgotten my birthday was next weekend. I'd thought he was concerned we wouldn't be able to celebrate it together on the day, but it had obviously completely slipped his mind. Perversely, I didn't remind him.

Jamie confirmed it when he called me as I was heading to the airport on Friday morning. 'The offsite's been extended for the weekend,' he said. 'We didn't get through as much of the agenda as they wanted to, so I'm stuck here. It's just as well you didn't change your plans for me, hey?'

He laughed, but I didn't laugh with him.

'I probably won't get a chance to call again,' he said, 'so I'll see you on Sunday night, okay?'

Yes, he'd forgotten my birthday. Any lingering guilt I had about going away with Alice and leaving him behind for the weekend vanished.

'That's fine,' I said. 'I'll see you then.'

As it turned out, Tommy was able to come with us. Our discount flight was late to land, but Laura was waiting at Sunshine Coast Airport for us with her latest baby in her arms. Tommy and I hung back while Alice gave her a hug and made appropriate interested-aunt comments.

'Oh, hasn't he grown? I really think he's starting to look like you, Laura.'

'Cut the crap, Ally, I know you have little interest until they're toilet-trained,' Laura said. 'But it's nice that you try.'

Alice grinned. 'Laura, this is my boyfriend, Tommy – I've told you about him. And you remember Callie, don't you?'

Laura held her hand out to shake Tommy's. 'Pleased to meet you, Tommy. You're very welcome.' She turned and hugged me as closely as the baby between us allowed. 'I'm so glad you could come, Callie. It's been way too long.'

Laura looked great. Her wavy brown hair had

been chopped and cropped so it could be styled with her fingers, and seemed to move with her. And dressed casually in three-quarter-length khaki pants, flip-flops and an oversized linen shirt, without a scrap of make-up, she looked every inch the Earth Mother. It suited her. While we waited for the luggage I told her so.

'You think?' she said. 'All I see when I look in the mirror is a bum that is definitely wider than it was last year, boobs that Mr Gravity has not been kind to, and hips that are very definitely child-bearing.'

I laughed. 'What I see is tanned and line-free skin, and curves you could run a grand prix on.'

'Thankfully Mick has always liked those bits – although perhaps just a little too much?' She looked ruefully down at baby number five.

'What's his name?' I asked.

'Matthew. We figured if we named him after my absentee brother, he might decide to visit once in a while.'

Up until a few weeks ago, it had been years since I'd heard Matt Delaney's name. Lately it seemed as though I couldn't escape it.

'Are you going back to try for a girl?' Alice asked.

'Are you happy to walk from the airport?'

'That's a no then?'

Laura threw Alice the sort of exasperated look that big sisters learn very early in life.

'Seriously though,' Alice went on, 'you really do

look great. You inherited Mum's olive skin, whereas both Matt and I burn easily – although at least he tans. I have to do the whole slip-slop-slap thing before venturing near anything that resembles sun. It's probably lucky I live in Melbourne.'

'Yes, but you got that fabulous red hair. I just got brown.'

Bags retrieved, Laura loaded us into her people-mover for the short drive to her house. 'We'll drop in so you can see the boys before the party tonight,' she said. 'Then I'll take you around to Mum and Dad's.'

Alice's parents had moved from their Brisbane home into the Mooloolaba holiday house permanently a few years back – about when it became clear that Laura wasn't going to be content with a small family.

Mick had built Laura's dream house – a restored Queenslander – on one of the high points in Buderim. You could see across to the coast and all the way up to Mount Coolum. He'd swapped the carpets for highly polished western red cedar boards, and replaced the aluminium windows with reclaimed materials and shutters. A wide verandah designed to catch the sea breezes wrapped around the exterior, and the house was perched high on the pedestals that gave Queenslanders their charm and practicality.

The living area was completely open plan, because, Laura explained, it meant fewer doors for the boys to either forget to shut, slam shut, or slam into. The central point of the space was a kitchen with benches fashioned from the same red cedar as the floor, and a large red Provençal-style oven and stove providing colour and warmth.

I heard the thunder of feet running down the hall from the bedrooms: the boys. I had a feeling I'd be deaf by the time the weekend was over, and was glad we were staying with Alice's parents.

'Ally!' Newton (number four) stopped in front of his aunt for a pick-up, an aeroplane hug and a present. Alice might have pretended otherwise, but she was a generous aunt.

The other three hung around waiting their turn. Kyle, the eldest at twelve, was too cool to show his excitement, and way too cool for a kiss, but just cool enough for a hair ruffle and a jacket in the colours of his favourite footy team.

Fraser, next in line, was skinny and blond and the spitting image of Mick. He didn't know quite how cool he was yet, and wasn't as into football as his brothers, so got a kiss and a magic kit.

Quinn was middle child personified. With Laura's brown hair and olive skin, and his dad's piercing blue eyes, he was too busy trying to grab Kyle's jacket to say hello. Luckily Alice had a matching jacket for him.

Once the boys had said their hellos and got their presents, they ran off as loudly as they'd arrived.

'The joys of school holidays,' said Laura, a tired

smile on her face. 'I'll put the kettle on. Mick will be out of the office soon – he's just on a call.'

'Here,' I said. 'Let me take Matthew for you.'

Laura handed the baby across, and I cuddled him to my chest, inhaling that sweet smell only babies have.

'Oh god, don't let Callie near the baby!' Alice said. 'She's likely to take him home.'

I pulled a face at her, and asked Laura, 'Does Mick usually work from home?'

'Not normally. He's taken a half-day on account of the party tonight.'

'What does he do?' Tommy asked, finally finding his voice.

Alice answered. 'He's got his own building company and mostly does renovations and restorations of Queenslanders – houses similar to this one, designed to capture the breeze and disperse the heat. He saw a gap in the market soon after he finished doing this one up, and now he's in quite high demand.'

'We've got clients down in Brisbane, and up as far as Maryborough and Hervey Bay,' Laura added.

When Mick joined them, the noise started again as the boys grappled to be first to greet him and show him the presents Alice had brought. He had a smile and a hair ruffle for each of them, giving them his full attention before greeting Tommy and me.

'Pleased to meet you,' he said, shaking Tommy's hand. 'And little Callie. How long has it been?' He hugged me briefly.

'I don't know, Mick. A while, I guess.'

'Too long. That's how long!'

Mick, for all his blokey gruff exterior, was one of the most kind-hearted men I knew. Not that much taller than Laura, he had the type of strength that could only be gained from hard physical labour – something he'd done nearly every day of his adult life. Tanned, blond and blue-eyed, he looked years younger than the forty we were celebrating tonight. He and Laura were childhood sweethearts and had been together since she was sixteen and he was nineteen. After they'd been dating for a month he'd announced he was going to marry her. She'd replied that she didn't intend ever getting married, and they broke up briefly when she started uni, but Mick never gave up and eventually she said yes. Alice said he was as devoted to Laura now as he had been when he first fell for her.

Part of me envied that, and I wondered if anyone would ever feel that way about me. Jamie was certainly being attentive these days, but I couldn't imagine him ever looking at me the way Mick was now looking at Laura. Or being as genuinely attentive to his boys as Mick was.

In the early days of our relationship I'd asked Jamie whether he wanted children, but didn't get a clear answer. He'd said something like, 'There's plenty of time to be thinking about things like that', and then distracted me in the best way he knew how.

Back then, I'd thought there was plenty of time too. Now, cuddling baby Matthew, I wasn't so sure. It felt like time was running out. But try as I might, I couldn't see Jamie's face as the father of my children.

CHAPTER FIFTEEN

After a lunch of sandwiches, and leaving Mick with the kids, Laura piled us back into the car for the short drive down to the beach and the Delaneys' house.

I hadn't been here since the summer that school finished. I'd stayed here with Alice's family for a couple of weeks in the time between when the schools went back and university started.

Back then this was still a holiday house and Alice's father would work in Brisbane during the week and drive up to join us every Friday night. Laura had finally given in and said yes to Mick and they were away on their honeymoon. Mrs Delaney mostly pottered about in the garden and sunbaked, so Matt, Alice and I were left to our own devices. Matt spent most of his time in the surf with his mates, and Alice and I ran free.

That holiday was the first time Tiff wasn't with us. Her parents had separated midway through our final year at school, and her mother had moved to Perth where the head office of the company she was a director of was based. To avoid her father, who was still wondering what had gone wrong, Tiff had managed to find herself a job for the entire summer break, so wasn't able to join us.

Despite Tiff's absence, it was the type of summer holiday that was hazily perfect. Long hot days filled with sun, surf and flirting. At eighteen, I felt very grown-up – as if I was on the brink of something. Alice was playing a couple of boys off against each other as she decided which one she preferred, but I only had eyes for Matt. I tried not to be too obvious about it, but he was impossible to ignore. Tall, tanned and lean, with the types of muscles that were made on a surfboard, not inside a gym.

There were plenty of girls only too eager to show their appreciation of him, but he always had a twinkle in his eye and an easy grin for me. He'd ruffle my hair as he went by and say, 'Hey, Calliope, all okay?' He was the only person, other than my mother, who ever called me by my given name and it felt like a secret just between us.

Alice's parents greeted me as a long-lost almost daughter. 'Why has it been so long, Callie?'

'I don't know, Mrs Delaney. You know how it is.'

'It's Jane and Tony now – you're too old for this Mr and Mrs Delaney rubbish. Now, I've put you in Laura's old room, and Alice and Tommy are in her old room.'

'Great. So Callie gets the double bed and we get the singles? That's not fair.'

I couldn't help grinning as I watched Alice regress to a teenager. 'It's okay, Jane,' I said. 'Alice and Tommy can have Laura's room. I don't mind the single bed. It'll be just like it was the last time I was here.'

Sleeping arrangements sorted, Jane filled us in on the schedule for the rest of the evening. 'We'll need to be dressed and ready to leave here by five so we can finish setting up the function room. Laura, Mick and the boys will be there by six so we can get the boys something to eat before everyone else descends. The rest of the guests will arrive around seven. We have a DJ, and mostly cocktail or finger food. If anyone wants more than that, they can go downstairs and get it themselves. Tony and I will take the kids home once they've had enough at about nine. We need to duck down now to make sure the food and cake are under control, so we'll leave you guys to it.'

Once they'd gone, Alice and Tommy started making eyes at each other as if they'd like some alone time, so I walked the short distance down to the beach. When we'd driven along the Esplanade earlier, I'd seen evidence of the developments that had sprung up in the years since I'd last been here, but the beach itself hadn't changed.

Taking my shoes off and rolling my jeans up to the knee, I went down to the water's edge and walked along the hard sand, leaping back every so often as a wave caught me unaware. Even in July, the middle of winter, there were people on the beach and in the water.

That last summer we'd spent nearly every waking

hour down here, lazing about on our towels on the sand, or gathered in groups up on the grass. Alice needed to be careful of the sun, but in true Alice style managed to turn her floppy hat and cover-all into a boho fashion statement that the rest of us aspired to. I remembered wishing I had the confidence of the girls who fawned all over Matt with their skinny bodies and skimpy bikinis. My breasts and bum were slightly too big for fashion. When I'd recently looked back at the photos from that time I thought I'd looked sexy and vital, but back then I'd felt lumpy, uncomfortable and inexperienced.

But none of that had seemed to worry Matt that night on the beach. He'd told me he liked the way I looked. And when he gazed at me the way he did, and touched me as he had, I'd believed him.

My heart had skipped a beat earlier when Alice had asked Laura whether Matt would be there tonight. I'd held my breath for a few seconds, releasing it only when Laura replied that she'd invited him but hadn't heard back. 'But there's nothing new in that,' she'd said. 'He never replies. One day he'll surprise us all by just turning up.'

By the time I got back from the beach, Alice and Tommy had resurfaced. And Jane and Tony returned soon after. Tommy parked himself in front of the television next to Tony so they could get to know one another, while Alice and I took a bottle of wine into her bedroom and helped each other get ready the way we used to as teenagers.

I'd chosen to wear a vintage rose-coloured fifties-style dress that sat just off my shoulders, nipped in tightly at the waist, dipped quite low to just above my breasts, and flared out to a relatively full skirt. I intended to dance so paired it with sensible ballet flats. Alice pinned my hair into a messy up-do, and we rimmed my eyes heavily with a smoky liner. The whole effect seemed too much for a beachside party, but Alice assured me that everyone was using it as an excuse to dress up.

She'd scrunched her red curls so they appeared even more riotous, and was wearing a black floral-patterned chiffon maxi-dress that dipped dangerously low in front and was split just as dangerously high. There was so much fabric floating around her as she walked that you weren't quite sure just how high the split went. She'd paired it with high-heeled black boots, and accentuated the almond shape of her eyes so they were more cat-like than usual. On anyone else the combination would have been way too much, but on Alice it was perfect.

Tommy's eyes were wide when he saw her. 'Wow!'

Tony shook his head with the sort of exasperation common to the father of a daughter who'd had her own ideas about fashion from a very early age.

Alice grinned and kissed his cheek. 'I love you too, Dad. If we're all ready, let's go and get this party started,' she announced, linking arms with Tommy and me.

•

I'd just come off the dance floor and was talking to Tommy when I felt a prickle at the back of my neck, as though someone was watching me. I turned and there he was. Tommy was still talking, but I couldn't hear a thing. Nothing existed except the man striding across the room towards me. Matt Delaney.

'Well, well, well,' he said. 'Little Calliope Jones — and looking very grown-up.'

I felt the warmth of his gaze as it slid from my face to my feet, and back up my body, lingering ever so briefly on my breasts. Briefly, but long enough that my nipples tingled under the bodice that suddenly seemed too small. Fourteen years might have passed since I'd seen him, but the effect he had on me was the same. The only difference was that now I knew what the butterflies in my belly and warmth between my legs meant.

I looked up into his face. He'd changed, but not so much that I wouldn't have known him. His face was leaner and his jaw firmer, and although he had a few lines around his eyes and the beginning of faint creases in his forehead, his eyes still twinkled as if he'd just stopped laughing. He seemed taller, but then to me he'd always seemed tall, and his shoulders were broad under what appeared to be a very expensive suit. He'd definitely filled out where he needed to. His lilac business shirt was unbuttoned enough for me to see a few hairs peeking out, and his tie was hanging loosely from his hands.

An image of him using the tie to bind my hands together so he could ravage me shot through my brain before I could catch it. Oh, Callie, I scolded myself, this is going to be a very long weekend if you react like that. *Remember Jamie. Remember Jamie.* Maybe if I repeated it often enough and didn't look into his eyes, I'd be okay.

'Hi Matt,' I said, and stepped forward so he could kiss my cheek. I looked up into his eyes and felt the bottom fall out of my world. He was looking at me the way he'd looked at me that night so long ago. The years disappeared and I was eighteen again and he was twenty-one.

Look away, Cal, I told myself. Look away now.

'Is that really your name?' Tommy was asking. 'Calliope?'

'It certainly is,' answered Matt, his gaze still caught in mine, his eyes creasing around the edges as his grin grew wider. 'She was named after that Manfred Mann song, "Blinded by the Light".' Tommy looked blank. 'Come on, man, surely you know it? It's the one where the calliope crashes to the ground.' He held his hand out to Tommy. 'You must be Alice's Tommy. I'm Alice's big brother, Matt.'

Alice chose that moment to come back with fresh drinks. She rested them on the nearest table and threw her arms around Matt. Then she drew back and punched him, quite hard, on the arm.

'Ouch,' he said, rubbing the spot.

'That's for staying away for so long.' She punched him again. 'And that one was for not telling us you were coming.'

He grinned at her. 'I wanted it to be a surprise. Besides, I wasn't sure if I could get away. Things have been pretty manic at work.'

He rubbed at his forehead and, despite his smile, I saw there was a tiredness about his face that I wanted to stroke away. *Remember Jamie. Remember Jamie.*

'Anyway, I made it, although I have to head back early on Sunday to make my Monday meetings,' he said.

'Yeah, yeah, whatever.' She grinned to let him know she was glad he was here. 'Have you introduced yourself to Tommy? And surely you remember Callie?'

He grinned down at me again. 'Of course I remember Callie. She's the real reason I'm here – nothing to do with Mick's fortieth.'

I knew he was joking, but even so my heart fluttered in my chest and I had to stop myself pressing my hand there to keep it from bursting out.

'Tiff told me Callie would be here,' he added. 'So I had to come.'

Tiff . . . Tiff and Matt – they'd had a thing. Did they still? I searched his face for a hint, but found none. He wouldn't flirt with me if there was something between them, would he? Of course he would – he was Matt Delaney. He could flirt with an iceberg.

'I was just telling Tommy that Cal's named after the crashing calliope in the Manfred Mann song,' he went on. 'But he had no idea what I was talking about.'

'You know very well that's not where my name comes from,' I said.

'Perhaps, but I always forget the real reason, and this one is more fun.' He smiled at me and it felt as though it was our private joke fizzing in the space between us.

'If it's not from a song, then where is it from?' asked Tommy.

Alice had disappeared again – presumably to get Matt a drink.

'Yeah, Cal, where's it from?' Matt asked. His head was cocked to one side and he was enjoying the discomfort he knew I felt about explaining my name.

I sighed. 'Calliope was the eldest of the Muses in Greek mythology. My mother was studying Greek ancient history at the time.' I shrugged. 'My younger sister's called Clio – she's another of the Muses.'

'Muse?'

Alice was back. I thought I saw her wink at Matt as she handed him a beer. 'No, Tommy darling, muses lurk about in murals, and burst out of them wearing flowing dresses and roller skates to inspire ordinary men to fall in love with them and create extraordinary things.' He still looked blank. 'Like in *Xanadu*. Surely you saw the movie when you were a kid?'

He shook his head. 'Not that I remember. I was more into *Star Wars*.'

Alice smiled. 'Of course you were. I wonder if anyone other than us actually saw the movie? Maybe they just bought the soundtrack.'

'Is that what you do, Cal – burst out of a mural in a flowing dress to inspire ordinary men to fall in love with you? Like a shooting star in the middle of a million dancing lights?' Matt's eyes were twinkling as he misquoted a line from the song, even though there was no smile on his face.

He moved closer and clinked his glass with mine. *Remember Jamie.*

'The Muses were supposed to be the daughters of Zeus,' I said. 'There were nine of them and each one was responsible for something in the arts. I think that's the only part of the story that *Xanadu* used. Calliope was in charge of inspiring poets. And also, apparently, the lover of the war god, Ares.'

'Aries – like in the sun sign? Why didn't I know that?' asked Alice.

'I'm an Aries,' said Matt, moving even closer.

'But what's the calliope in the song you were talking about?' asked Tommy.

And that's when I heard it – the opening bars of 'Blinded by the Light'. I glared at Alice, who was grinning widely.

'I do believe this is our song,' said Matt, grabbing

my hand and dragging me onto the dance floor. Alice took the wine glass from my hand on the way.

Matt pulled me to him briefly before sending me twirling away again. I could feel the wide skirts of my dress rising as I spun around.

'Remember the last time we danced to this?' he said.

'I do.' I gasped as I hit his chest again.

This time he held me there, one arm around my waist, the other grasping my hand to move us around the floor. 'So do I. We were here at the surf club. You'd been staying with us, and it was the last night before I left to go backpacking for six months.'

'I remember.'

He pulled me in closer, his chin resting on the top of my head. My body was melting to fit against his, and my breasts were squeezed hard against his chest. I knew that if I looked down I'd see their pale globes pushing up against the bodice of my dress.

'We danced to this song, and then we went outside, down to the beach, and sat on the sand and talked,' he said.

I closed my eyes, remembering. It was before they'd put the lights up along the beachfront so it was dark, but the sand was soft. I'd heard soft giggles coming from a little way down the beach and had guessed we weren't alone out there.

'We talked for a long time,' he said softly, before

pushing me away to spin me around. He sang along with the chorus, badly, making me laugh, then pulled me back into him. 'It was a good night. Possibly the best night of my life,' he whispered.

I stopped dancing and looked up at him, my breath freezing in my throat, my heart crashing around like the calliope in the song. The twinkle had gone from his eyes.

'Me too,' I said. 'And the next morning you were gone.'

And I've never stopped wishing you'd stayed. Of course I didn't tell him that. I hadn't realised it myself until this moment.

'Cal, I –'

He didn't get to finish, because Laura grabbed his arm and hugged him close.

'Sorry, Cal, it's been too long since my little brother came home.' She released him and thumped his arm in the same place Alice had punched him. 'How dare you sneak into our party and not tell us you were coming! I send you invitations to these things, but don't really expect you to show up – and yet here you are. I'm so glad to see you!'

He rubbed his arm and grimaced. 'You too, sis. How many kids have you got now?'

'Only five, smart-arse.'

'Five! Man, didn't Mum and Dad give you the talk? Or maybe Mick's dad didn't tell him about keeping it wrapped.' He shied away to deflect another blow.

'Oh, ha ha. Mick only has to look at me and I fall pregnant. And don't you dare say anything,' she warned when Matt seemed about to speak, the twinkle back in his eyes. She gestured towards the tables at the back of the room. 'Anyway, the boys are over there with Mum and Dad. And Mick's probably somewhere near the bar. I'm sorry, Cal, but I'm going to drag him away for a few minutes.'

'That's fine,' I said, smoothing down the skirt of my dress. 'I'll catch up with you later, Matt.' I tried to make the words sound off-hand, as if I didn't really care.

'Oh yes, you will,' he whispered in my ear before Laura pulled him away.

Feeling a little like a shag on a rock in the middle of the dance floor on my own, I wandered back to where Alice and Tommy looked as though they were in the middle of an argument. Or if not an argument, then at least a very animated discussion.

'Sorry,' I said, backing away. 'I'll leave you two to it.'

'You don't have to go, Cal. Tommy was just saying how he wants to go to Bali to do some diving off one of the islands, and I just happened to mention that there's an astrology conference on in Ubud at sort of the same time.'

'And I suggested she could go to the conference, I could go diving, and we could have some time before and after on holiday together.' Tommy's face fell as he tried to understand how that could have upset Alice.

'And I told him I don't do conferences,' Alice said. 'It's a rule of mine. I'm not great with a lot of people in confined spaces.'

'I don't know, I think it sounds like a great idea,' I ventured. 'You've been saying for a while that you want to go away. And don't forget it's yes month. I had to push myself out of my comfort zone to go belly dancing, and to your trivia night, and to come here. So you, my dear, can go to that conference. A little networking will do you good. You've been saying for ages that you need to get to know other people who speak your hocus-pocus language. This is your chance.'

'Hmmmm. I'll think about it,' Alice conceded.

'She'll do it,' I told Tommy.

'You'll love it,' he said. 'I'll make sure you do.' And he smiled at her with adoration in his eyes. He really was quite sweet.

I excused myself and went to the bar to get another glass of wine. I could see Matt in a corner with his parents and some of their friends. He'd taken his jacket off and rolled the sleeves of his shirt up, and was telling a story with his hands in the way I remembered. He looked a long way from the cool sophisticated executive Tiff had described.

My tummy lurched again as I recalled Tiff saying that Matt, or someone just like him, would be her perfect man. Someone who'd put his career first and didn't want children. As tempting as he was, if Matt Delaney didn't want children, he could never be my perfect man. I just had to convince my heart of that fact.

I took my wine out onto the balcony, and looked past the lifeguard's tower to the beach. These days it was lit up like a football field. To get any privacy you'd need to go right down the other end of the beach, away from the Esplanade. Not that I was in any need of such privacy tonight.

I could almost see Matt and me sitting down there on the sand, talking for longer than I'd thought it was possible to talk to anyone for. He'd told me about where he was travelling, what he'd be seeing, and about his dreams for the future. I'd told him that I wasn't sure about the economics university course I'd enrolled in; that I was doing it to keep everyone happy and really wanted to study English literature. I'd told him that I didn't know what I wanted to do with my life. And I'd told him that I wanted him to kiss me. He said he'd been wanting to kiss me all summer. So he did. And it was more than I'd ever dreamed it could be.

We talked some more, and we kissed some more. Then we slept, there on the sand, my head on his chest, his arm holding me close. We woke at dawn, the sky turning pink in the early morning light, the colour mirrored in his eyes. He kissed me again, and we sat wrapped in each other and watched the sun come up. Then we walked home, hand in hand, and crept back to our respective beds – me to the twin bed in Alice's room, and him to the granny flat in the backyard. When I woke, he'd already left for the airport.

That's all we did – kissed and talked and slept – but it was the best night of my life too.

CHAPTER SIXTEEN

Matt found me out there on the balcony, sipping my wine, looking at the waves and remembering another night long ago.

'You know,' he said, 'it was just over there – just behind the lifeguard's tower.'

I nodded, not even pretending to misunderstand.

'I should have written or something,' he said.

I didn't tell him that I'd hoped he'd contact me. That somehow he'd got my address so he could send me a postcard, or something. Anything so I knew he hadn't stopped thinking about me, just like I hadn't stopped thinking about him.

Instead I shook my head. 'No, it wouldn't have mattered. We were both too young. You were travelling, and I was going to Sydney for uni. It was a perfect night, and that's where it needed to end.'

I shivered as the chill of the night came through the fabric of my dress. He saw, and put an arm around me to share his warmth.

He gazed out past where the waves were breaking.

'Don't you ever wonder though? You know . . . what if?'

I turned to look at him and immediately wished I hadn't. 'Yes,' I whispered.

'Me too.' He spoke the words a hair's breadth from my lips, and they hovered there between us for a heartbeat, maybe longer.

Then, with a groan, he leaned in to taste my top lip, then my bottom lip. I met his mouth with mine, my palms on his chest, his arms reaching around to hold me fast against him. This kiss was nothing like the easy magical kisses we'd shared all those years ago. It was full of longing and desire and an intensity I'd never felt before – and it scared the hell out of me. Before it all got too much – or too much more – I pushed him away.

With my hand against my mouth – whether to hold the kisses in or to wipe them away, I wasn't sure – I backed away. 'No, this can't have happened.' I shook my head. One tear came out, and then another. 'We can't have just done that.'

'Cal . . .' He moved towards me again and gripped my shoulders. 'What's wrong?'

'What about Tiff?' I blurted out. 'Oh my god! What sort of a woman does that make me? I just kissed my best friend's lover!'

The tears came more persistently. I knew Tiff was sort of dating Jake, but she'd also sort of been dating Matt too. Hadn't she?

'What on earth are you talking about?'

'You and Tiff – I know you've been . . . well, together.' I couldn't look at him. If I did I'd be lost again. 'Even if it was just a sometimes thing, there's the code, you know. The one where you don't go around kissing your best friend's lover – or whatever you were.'

'Callie, listen to me. Tiff and I . . . yes, we've hooked up a few times, but there's nothing between us any more. There never really was. We're just good friends – without the benefits.' I could hear the smile in his voice. 'You haven't done wrong by Tiff, and nor have I. Despite what you might have heard about me from my sister, I don't make a habit of going around kissing other women when I'm in a relationship.'

His words made me cry harder. He might not have cheated, but I had. *What about Jamie?* whispered another voice inside my head.

'Hey? It wasn't that bad, was it?' He was attempting a joke, but his voice sounded worried. 'Please look at me, Cal.'

He tipped my chin up so I had no choice but to look into his eyes. They weren't twinkling any more. They were as dark as the ocean below us.

'No, the kiss was . . . well, you know how it was. Spectacular.' My smile was watery. 'But I'm with someone – I'm with Jamie. And I've kissed you. You mightn't be in the habit of kissing other women when you're in a relationship, and nor am I. But I just have. So what sort of a person does that make me?'

'Oh, Cal.' He put his arms around me and hugged me to his chest.

I sniffed and burrowed deeply into him. I was sure that by now my face was the same colour as my dress, and my nose and eyes a shade darker.

'I'll cover your shirt with make-up,' I said.

'It's okay. At least I'm not wearing white.'

'I guess.'

'Look, I knew you were back with Jamie,' he said after a few seconds. 'Tiff told me when I saw her last week. And I kissed you anyway. So what sort of a man does that make me?'

'But –'

'I kissed you because I wanted to kiss you. In all the time that Tiff and I have been friends, she's never really mentioned you. I knew obviously that the three of you had stayed close, but we didn't really talk about our lives outside of work. And, well . . .'

'The benefits thing?' I said.

'Yes. The benefits thing. But when that stopped, we really started talking, and Tiff mentioned you. For some reason, I haven't been able to stop thinking about you ever since. Or about that night, and what might have happened if I'd stayed. So yes, I knew about Jamie, and I still wanted to kiss you.'

'Oh.'

'And then tonight when I arrived, there you were under the lights.' He smiled weakly. 'It sounds corny, but you looked just the shooting star in the song.'

I lifted my head and looked up at him. He gently brushed away a leftover tear and tucked my hair behind my ear.

'And, just so you know, I'm going to kiss you again. Don't say I didn't warn you,' he whispered as he cradled my face in his hands and lowered his head to mine.

He pushed me into the wall, into the darkness, his hardness insistent against my belly as his tongue plundered my mouth. If there was any resistance left in me, I let it go and gave myself up to the wonder of his kiss, moaning softly in the back of my throat, my hands reaching around his back to pull him even closer.

'Umm, sorry . . . Callie, is that you? And Matt? Oh wow, I didn't see that coming.'

Alice. Shit.

Matt released me, and turned away so he could adjust his trousers and shove his shirt back into his waistband.

I felt the blood that, for a few delightful moments, had been diverted elsewhere rush to my face, and averted my gaze as I straightened my dress. The whole time I could feel Alice's gaze on me. Oh god. She'd caught me kissing her brother. She had to have a rule about that. I knew she had a rule about kissing someone else when you were in a relationship. Well, if she didn't, she should have.

'Your timing, as always, Ally cat, is impeccable,' said

Matt, grinning and once again completely presentable.

'I'd say my timing is spot-on,' replied Alice, looking at me with concern. 'Are you okay, Cal?'

'Yes, I'm fine. I think I need the bathroom though. Excuse me.'

Unable to look at either of them, I scuttled off in the direction of the toilets, and locked myself in a cubicle.

How stupid could I be? Matt Delaney. Alice's brother. Tiff's sometimes lover.

Then there was Jamie. Jamie who, only a few weeks ago, was the one I'd said I wanted. He'd left me because I couldn't trust him, yet here I was carrying on with Matt Delaney as if I was still eighteen and fancying myself in love for the first time. Jamie was at an offsite being the perfect boyfriend, and *I* was the one who couldn't be trusted.

Oh, but those kisses. Matt had kissed me as if he'd been waiting to kiss me for over fourteen years. And I'd kissed him back as if I'd been waiting for him too.

I lowered my face into my hands, feeling the heat of my cheeks against my palms. And Alice saw us. Could this be any worse?

'I know you're in there, Cal.' Alice knocked on the door of my cubicle. 'You can't stay in there all night, you know.'

'I'm going to stay here until I wake up and realise it was all a terrible dream,' I muttered into my hands.

'Kissing my brother was that bad? He must have lost his touch.'

I could hear the grin in her voice and groaned.

'Cal, please come out. Please, sweetie.'

I flushed the toilet and opened the door. In the mirror above the sink, my face seemed paler than usual, with two spots of colour high on my cheeks. My make-up had seen better days, and my hair – the least said about that, the better. It had come out of the loose up-do and was a messy tangle around my face, as though I'd just crawled out of bed. My lips felt swollen and pink, and all traces of gloss had gone. I looked as if I'd been kissed thoroughly.

Alice smiled as she watched me touch my mouth. 'Hello . . . I'm still here.'

I looked away from the mirror, unsure of what I'd see in her face. 'I know what you're going to say, and I'm sorry. I have no idea what . . . I couldn't . . . Oh god, I don't even know what to say to you.'

'Sweetie, it's okay. Seriously.' She hugged me. 'You and Matt have always been unfinished business. Ever since that summer.'

I pulled back and stared at her, my mouth open. 'You know about that? You never said!'

'Of course I knew. I heard the pair of you sneak in that morning. Don't forget we were sharing a room.'

'But I thought you were asleep.' I'd been so quiet and careful.

'I was pretending. And I saw your face the next morning when you got up and realised he'd already left. What happened that night, Cal?'

'Nothing, everything.' I saw her eyes widen. 'Not that! We just talked and kissed, that's all. He didn't take advantage of me or anything like that – although I wish he had.' I paused. 'Why didn't you say anything?'

'I thought you'd tell me if you wanted to. Then before I knew it, you were dropping out of uni to follow that guy to Melbourne. What was his name?'

'Justin.'

We'd met in my first week of uni in Sydney, and he'd taken my mind off Matt – and my virginity. We were together the whole of first year, but didn't last long after we moved to Melbourne. I vaguely remembered thinking that I'd do anything to get him back – until I started seeing Michael. And so the pattern repeated. Jamie had lasted the longest, but he really wasn't any different to the others. None of them were Matt. Matt, who was Tiff's perfect man because he didn't do relationships and didn't want children.

'I asked Matt about you once,' Alice said, 'and he refused to talk about it. That's when I knew you were different.'

'The only thing different about me is that I'm your friend and I didn't sleep with him.'

She shook her head. 'No, Cal, you're different.'

'Well, whether I am or not, I'm with Jamie. What I

just did was wrong.'

'Did it feel wrong?'

I shook my head, and felt the smile come right up from my heart and spread over my face. 'Oh no, it felt so right. But that doesn't make it right.'

'Okay,' Alice said, 'here's the deal. Sometimes rules need to be broken. Maybe this is one of those times. Tonight, tomorrow – it's an interlude. It's your birthday tomorrow, and Matt's leaving on Sunday morning – and so are you. Enjoy it, see what happens. It might help you work out how you really feel about Jamie.'

'What do you mean by that?'

'Do you love him?'

'Jamie?'

'Yes, Jamie.'

I thought for a second.

'Be honest, Cal.'

'I don't know,' I conceded. 'Things are different this time.'

'Do you love my brother?'

'I used to, but that was so long ago. I have no idea how I feel now – he's taken me by surprise.' I giggled, and misquoted Manfred Mann. 'Matt's always dazzled me. With him it's been like looking into the eye of the sun.'

Alice laughed. 'Oh, but darling, that's where the fun is.' She picked up and held one of my hands. 'Seriously though, let go of the "shoulds" for a couple of days and see what happens. It's yes month so you have no choice.'

'When you put it like that,' I said. 'But what do I tell Jamie?'

'That, my dear, is entirely up to you. Tell him, don't tell him – it's your call. This will be our secret.'

When Alice and I resurfaced, my face as repaired as I could make it, Mick was relaying a tale from a wedding he and Laura had recently attended.

'These chicks from Sydney, they ask me what I do, right? I tell them I'm a builder, and one of them's like, "How hard is it to build a house?" So I say, it's not rocket science, mate. All you do is dig a few holes, pour some concrete down, build up a wall and repeat the process until it's as big as it needs to be, which is when you put a roof on.'

As he told the story, one hand held his beer, while the other was buried deep into his jacket pocket. Mick always looked as if he was burrowing in against the cold – even in summer.

'So the chick that asked seems pretty impressed. Her friend, who looks like she's some stuck-up city bitch with a checklist a mile long – you know the ones who won't look at you unless you do the right job and earn the right money? I think she likes tossers. She talks like the girls who like tossers talk, with that really pretentious put-on posh drawl?'

He mimicked it. Yep, I'd heard it in many a fashion store and café in *that* part of Melbourne. Although, she didn't speak like *that*, his mention of the checklist reminded me of Tiff.

'Anyway, this chick thinks she's pretty hot, and she asks me what university I went to. I'm like, you're fucking joking, aren't you, mate? And then she says something like a builder isn't worth anything because he's got no education.'

I could see where this was heading. Mick, who was one of the smartest men I knew, had always had a bit of a chip on his shoulder about his trade.

'I ask her what she does, and she tells me she teaches geography. Now, you know I have a heap of fucking respect for chalkies, so I'm treading pretty carefully here. And then she tells me that if she'd been my teacher, maybe I would have ended up getting better marks and been able to pursue a more worthwhile profession. And I'm like, what the fuck?'

Oooops. Mick had actually started a law degree, but he'd got hooked on building during a summer job and never went back.

'I asked her if she's been to any of the places she teaches the kids about, and she says she can't afford to travel during school holidays. So I tell her she can ask me anything about any of those places as Laura and I have probably been there. And she makes some comment about how I must have saved for ages, so I scull my beer and tell her I earn at least three times, possibly four, what she does, so who's the smart bitch now?'

I choked on my wine. Everyone else knew better than to take a sip when Mick was at the punchline to a story.

As Mick talked, Matt had moved around until he was by my side. 'You okay?' he asked softly.

I turned and faced him, braving his eyes. 'Yes. All good. I'm sorry, I completely overreacted –'

'It's okay, Calliope.' He smiled at me. 'I didn't even think about how you might be feeling about it. But I'm not sorry.'

I took a deep breath. 'No, I'm not either.'

He smiled then, the twinkle back in his eyes. 'What happens now?'

I smiled back. 'I have no idea, but I suggest we start back at the beginning and maybe catch up on what we've been doing since we last saw each other.'

'And then?'

'And then maybe you kiss me again.'

'Is that all?'

'For now.'

He nodded slowly. 'I can work with that.'

CHAPTER SEVENTEEN

'Morning, sleepyhead!' Matt burst into the room and planted a kiss on my forehead. 'Happy birthday, Calliope! Do you want me to sing?'

'No,' I groaned.

'Well, get that cute arse out of bed before I come in after it.' I paused long enough that he grinned wickedly and said, 'That's a tempting thought, isn't it?'

After the long drugging kisses we'd shared last night, it certainly was tempting. He'd promised me we wouldn't go any further, but oh, how I wished he'd broken that promise.

'Did you know you have a very expressive face?' he said. 'Sometimes I think I can see straight into your mind.'

'No!' I rolled over and buried my face in the pillow.

'And now you're giving me a great view of your delectable bottom.'

He laughed as I pulled the doona up higher.

'Is she up yet?' Alice bounced into the room, sat on the edge of the bed and attempted to pull the doona down.

'Careful, I could be naked under here,' I complained and gripped it tighter.

'In my dreams,' muttered Matt.

'Behave yourself.' Alice thumped him on the arm, in exactly the same spot she'd hit him last night.

He rubbed at it ruefully. 'One weekend with my sisters and I'll be going back to Honkers black and blue.'

'Whatever.' Alice gave him a disdainful look. 'Come on, Cal, enough mucking about. We're taking you out to breakfast, followed by a walk up the coast path, and then back to Laura and Mick's for lunch. It's not every day you turn thirty-three and we don't have time for you to waste lying in bed.' Orders issued, she left the room.

Matt took the spot she'd vacated, and smoothed the hair off my face, gently tucking it behind my ears. 'Last night was fun, Cal.' He bent down and kissed my lips. 'But frustrating as hell.'

I could feel my cheeks blazing. 'I know. Me too.'

He grinned. 'Good. I'm glad you suffered too. And now it's time you were up.' He ripped the doona off me, and his eyes darkened as he took in the singlet and boxer shorts that were my sleeping attire. 'I'm not sure whether I'm glad I did that or not.'

His voice had lowered almost to a groan, and I felt my nipples hardening under his gaze. He swallowed once, then again, his hand reaching out almost of its own volition to cup my breast through the thin fabric.

His thumb grazed my nipple, his eyes holding mine as my breath quickened and the fire deep within me came to life.

My hands itched to reach up and pull him down towards me, but Alice chose that moment to yell through the half-open door, 'Are you up yet?'

'I most certainly am,' Matt said softly, his hand dropping away from me.

'I heard that!' Alice popped her head around the door. 'Man, you're so immature.' I'd pulled the doona back up to cover the evidence of my desire, and she raised her eyebrows at me. 'Come on, get your arse out of bed. And you, big brother, let Callie get dressed in peace.'

'But the view's so good in here,' he said, his eyes lingering on my lips.

Alice shook her head and grabbed his arm to drag him from the room.

I stretched my legs out in the bed, wanting to hold that deliciousness in my belly for just a few minutes longer, but Alice wasn't having any of it.

'Up!' she ordered.

We walked down the Esplanade for breakfast, choosing one of the many cafes on the strip. Alice and Matt bantered in that good-natured way siblings who actually like each other do. Tommy and I sat back and laughed at them. It gave me a good opportunity to look at Matt in the daylight. Dressed casually in jeans, trainers and a long-sleeved T-shirt, he looked nothing like the sophisticated professional he'd been when he arrived last night. Now he was more like the boy I'd fallen in love with all those years ago.

He caught me looking at him and leaned in to whisper, 'Do I pass?'

'You know you do,' I whispered back.

Under the table he reached for my hand, grinned at me, and began teasing Alice about something she'd just said.

Later we strolled along the coast path over the headland. Matt and I sat on the chair above the rock wall and watched the surfers while Alice and Tommy walked down to the surf club. He put his arm around me and I leaned into his shoulder, feeling more comfortable and happier than I could remember feeling in years. I knew it was wrong, but for one weekend I was breaking the rules.

'I want to kiss you again,' he said into my hair.

'Yes, please.'

I lifted my face and met him halfway. But his lips had no sooner touched mine than we were interrupted by the ringing of my phone. I groaned and reached in my pocket for it, and groaned again.

'I'd better get this. It's my parents.'

He smiled and pulled back, but kept one arm around my shoulder.

'Happy birthday, Calliope.'

'Thanks, Mum.'

'Hold on, your father wants to say a quick hello. He's on his way out for a run.'

'Happy birthday, love.'

'What are you training for this time, Dad?'

My father was always on a health kick of some description, and first to jump on whatever the latest superfood was. I sometimes thought he was on a quest for eternal youth. Usually occupied with her own interests, Mum tended to just let him get on with it, but drew the line at being expected to comply with whatever dietary regime he was flirting with at the time.

'I did the Gold Coast marathon at the start of the month, and I've got the Sunshine Coast one at the end of next month.'

I laughed and shook my head. 'I can't keep up with you, Dad.'

I heard his smile through the phone. 'I'll hand you back to your mother. Make sure you come and see us soon. It's been far too long and the weather here's much better than that rubbish you get down there.'

'I will, Dad.'

I heard him kiss Mum goodbye and then she was back. 'What are you up to today? Is Jamie spoiling you?'

I closed my eyes briefly and edged slightly away from Matt. 'No. Actually he's away on a work offsite, and I had a last-minute invite from Alice to join the

Delaneys for Mick's fortieth birthday.' I screwed my face up as the lie came out.

'The Delaneys? On the Sunshine Coast?' I grimaced as I waited for her next comment. Brisbane was just an hour or so's drive away. 'Are you going to make it down here?'

'Not this time,' I said. 'It really was a last-minute thing and I don't have access to a car.' I could see Matt grinning as I reached for excuses. 'And we're flying out early tomorrow. I'll make sure I come up soon for a long weekend. Go baby-supply shopping with Clio maybe.'

Where had that come from? God knows the last thing I wanted to do was go around baby shops with Clio.

Mum's tone softened. 'That would be nice. Bring Jamie too, it's been such a long time since we saw him. Is it all still going well?'

I looked at Matt. He was close enough to hear Mum. He dropped his arm from around my shoulders and raised his eyebrows as he waited for my answer.

'It's early days still.' I stood and walked across to the rock wall. From the shade of a pandanus palm I watched the waves roll in below. 'I'm not yet sure how –'

'Hold on, Calliope. I think that's your sister.'

I waited, hearing screen doors open and shut noisily in a Brisbane suburb just an hour away.

'Happy birthday, Cal! Wow, thirty-three – how does that feel?' Clio didn't wait for my response. 'Mum said you're at the Delaneys' but you don't have a car. Maybe I can get Owen to drive me up? I'd love to see you, especially on your birthday.'

I looked over to where Matt was still sitting watching the surfers. I didn't want anything to cut into the limited amount of time we had together – not even my family. He looked up and our eyes met. Clio was still talking, but I was no longer listening. I wanted to feel Matt's arms around me again, the touch of his lips against mine. I didn't want to spend a single minute apart from him, not when we had so few minutes left together.

'Cal!'

'Sorry, Clio. What were you saying?'

'Just that I've remembered I'm supposed to be catching up with some friends for lunch. I could always –'

'No, love. Don't change your plans. I told Mum I'll be up soon and we can catch up properly. Besides,' I laughed, 'by then you'll be huge and needing maternity clothes.'

Matt came up behind me, wrapped his arms around me and rested his chin on top of my head.

'Absolutely,' she said. 'We can go shopping!'

'It's a date. Anyway, I'd better go – Alice is waiting for me.' Another lie.

'Okay. Talk soon. Love you, Callie.'

'Love you too. Give Owen a kiss for me.'

'I will. Here's Mum.'

'Make sure you come up soon,' Mum said. 'We love you.'

'I promise. Love you too.'

I wriggled against Matt as I put my phone back in my pocket, and felt his body respond.

'Hey,' he said. 'Not so much of that, okay? I'm barely holding it together here.'

I giggled. 'So it would seem.' I relaxed in his arms and we stood like that for a few minutes. 'Matt, about Jamie . . .'

He turned me in his arms. 'No, let's not talk about him. Not now. Today is a Jamie-free zone.' He tilted my chin so our eyes met. 'Okay?'

I thought back to what Alice had said last night. These few days were an interlude, and one I didn't want Jamie to intrude into. I nodded.

He dropped a quick kiss on my mouth. 'And now, with her usual impeccable timing, here comes my sister.'

Lunch at Laura and Mick's was as noisy and fun as I'd expected it would be. After the hellos, the men disappeared downstairs to where Mick had the barbecue going, and Laura, Alice and I made salads and drank wine. Neither sister asked me about Matt, although I could tell Laura was dying to. At one point she opened her mouth to say something and Alice nudged her so firmly that she spilled her wine.

'Apparently I'm not allowed to ask you about

Matt,' was all she said.

I blushed and Alice scowled at her.

'But feel free to tell me whatever you want to,' she added, causing me to blush again.

Jane and Tony arrived then with more meat, so we all trooped downstairs to where the cooking was happening.

Matt was obvious in his attentions to me during lunch – leaning across to touch my arm when he spoke to me, taking my hand every so often to hold it or raise it to his lips for a quick kiss, resting his thigh against mine under the table so I could feel every long line of it. All the nerves in my body seemed to rush to my left leg to be nearer to him. Every touch, glance and light kiss felt like a promise, and every bead of heat in my body seemed to be pooled between my legs, waiting for his touch. I was consumed by the need to be alone with him.

After lunch, Matt led the kids into the backyard for a game of touch football. He was so naturally good with each of the boys that I found it difficult to reconcile what Tiff had said about him not wanting his own kids.

Later in the afternoon, when I was holding baby Matthew, who'd fallen asleep in my arms, Matt came and sat beside me. 'You look beautiful,' he said, his gaze sending sparks along my bloodstream. I didn't know what to say, so I said nothing.

'I want this life one day,' he said, looking over to

where Tommy, Mick and Tony were teaching Newton how to place a ball on the mound for a goal kick. 'This whole thing – the kids, the family, the whole suburban extravaganza. And I want someone to share it all with.'

As he said the last, he looked into my eyes again, all signs of the twinkle gone.

'Tiff said you didn't want children,' I blurted out.

'Really? Well, I do.'

Newton kicked the ball, and it hit my chair and disturbed baby Matthew. As he woke he also realised his nappy was wet and let out a wail.

Matt took him from my arms. 'Come on, little fella, let's find your mother and get this bum of yours dry.'

I watched him go, imagining for one brief wonderful moment that it was our child he was holding. What on earth was I doing thinking about having another man's babies?

Still, if I was really honest with myself, my mind had always needed to work extremely hard to place Jamie in my family portrait. He'd be a largely absentee dad, I'd decided, and used to think that would be alright – plenty of men had little interest in babies but still loved and provided for their families. But after seeing the way Mick was with Laura and his children, I didn't want to settle for 'alright'. I wanted it all, and with someone who wouldn't be satisfied leaving the parenting to me.

Matt returned with a freshly nappied and happily gurgling baby. He smiled widely at me as he carried

Matthew over to where Tommy, Mick and Tony were standing. Matt would be a hands-on father, I knew. One who was completely involved.

The fantasy knocked on the door of my brain again, and this time I let it in – just for the weekend.

When we got back to the Delaneys' later that afternoon, Tommy and Tony planted themselves in front of the television to watch sport. Alice was in the garden with her mother, checking out the new vertical planter she'd installed, so I went into my bedroom for some time alone. I needed a rest from the multitude of feelings the day had brought up. I propped some pillows behind my head and settled down to lose myself in a book.

Matt found me there, and sat on the narrow bed beside me. 'What's wrong?' he asked.

'Nothing,' I lied.

'It's this, isn't it – us? Is it too much too soon?'

I looked into his open face and nodded slowly. 'Yes. I'm a little overwhelmed.' It was all too much; he was too much. But at the same time it felt like it wasn't enough.

'Good,' he said. 'I don't want you to have any time to think. You can let the real world in when you get home – you'll have plenty of time then to overthink what's happened between us.' He grinned. 'Which gives me a few hours more to ensure that you have something to overthink.'

'But Jamie,' I protested weakly.

'I've told you before – I don't care about Jamie.' His hand idly stroked circles on my arm, sending spirals of sensations through my body, and his eyes burned into mine. 'I want so badly to kiss you right now. I want to kiss you until you can't say his name, let alone think it. But I'm not going to.'

'Why not?' I wanted that too – so very much. I wanted so much more than his kisses.

He smiled slowly as he watched the expressions move across my face. 'Because I'm so wired that I think I'd lose complete control of myself on this single bed – and that's something I'm not going to do with my parents and my sister on the other side of this thin wall.'

'Oh.'

'And if I'm reading the signals correctly, you're feeling much the same. Am I right?'

I nodded and he smiled again, but it wasn't in triumph, only acceptance and the joy of a mutual attraction.

'So, here's what's going to happen. I'm taking you to dinner tonight – just us. And after dinner, we're going to sneak back here to my room in the granny flat, not this tiny bed, and I'm going to make love to you. No promises, no expectations, no ties. What happens after that is your decision, but I'm hoping that when we're both back here for Mum's sixtieth birthday in September, you'll have had enough space and time to decide you want to be with me – and only me.'

'But –'

He put a finger to my lips and shook his head slowly. 'No. No thinking. You can do that tomorrow.'

I took the tip of his finger into my mouth and nipped it before sucking gently on it. Oh god, I wanted him so badly. I swallowed hard and felt my breath coming too fast. He closed his eyes and rested his forehead against mine, his breathing also laboured.

'Christ,' he muttered. 'I want you so much right now.'

'Me too.'

I lifted my head and covered the distance between us with a sigh that came from long ago. He gave up and pushed me back onto the bed, plundering my mouth in the way we'd both been waiting all day for. His hand found its way under my shirt and into my bra. I moaned and threw my leg over his to force his hardness into me, grinding myself against him, so close to coming that I knew he'd only need to touch me there, just once, for me to combust.

'No, Cal.' He forced himself away from me and sat on the side of the bed, panting. 'Not like this. You deserve more than this – you deserve the granny flat.' He grinned then, and I laughed with him. 'You deserve so much more than the granny flat, but that's all I can offer you right now.'

He reached down and arranged my clothes for me, before tidying himself up. 'Be ready at six thirty –

remember we Queenslanders like to eat early.' Then he kissed my lips briefly and let himself out of my room.

I rolled into a ball on the bed, forcing my fist between my legs in an effort to soothe the ache he'd left there. Before I could give in to the temptation, I got up and went outside in search of Alice and Jane.

CHAPTER EIGHTEEN

Alice grinned when I told her I was going out with Matt that night. 'An interlude, right?' she asked.

'That's all it can be,' I said.

'We'll see.'

We went to an Italian restaurant on the Esplanade opposite the beach. Matt took my hand as soon as we left the house and held it as we walked. We ate pasta and drank wine and filled in the gaps of each other's lives over the past fourteen years.

He told me about his life in Hong Kong and how much of Asia he'd seen. It all sounded so glamorous, but he said he wasn't happy in his role any more. 'It's not the job. I think it's time I came home. This sort of life is for when you're younger and hungrier than I am now. It's really quite shallow – which is one of the things I used to love about it. But now? Now I think I need more depth, and I can't have that while I'm living a half-settled life.'

He asked me about my job and I told him about the call centre and the casual dress policy. He laughed when I said our HR director thought it was an expression of personality for people to wear ugg boots and studded stilettos to work.

'I really need to leave,' I said. 'Even if this job with Helium doesn't come off, I'll look for something else.'

We talked through the role I was going for and he offered me some pointers for the interview.

I told him about Hen and how I needed to kick her out and find my own place. I even told him about the time she'd spray-painted her laundry basket on the balcony with white enamel paint and hadn't bought any turpentine for the clean-up. 'Then she just left. There was white paint on the taps and dripped all across the tiles. It took me forever to clean it up.'

He laughed and I did too. 'She needs to go, Cal, you know she does.'

'Yeah, that's what Tiff says too.' I snuck a look at him as I mentioned Tiff's name, but his expression didn't change.

As the restaurant staff started packing away tables around us, Matt called for the bill. 'They're giving us the hint,' he said. 'I didn't realise it was that late.'

'Me neither.'

'Happy birthday, Cal.' He leaned across the table and kissed me gently, setting the butterflies in my tummy free again. 'I've had a really good night.'

'I have too.'

'Come on.' He pulled me to my feet. 'Let's go home.'

We both giggled as we tried to open the front gate without it squeaking, and giggled some more as we crouched down and crept past the living room window, even though the house was in darkness. All giggling stopped though once we reached the granny flat.

Matt put down his wallet and keys and turned to me. Cupping my face, he smoothed my hair behind my ears and kissed me. Briefly at first, pausing to look at my face as if he were memorising it. One heartbeat. Then two. Three. Then he captured my lips, taking his time, tasting me, teasing me. My arms went around his neck and I pulled his head down so I could have all of his mouth. He walked me backwards until I was leaning against the door, but still his lips didn't leave mine.

My hands were under his shirt. He pulled back, breathing hard, and pulled his T-shirt over his head. I was already sucking and nipping at his nipples, needing to inhale him, needing more of him.

He groaned low in the back of his throat as I reached for his belt buckle. 'No, you don't,' he muttered, taking over the task. 'If you touch me now, this is going to be over way too quickly.'

I moaned my frustration.

'I know, my darling, I know,' he whispered as he pulled my top over my head and reached behind me to unclip my bra. He pulled back and looked. 'You're even more beautiful than I dreamed you'd be.'

He bent his head to take one nipple into his

mouth, his hands busy undoing my jeans, and sliding them and my knickers down my body. I stepped out of them and pushed him backwards until we both toppled onto the bed.

Once we were there, me straddled over him, I froze. Just for a second. I didn't know if it was wonder, or fear, or something else, but I wanted to remember this moment, the seconds before we were joined, when we both knew there was no turning back.

'You sure?' he asked.

'Uh-huh.' I began to move, rubbing myself against him, my eyes half-closed as I felt the wave building within me.

He groaned, 'Condom. Top drawer.' As I reached across to open the drawer he stopped me. 'No, wait, there won't be any in there. It's been too long since I was home.'

'Please tell me you have one?' I moaned. I was so close.

'I do, but in my wallet – all the way over there, near the door.'

He sounded so pained that I couldn't help giggling.

'You'll pay for those giggles,' he growled, gently pushing me onto my back so he could get up.

'I certainly hope so.'

I lay there and watched him walk across to where he'd left his wallet, drinking in every long, hard, beautiful line of him. He watched me watching him and smiled.

'You're lovely,' I said.

'You're like a dream I never want to wake up from,' he said when he was lying beside me again, propped up on one elbow. 'Now, where were we before you so rudely interrupted us with your giggles?'

'My giggles? I thought it was your lack of preparation.'

'Really? My lack of preparation, hey?' He moved down the bed until he was kneeling between my legs. 'Are you saying I wasn't ready?'

He leaned forward and lapped at me, just one long stroke of his tongue. Oh. God.

'Or . . .' He licked me again. 'Maybe it's you who wasn't ready?'

He bent his head and sucked hard on my clit. The orgasm that had been building all day hit me with a force that had me crying out his name and left my head spinning. And still he lapped at me.

'Hmmm, I'd say you're definitely ready now.'

As he filled me, inch by delicious inch, his eyes never left mine. Not even when I whimpered as he withdrew almost completely before thrusting into me, not even when mine closed as the second wave hit, and not even when he followed me seconds later.

We talked a lot in-between lovemaking. Matt overwhelmed me with his honesty, his passion and his complete openness.

'I don't want to play games with you, Cal. This is special to me; you're special to me. In fact, I think you could be the one I've been looking for since I last let you go.'

Then he held me close to him and we slept.

We woke again sometime before dawn, turning to each other in the dark, our lovemaking slow and almost painfully tender.

Lying in each other's arms afterwards, Matt suddenly flung back the covers and sprang out of bed. 'Come on. We're going to watch the sunrise.'

'Really? It's the middle of the night.'

'Nope, we have enough time to get to the lighthouse and watch it come up over the horizon.' He sat on the bed and leaned down to kiss me. 'I don't want our last few hours together to be spent sleeping.'

My eyes filled with tears and I turned my head into the pillow to hide them.

'Hey,' he said softly. 'This isn't an ending. I meant every word I said to you last night.'

I didn't come out from under the pillow. I knew that this weekend was supposed to be an interlude only, but last night had been so magical that I'd allowed myself to pretend that it could be real. Matt's mention that we only had a few hours left together was a reminder that we each had lives to go back to.

'Last night we changed each other's world, Calliope – now we just have to work out how to live there. You have things to sort out and decisions to make, and so do I. But right now I want to watch the sun come up with you. We're going to make the most of every second we have until I have to get in that car to drive back to Brisbane to catch my flight out. Every. Single. Second.'

He punctuated his words with kisses so sweet that I put my arms around his neck to drag him back into bed with me.

'No.' He pulled himself away reluctantly. 'We're going to see this sunrise, so get your arse out of bed.'

I dressed in the jeans I'd had on last night and a hoodie he found in his wardrobe.

'Man, you look sexy as hell in that.' The look in his eyes told me he was rethinking his determination to see the sunrise.

I pushed him away gently. 'No, mister, you had your chance. You wanted a sunrise, so a sunrise is what you'll get.'

Rather than going down to the beach, we drove to the lighthouse on the point. 'It faces due east here,' he said. 'And not as many people know about it.'

He took my hand as we walked the short distance from the car park to the lighthouse reserve. Looking back down to Mooloolaba, the sky was tinged all shades of pink and orange from apricot through to magenta.

As I stood marvelling at the colour, he wrapped his arms around my middle, pulling me back into him and breathing in deeply. 'Do you remember the last time we watched the sunrise together?'

I nodded, my words stuck in the base of my throat.

'I wanted you so much that night, but I knew it would be unfair of me to make love to you and then leave. I don't know that I'd have been able to go away if we'd made love that night.'

'That night was so special because we didn't,' I said. 'We were both too young. Our timing was just wrong.'

'And now? Is our timing right now?'

'I don't know,' I said honestly. 'What if it feels so perfect because it's a fantasy?'

'And what if it isn't a fantasy?'

I turned in his arms to face him, and saw the hope shining in his eyes.

'Then that would be exceptional indeed,' I whispered.

'Wouldn't it just?'

As the sun made its way over the horizon in a blaze of golden glory he kissed me, and for that moment I believed that the dream he'd talked about could be real.

CHAPTER NINETEEN

The guilt began as soon as I buckled my seatbelt on the plane, and continued for the entire flight and the drive home. Alice tried to talk to me about it, but I pushed her away.

'I did warn you what he's like,' she said. 'When Matt decides he wants someone, she doesn't stand a chance. It's such an Aries thing – the whole hunt you down and throw you over his shoulder to take you home approach. You don't have time or space to think – it's a complete takeover.'

'You've seen him like this a lot?' I asked.

The things he'd said to me, the way he'd looked at me and held me and made love to me – it had been a whirlwind, but I'd believed him. It felt worse to be just one of many.

She thought for a few seconds, wrinkling her nose as she cast back through her memory. 'No,' she said finally. 'Not like this. I think he might just have stopped playing games.'

I nodded as if I understood, but I didn't understand

anything that had happened over the past couple of days. Like he'd said, it was as if I'd been taken from my world and dropped into another one – a place I knew nothing about. Alice and I used to laugh at the tourists who tried to bodysurf when the surf was dumping. You could go deeper and ride those waves to the top, or stay in the shallows and play in the foam. But where the waves shredded – we called that 'the kill zone'. That's what looking into Matt's eyes felt like, it was what making love with him felt like – when the wave dumped you, and your breath was knocked out of you, and you didn't know which was up and which was down.

I wanted to go deeper, but I was scared. I was in the kill zone, not knowing if I was upside down or the right way up. All I knew was how he'd made me feel.

'What are you going to do about Jamie?' Alice asked.

'I have no idea.'

'Do you want to talk it through?'

'No. I think I'd prefer to sit here and beat myself up for being the faithless cheater I am.'

I turned my back and squeezed as close into the window as I could, ignoring her and Tommy for the rest of the flight home.

Jamie called around on Sunday night. He was full of apologies for not having phoned me over the weekend.

'I'm sorry, I just didn't get a second to myself. This

whole thing about future-proofing the business didn't leave any time for anything else.'

His arms were outstretched, but I didn't fall into them. 'You couldn't even find five minutes to call and wish me happy birthday?'

I watched as the thoughts ran across his face. He really had forgotten. I pushed aside the fact that I'd scarcely thought about him until I was on the flight home this morning. Somehow it made it worse that while I wasn't thinking about him, he hadn't been thinking about me either.

'Oh god, Cal, I'm so sorry. We were under so much pressure to come up with strategies – it just slipped my mind. I'll make it up to you, I promise.'

He pulled me close to kiss me, his mouth and tongue moving against mine, but this time I didn't melt. I knew it would be make-up sex, intended to take my mind off his neglect, and I didn't want that.

All I could think about was Matt and the open generosity of his kisses. Kisses that weren't intended to distract or influence, or exercise any sort of control over me. Matt's kisses were given purely because he wanted to kiss me, to please me. I tried to shut him from my mind, but couldn't. When I closed my eyes, I saw his.

I drew myself back from Jamie. 'I'm sorry, I'm really tired. We had a couple of late nights over the weekend, and I didn't sleep well in Alice's single bed.'

I laughed to take the sting out of the rejection, but I couldn't meet his eyes in case he saw the truth in mine.

'You don't want me to stay and make you feel better?' he asked.

'No, not tonight. I'm sorry, I feel like I'm out on my feet.'

'Okay, tomorrow then. We'll go out for a special dinner.' He hit his forehead with the back of his hand. 'Actually I can't tomorrow night – I have to work late. Tuesday night?'

'Sorry, I have belly dancing.'

'Can't you miss it just this once? I'll make it up to you.' He pulled me towards him so I could feel just how he was going to make it up to me. 'After all, it's only a dance class, and you still haven't given me a demonstration.'

Once upon a time his suggestive tone might have been enough to make me cancel my entire schedule for him. Now it just made me angry. I pushed at his chest until I was out of his arms.

'I've never asked you to skip something you've committed to, so please give me the same respect. It might be just a dance class, but it's my dance class and it's for me and I want to go. Much the same as your running training is just running training, but I understand that it's something you want to do.' I took another step back from him. 'Don't expect me to change my arrangements to make up for you forgetting my birthday.'

He stared at me for several seconds, probably expecting me to back down and fall into his arms. Not this time.

'You're right,' he finally said. 'You're tired. We'll have dinner on Wednesday night. Does that suit?' I nodded, and he pulled me towards him and kissed me. 'I'll call you tomorrow, okay?'

I nodded. 'Yes, I'll talk to you tomorrow.'

After he'd left, Hen wandered out of her room. 'Trouble in paradise?'

'Oh, shut the fuck up,' I snapped. 'And as you're out of your cave, you can make yourself useful and clean your mess up.' She opened her mouth to argue and I held up a hand. 'I don't want to hear it. In fact, as well as cleaning up the mess you've left in the kitchen, do something with the pizza boxes in the lounge room too.' I took a breath. I was on a roll so I might as well make the most of it. 'And then you can find somewhere else to live. I want you out of here in a month.'

She stared at me with her mouth open. It wasn't an attractive sight.

'Don't take your fight with lover boy out on me,' she snarled.

I straightened myself to my full five foot three and looked up at her. 'This has nothing to do with Jamie. It's because you're lazy around the flat, never clean up, never wash up, are always late with your rent and share of expenses, and because I don't want to live with you any more. That's all. Oh, and because I don't like you.'

I turned my back and walked away.

'I don't like you either,' she shouted after me.

'I know. And I don't care.' And I meant it.

Jamie sent a huge bunch of roses to my office on Monday. The card read: *I couldn't buy the entire store, so had to settle for these. With my love – all of it, Jxxx*

His words should have softened me, but instead they fired up the guilt that had kept me awake most of the night. The worst part was that I didn't feel guilty for what I'd done with Matt; I felt guilty that I *didn't* feel guilty. By 5 am I'd decided that I couldn't be with Jamie and yearn for someone else. Even if my weekend with Matt did prove to be a delightful fantasy, it had shown me that I was more in love with the memory of how Jamie and I used to be in the early days than I was with him now.

Tessa was right: I'd gone back in order to go forward. I'd been alone before, and I wasn't afraid to be alone again. I resolved to tell Jamie on Wednesday night that we were over.

Kerry gasped when she saw the size of the arrangement. 'Wow! Are these "I love you" or "I'm sorry" flowers?'

'I think they could be the equivalent of the make-up sex we didn't have.'

'What did he do? They look like a pretty big apology.'

'He forgot my birthday.'

'Ah.' She turned away, but not before I saw the thought in her eyes.

'You don't have to say it,' I told her. 'I know it's not a good sign after we've only been back together such a short time.'

The job at Helium was finally advertised on Monday too. I immediately sent through my resumé and application.

Marion called during the afternoon to let me know she'd received it and that the interviews would be taking place in a couple of weeks.

'Pip will do the initial interviews, but Alex wants to talk to each of the shortlisted candidates himself,' she said. 'He's away on and off until the end of the month, so you might need to be flexible when it comes to interview times. His diary can all too often be a moving target.'

I laughed as I knew I should. After talking through the possibilities of the role with Matt on Saturday night, I was even more determined to give it my best shot. The more I thought about it the more convinced I was that the role couldn't be more perfect for me.

I said as much to Marion. 'It probably sounds like I'm just saying that,' I added, 'but I can assure you I'm not. It's an opportunity that I don't want to waste.'

'It's why I thought of you in the first place,' she said. 'It's right up your alley.'

On Tuesday night at belly dancing, I finally nailed the shimmy-walk.

After thirty minutes spent on basic steps and choreography, Tessa announced the arrival of a local drumming band who'd be accompanying us for some free dance time.

'I'm going to turn the lights down so you can't see yourselves in the mirrors,' she said. 'I want you to feel the music beating in your chest and hips and allow your body to follow it. Don't think about the next step, just go where the music leads you. Close your eyes if you want.'

At first I just moved around on the spot. Without being able to see the mirrors, my arms felt graceful, my middle finger held out and my hands rolling, leading my arms into the air and back again in a snake-like movement. My shoulders followed, and my hips lifted and dropped, sliding and rolling in time to the beat I could feel as well as hear.

I closed my eyes, and as I danced I allowed myself to think about Matt – really think about him. I replayed the things he'd said to me, the way he'd made love to me, how it felt to be curved into his body while we slept. I saw again the sunrise, the blast of colour and the kiss that promised a new start without an ending.

I began to move around the floor, and as I did my

mind went back to our goodbye on Sunday morning. He'd kissed me and held me tightly, not caring that his entire family was watching. When we came up for air, he guided me away from them all and said, 'I know this has been quick, and it's probably too much for you to take in. But it feels right. Take the next few weeks to sort things through. I won't contact you in that time, or try to influence you in any way, but know that I'll be thinking about you. Then, when we're both back here for Mum's birthday, we'll talk properly.'

'You seem confident I'll choose you.' I tried to laugh as I said it, but the words came out all choked.

'I have to believe you feel the same way I do,' he said simply. 'But I also get that you might need space to realise that – as hard as it's going to be not hearing your voice over the next six weeks.' He kissed me again and rested his forehead against mine.

'I miss you already,' I whispered.

'Good,' he said. 'See you in September, Calliope Jones.'

As the drumbeat ran through my body, it pushed away the doubt and the guilt. It was Matt I loved. It had always been Matt. He made my heart sing.

I was brought out of my drum-induced daze by Kerry's voice. 'Oh my god, Cal! You did it! You nailed the shimmy-walk!'

'So I did!' I felt the smile spread across my face.

'But how?' asked Kerry.

'Tessa was right. It happened when I stopped thinking about it. I closed my eyes and just felt the music.'

Once I'd started, it seemed I couldn't stop. Even when we went up to the rooftop with our drinks after class, I shimmied around the perimeter, returning to our table with what we giggled was the 'excuse me' move, because it was the way you'd roll your hips forward if you were squeezing through a tight crowd with a tray of drinks.

Tessa clapped when I sat down. 'You've certainly got the bug,' she said.

She saw my answer on my face.

I grabbed Kerry's arm. 'Come on, you can do it too. You know the steps, you're just thinking too hard.'

'I don't know . . .'

'Stand behind me and put your hands on my hips and close your eyes. Tessa, has she got them closed?'

'She has.'

'Good. Now feel the beat again in your chest, and feel my hips through your hands.'

We moved around the rooftop like that for a few minutes – me shimmy-walking, Kerry following. When her hands dropped away from my hips, I knew she had it. Her wide smile said the rest.

Jamie, as promised, took me out to dinner on Wednesday evening. He'd made an early booking at a restaurant in the city I'd always wanted to eat at but couldn't justify on my salary. Mindful of the expense, I tried to talk to him before we ordered, but he wasn't having any of it.

'No, Cal. Whatever you've got to say can wait until after dinner. Let's just enjoy this, hey?'

After a meal that was no doubt every bit as fabulous as I'd imagined a meal here would be – if only I'd been able to taste it – he again apologised for forgetting my birthday.

'You have no idea how sorry I am. I got so tied up in work, I forgot everything else.'

'It's okay,' I said, meaning it. 'It's no big deal. It's not as if it was a special birthday.'

Even though it ended up being the most special birthday of my life.

'It's not okay. I really didn't want to fuck up this time. So . . .' He reached into the inside pocket of his jacket.

I went icily cold. Surely he wasn't going to make the sort of declaration that would have had me in grateful tears only a few weeks ago.

'I got you this,' he said, handing me an envelope.

I let out the breath I'd been holding and opened it. It was a travel itinerary: two air tickets to Phuket and seven nights in the resort we'd stayed in last time we were there. Leaving in just over two weeks.

He watched me reading and waited for my reaction. I was probably supposed to jump for joy and throw my arms around him, but I couldn't. I held the envelope as if I were afraid of its contents. In a way I was. Going with Jamie to Phuket represented a commitment to him that I no longer wanted to make.

'This is lovely,' I said, 'but I have the interview at Helium that week. And I'd need to arrange time off work. Plus, I promised my parents I'd visit in a couple of weeks.' Matt's face swam into view and I shoved it aside. 'In fact, we really need to talk about –'

He didn't let me finish. 'You must have heaps of holiday time owing. And let's face it, you probably weren't going to get that job anyway.' He ignored my gasp and smiled at me. 'You can see your family any time – you probably should have done it last weekend when you were only an hour away. Stop trying to think of excuses and say you'll come, Cal. We were happy when we were there last time, and I want to prove to you that we can be happy again. This is it for me – you're the one I want to be with. I thought I was the one for you too.'

I smiled weakly at him. Until recently I'd thought the same.

He reached across and stroked my cheek down to my jaw. 'I love you, Cal. I can't imagine life without you. Let me prove it to you.'

Oh god. Where did that leave me?

'Jamie, I don't think –'

'Please,' he said. 'After I hurt you so badly, I don't blame you for hesitating now, but the thing is, I was lost without you and I don't think I could hold myself together if it happened again.' Oh god, was that a tear in his eye? 'You're not planning on leaving me, are you?'

Yes, it was a tear, and it was followed by another. He let them slide down his face without attempting to stop them.

I could feel my expensive dinner swirling around in my stomach. How could I tell him now that not only did I not want to go to Phuket with him, I wanted us to break up? Christ, this was a mess. I rubbed absently at my forehead as I struggled for something to say.

'You are,' he accused. 'You're planning on leaving me! I can tell from how you're not saying anything.' He reached for my hands. 'Please, babe, it's just a week. Seven days.' He smiled weakly. 'Say you'll come. All I'm asking for is one more chance. And if by the end of that time you're still not convinced we're meant to be together forever . . . well, I suppose I'll have given it my best shot.'

I swallowed hard as my soufflé threatened to make a reappearance, and looked down at our joined hands, then back up at his eyes. They were still glistening with emotion. How could I contemplate saying no? I'd had five years with Jamie, and just one night with Matt. What was I thinking? I wasn't thinking – that was the problem. My hormones were doing it all for me. I was sure that Alice would have a rule for making rash decisions under the influence of lust.

'One more chance, Cal. After all we've been through – and all we went through when we were apart – surely we're not going to break up over a forgotten birthday? Please say yes. Let me show you how special you are to me. Let me love you the way you deserve.'

He was saying everything I'd yearned for him to say, laying himself open before me in a way I'd never thought him capable of. Did I have the right to break his heart when he was trying to do everything I'd wanted him to do – except forget my birthday, of course. Although my hesitation was nothing to do with my birthday, of course. It was all to do with one night in another man's arms.

'Please, Cal. I'm begging you.'

Oh god, I couldn't do it to him. It was seven days, that was all. Seven days in the sun to chase this madness from my veins. Besides, he'd already paid for the holiday.

I nodded. 'Okay, I'll come.'

He smiled with relief and squeezed my hands tight. 'You won't regret it, I promise.'

His grip felt like a steel band, locking me to him. And when I looked into his eyes again, they were dry.

As we were walking down Bourke Street in the cold, Jamie took my hand and smiled at me. 'I'm sorry, I forgot to tell you – I have to go to Sydney again tomorrow. Hopefully just for the day, but it could be overnight.'

'Again? You only just got back from the offsite.'

'I know, babe, I don't want to go either.' He gently moved me out of the drizzle and into a shop doorway. 'It kills me to be away from you.'

He kissed me – a long slow kiss deserving of an audience, or a camera crew. The sort of kiss that should have removed all doubt from my mind, but left me wondering why he was trying to distract me.

'It's only a couple of days,' he said when he raised his head. 'And in just a couple of weeks we'll be in Phuket. I want to lay you on the sand and kiss you all over.' As he spoke he was nuzzling down my throat in the way that used to make me swoon. This time the move felt rehearsed. 'Then we'll make love slowly – the way you like it – as the waves lick around our bodies.'

He'd wrapped his coat around me, and one hand found its way to my breast. Only a week ago I would have been struggling to remember what it was I wanted to ask him about the offsite. Now he left me cold – and I felt awful about it.

'Aren't the beaches too busy for that?' I asked.

'I'll hire a boat to take us to a quiet one,' he said, and kissed me again.

I didn't want to make love with Jamie on a beach. Beaches reminded me of Matt. I screwed my eyes shut to concentrate on the here and now. Jamie. When he raised his head again, I saw that he wasn't looking into my eyes, but rather at a strikingly pretty dark-haired woman standing nearby. I'd seen that look on a woman's face before – my own – and knew what it meant.

Jamie kissed my forehead and said, 'Give me five minutes. I need to sort this out.'

He walked towards the woman and they spoke briefly, then he drew her under the awning out of the rain. They talked for a few minutes more, then the woman turned away from him and walked past the doorway where I stood. Although she didn't look my way, I knew she knew I was watching her. I could see that her face was wet, and I didn't think it was from the rain. Damn him.

Jamie watched her as she walked back down Bourke Street, then he pushed his hands into his pockets and returned to the doorway where I was still huddled.

'Who was that?' I asked.

His expression was blank.

'That woman. Who was she?' I said again.

'Oh, just someone from work.' His tone was dismissive.

'What's her name?'

'Does it matter?'

'Of course it matters. You've just told me that I'm the only one for you, yet she looked as though you'd broken her heart. What's her name?'

He sighed heavily. 'Emily.'

'She seemed upset.'

He reached for me and I backed away. 'I'm serious, Jamie. If I'm going to trust you, you need to be honest with me.'

He nodded slowly. 'You're right, but it's an awkward situation.' He grimaced and rubbed behind his head. 'The truth is, she has a thing for me. And before you and I got back together, I have to admit I was tempted.'

'What stopped you?'

He shrugged and turned briefly to watch Emily trudging away in the rain. 'Three things. Josh is in love with her, although he's never said so. I thought they were just friends, but I think something changed for him when he saw her falling for me.' He said it without a hint of conceit. 'I couldn't do that a friend. Besides, after the incident with Kylie, I've learnt my lesson about screwing with the crew.' His short laugh sounded embarrassed.

'And the other reason?' My voice was quieter now. His consideration for Josh had touched me.

He reached for my hands, his eyes glistening. 'You, of course. I love you, Cal. It's only ever been you. As for the others –'

'The others? I thought there was only Kylie. Just the once, you said.'

'It was only Kylie while we were together, but you know I was with other women while we were apart.' His look was patient, as though he was explaining a simple concept to a very slow learner. 'Anyone else was a mistake, because I was feeling weak at having let you go. Losing you for those few months – well, it showed me what's really important. It showed me who I really love.' He pushed me back into the dark of the doorway and kissed me hard on the lips. 'I love you, no one else. I can't lose you again. There's nothing between Emily and me. Nothing. It's all you – it's always been you.'

'But –' I started.

His hand crept under my jersey skirt and found the edge of my knickers. 'I don't blame you if you've been having a few doubts, but you know no one makes you feel like I do.'

'No,' I said, turning my face away from his mouth.

'What's wrong?' he murmured into my throat, his fingers still searching for an entry point into my pants.

'Not here. Not now.' I pushed him away and rearranged my wrap dress.

An expression slid across his face that could have been anger, but it was gone so quickly I thought I'd imagined it.

'Let's go back to your place then?'

I couldn't get Emily's face, her tears and her hurt, out of my mind. He'd said she meant nothing to him, but he clearly meant something to her.

'No,' I said, 'not tonight.'

'Are you sure?' He moved closer, forcing me back against the wall so I could feel his hardness pushing into my tummy.

I was suddenly angry. 'I said no, Jamie. I'm tired, and you've got an early start. Let's just leave it for tonight, okay?' I reached up and kissed him briefly. 'Here's my tram. I'll talk to you when you're back.'

I was almost home when his text came through.

Please don't be angry with me, Cal. I'm sorry I missed your birthday, and I'm sorry we ran into Emily. Phuket will be the fresh start we need. You won't be sorry you said yes. Jxxx

But I already was sorry.

CHAPTER TWENTY

'You're going where?' Alice sounded disbelieving on the phone. She had every right to – less than a week ago I'd been wrapped up in her brother.

'To Phuket with Jamie. It might mean I'll miss the Helium interview, but the big boss is away on and off for the next few weeks so it could be put off anyway. Plus, who's to say I'd even get the job. There'll be other jobs, but there won't be this chance again with Jamie.'

I knew I was babbling, attempting to justify the whole sorry mess to myself. I could almost hear Alice's brain ticking away. There were background noises too.

'Ally, where are you?'

'In the park with the dogs. Mac's away, so I've got Kevin at the moment. Hang on, let me get them both on leads so I can sit down and listen to you.' I heard her call for the dogs, and click leads back on to their collars. 'Okay, I'm with you now. Sit! Not you, Cal, the dogs. Right, so you're going to Phuket with Jamie. When? How? And most importantly, why?'

'Sunday after next. He sprang it on me last night.

He forgot my birthday and I think he felt he needed to make up for it –'

'Or something else,' Alice interrupted.

'Possibly,' I conceded, remembering Emily's sad face. 'Or maybe he guessed I'd . . . well, that I'd . . . you know?'

'Spent the weekend pashing with my brother?'

'Does anyone even say pashing any more? But yes, maybe he was picking up that something's different. I've been distant with him since the weekend.'

If I was being honest, I'd been distant before that too.

'Don't you mean he picked up that you weren't as into him as you used to be?' she said.

'Maybe. I was all set to finish things, but then he said he loves me and wants to prove it to me. He said he wants us to be happy like we used to be, like we were the last time we holidayed there. He even cried, Ally. You know what Jamie's like – he wouldn't want anyone to see him cry! I couldn't say no to him.'

'Okay.' Alice paused as she collected her thoughts. 'What I'm hearing is: you're feeling guilty about cheating on him with Matt; and he's feeling guilty about missing your birthday and so now he's manipulating you into remembering a time that actually wasn't as rosy when you were living it as it fucking seems now!'

'Alice!' She rarely swore.

'I'm sorry, Cal, but I'm not sure who I'm angrier

with at the moment – you for romanticising a relationship that included him taking you for granted and throwing you the occasional mini-break to get things back on track, or him for thinking he can waltz back in and fuck you up again, and you for letting him. Or you for not seeing the blinding obvious, which is you don't belong with him. For fuck's sake, you don't even want him any more! If you're being really honest, you'll admit that you haven't wanted him since you got him back. And what about Matt – what was that about? You couldn't have been with Matt if you still loved Jamie. That's not who you are!'

Alice also never yelled, but she was doing that now in the park – and probably scaring the dogs. She was certainly scaring me.

'You were the one who said it was just an interlude.' I wanted to raise my voice too, but couldn't – not in the middle of Collins Street.

'Christ, Cal. For a smart woman you can be so stupid sometimes. Of course it wasn't a fucking interlude. You two belong together. Matt knows it, and so do you.'

'But how can I be with Matt? It was one weekend –'

'You know it was more than that.'

Was it? Was it really something that was meant to be, or had we been trying to recreate something that almost happened a lifetime ago? I didn't know, and it was confusion rather than anger that made me yell back at Alice.

'I can't be with Matt. He's Tiff's perfect man – she said that, remember? And he lives in Hong Kong. Besides, I've been an idiot in the past and rushed in and I don't want to do that with Matt because I think he's the real thing and that means I need to take my time, even if taking my time means I might lose my chance to be with him. It's just he overwhelmed me and I feel so much it's fucking terrifying.' I didn't usually swear either. 'What if I'm mistaken and what seemed so special was nothing more than unfinished business for us both?'

'I understand you need to take your time,' Alice said. 'Hell, I watched my brother sweep you off your feet without giving you a second to think about it. I'd be just as pissed off if I thought you were rushing into things with him – if it goes wrong I stand to lose either my best friend or my brother. But does taking your time involve going to Phuket on a romantic holiday with another man? No, it fucking does not!'

When she put it like that. Oh man, I'd made a mess of things.

'I feel so bad for Jamie though. It wasn't that long ago that I wanted him back with every piece of me, and now I've got him it's different. It's all my fault – I should have listened to you and left him in the freezer. But then if I hadn't taken him out and stuck him back together and got back with him, I wouldn't have known that I don't love him any more, and I would've spent years thinking I did until it was too late to realise I didn't. And now I'm in too deep, and he says he loves me, and I feel oh so fucking guilty because the person I didn't know I still wanted, I really truly do, and he's on the other side of the world being Tiff's perfect man.' I'd screamed this all out loud, and now I burst into tears. 'Ally, I'm in such a mess. I feel like I owe it to Jamie to go away with him and give us a chance, but when he touches me I can only see Matt. And Jamie's done nothing wrong this time – okay, maybe he has with some girl called Emily – and part of me wishes he had. It would make me feel justified about cheating on him – because that's what I've done.'

She listened as I sobbed noisily into the phone, and waited while I got a tissue from my bag. 'Where are you, Cal? Not in the office, I hope?'

'No. I came downstairs.'

'So you're screaming at me and sobbing your heart out in the middle of Collins Street?'

'Not exactly. I'm sort of in a laneway, but yeah, I have had some strange looks.'

She giggled and I knew she was done with the yelling. 'I can imagine. Okay, let's break this down. You feel obligated to go on this trip that he arranged without any consideration of you or what you've got going on. Am I right?'

I sniffled. 'Yes, but he thought he was doing something nice for me, and to prove how serious he is about us being together.'

'Sweetie, Jamie Aldridge doesn't do anything without an underlying reason. We just don't know what that reason is yet.'

'He said he loves me and he'd be lost without me. He cried, remember?'

'And perhaps he does, but that's his problem, not yours. I agree with you – you had to get back with him to realise what you were in love with was the past and the thought of wedding bells and babies. But that doesn't mean you have to stay with him if he isn't who you want. And seriously, why the fuck did you take him back out of the freezer? I could have told you how that would work out.' She paused. 'Listen, I could give you the official astro talk about holding on to something long past its use-by date just because things were great for a couple of brief moments in the past. It's those minutes, seconds, whatever, that keep you hoping you can find that past again in the present, if you just hold on and love him more or better. But often it's not like that. I could tell you that – actually, I just did – or I could tell you not to think about Jamie's emotions, or even Matt's, but to think about yourself for a change. Don't go with Jamie because you feel guilty for sleeping with Matt, or you feel obligated. Go because you want a holiday, or because you really want to give this thing with Jamie a red-hot try and you truly believe those few days with Matt were just a fantasy.'

'And Matt?'

'You said it yourself, sweetie. You need some space before you can decide to be with him. And he deserves better than to be your rebound guy. He gave you until September, so use that time. But please don't make him your second choice or consolation prize. He doesn't deserve that.'

I nodded.

'Cal?'

'I'm nodding.' I paused. 'You know, you're really scary when you get going.'

She giggled. 'It's the red hair. It doesn't happen often, but when it does – man, you'd better not be in the firing line.'

I started to sneeze on Friday morning, and by the afternoon I'd taken myself home from work and was tucked into bed with boxes of tissues and various concoctions guaranteed to keep head colds at bay. Thankfully, Hen had made herself scarce since I'd snapped at her on the weekend. I couldn't have thought of anything worse than being sick with her friends partying in their big boots in the next room.

Jamie texted at about eight to see if I was home and needed company. I texted back that I was sick and wanted to try to sleep it off.

Do you need me to bring you anything?

I replied that I was fine.

How about I come and hold your hand?

I sighed and tapped out a response: *Thanks, but I don't want you to get this. Talk tomorrow.*

I put my phone down and thought about how this time last week I was with Matt on the balcony of the surf club. He was kissing me and turning everything I'd thought I wanted upside down. I closed my eyes and pictured his face – the twinkle in his eyes, and the way it disappeared when he looked at me in that way. Then his eyes became as dark and deep as the ocean, and just as dangerous.

My phone alerted me to a new text. It would be Jamie wanting to change my mind. I picked it up to tell him thanks but no thanks, but it was from Matt.

Hi, I was just thinking about you and how this time last week we were together. I wish we were again now. That's all. xxx

I felt the burn of tears behind my eyes. Before I could stop myself, I replied.

I was thinking exactly the same thing – that it was this time last week and I wish we were together now. xxx

I ached to call him, but knew I had no right to. Not while I was still with Jamie. Not while I hadn't decided what to do.

Jamie called around on Sunday night with flowers and chicken soup. I was feeling better, but when he reached for me I shrugged away.

'Sorry, I'm probably still contagious. I don't want you getting sick before we go away.'

He allowed me to pull away but kept hold of my hand. 'Are you sure that's all it is? I've barely seen you since you got back from Queensland.' He smiled. 'It feels as though you're keeping me at a distance.'

'Don't be ridiculous. You've been away too, and I've been sick the last couple of days.' I closed my eyes, immediately regretting my tone. 'I'm sorry. I'm not a great patient, and this cold has come at the worst possible time when I need to get things organised to go away. That's all.'

'You're sure you're not having doubts?' He smiled again, but it didn't reach his eyes and there was an edge to his voice. 'I can't apologise again, and I've told you how much this trip means to me.'

Desperation — that's what the edge sounded like. As if he was desperate to keep me happy.

I let out a breath and rubbed his shoulder. 'I'm not asking you to apologise again. I really am just not feeling well.'

'Okay,' he conceded. 'As long as that's all it is.' He led me over to the lounge. 'You sit yourself down and wrap up in this blanket. I'll heat the soup up for you.'

His kindness just made me feel worse.

While he was in the kitchen, a text came through on his phone. I glanced down and saw the screen. The caller was someone called Suse, and the message said, *Call me xxx.*

I took it through to the kitchen and held it out to

him. 'Who's Suse?'

'Who?'

'The message. She said to call her, and ended it with kisses.'

He laughed. 'Oh, *that* Suse. She's one of the women in the project office at work – a bit older than me. She's just started seeing this guy, James, and when she's had too many wines, I think she hits the wrong number. Jamie, James – it's an easy mistake.' He grinned. 'I tell you what though, they must have fun judging from some of the texts that have come to me accidentally. Phew, they're hot!' He glanced at the phone. 'I probably should tell her she's got the wrong man again.'

He picked up his phone and typed: *Hey Suse, wrong James. Callie's getting all worried. Lol.* He added a laughing emoticon and pressed send. 'There. I'll turn it onto silent so we're not disturbed again.'

He smiled at me, confident he'd convinced me, and began telling me about what he'd planned for us in Phuket. I didn't believe a word of his explanation, but smiled and pretended I did.

CHAPTER TWENTY-ONE

Belly dancing on Tuesday night was a relief from the gloomy fog I'd allowed to surround me, but even so I went through my steps out of habit rather than passion. My arms were doing what they were supposed to do and my hips followed suit, but my shimmy definitely lacked sparkle. I could blame the remnants of my cold, but I knew that wasn't what was bothering me. This time last week I'd been full of the promise of a future with Matt. Now, something I'd agreed to out of guilt was choking the joy out of me.

Kerry had asked Louise, another student, to have drinks with us after class. With shoulder-length corkscrew curls and olive skin, she was a pretty girl, but seemed quite shy.

'You don't mind, do you, Cal?' Kerry asked when I told her I wouldn't be staying around after class.

'Of course not – Louise seems nice. It's just that I'm still getting over this cold and I'm terrible company. Go and have a drink for me – and make sure you ask Louise where I can buy one of those fabulous purple coin belts.'

Tessa pulled me aside as I was packing up to leave. 'What's going on, Callie? You were on top of the world last week and tonight you seem as though you're carrying the world on your shoulders.'

I tried, and failed, to hide the tears that sprang to my eyes. 'I've made a real mess of things, that's all – and I don't know how to get myself out of it.'

She nodded slowly. 'I think I understand. Listen, give me a couple of minutes to pack up and you and I can go for a coffee.' She indicated to where Kerry and Louise were chatting. 'We'll let those two go on without us tonight.'

We stopped in at a café a few doors down Brunswick Street.

Tessa waited until our coffees had been delivered before saying, 'Okay, start talking. Last week your heart was singing and your shimmy was sharp. What's changed? I assumed things were going well with Jamie.'

I shook my head. 'That's the problem. He's done nothing wrong – except for forgetting my birthday. It's just that now we're back together I've realised I'm not in love with him. He, on the other hand, is saying and doing everything I wished he'd said and done before. He says he's afraid I'm going to leave him and break his heart – and the worst is, that's exactly what I was planning to do.'

'Hold on, didn't you say he got like this before when you started going to book club? He told you that was why he'd had the fling – because he was afraid he was losing you?' She paused to let that circle around my brain. 'Then once he had you where he wanted you, he backed off again. Are you sure he's not playing the same game this time?'

'But he cried.' His tears had dried up awfully quickly though.

Tessa watched me as I thought. 'You certainly seemed like someone who was in love last week,' she said.

I felt the blood rush to my face. 'Yes – just not with Jamie.' I took a breath. 'It's Alice's brother and we . . . well, you know . . .'

'Hooked up?' she guessed.

I nodded. 'When I went to Queensland with Alice. I cheated on Jamie, and I'm an awful person for doing it, but I can't feel sorry it happened – and I can't bear Jamie to touch me now.' I grimaced. 'And that's why I'm in so much trouble. I'd decided I couldn't be with Jamie and feel the way I do about Matt, so I was all set to tell him we were over and . . .'

'And that's when he cried and told you he couldn't live without you?'

I nodded miserably. 'And then he told me he'd bought us a week's holiday in Phuket so we could start again.'

'Are you going?'

I nodded again. 'It would seem so. He begged me

to go, said he needed one more chance to prove to me that he loves me. So I said yes. Then after we left the restaurant we ran into this girl who seemed really upset to see us together. He said it was because she has a thing for him but he hadn't touched her. He seemed so believable at the time, but I can't get her face out of my head. Then there was a text that came through from someone called Suse the other night. He had an explanation for that too. I don't know whether I want him to have lied to me so I can feel better about what I did with Matt, or so I have an excuse to back out of the holiday. Or should I trust him and give him the chance he's asked for? After all, it's only seven days.' I smiled ruefully. 'Seven days is nothing – and I get a holiday in the sun.'

'But what would Matt think about it? Is a relationship between you on the cards?'

'I think so. Of course I'm second-guessing that too. But even if there isn't a future with Matt, I don't think I want one with Jamie.'

Tessa rested her chin on the heel of her hand and tapped her fingers lightly against her cheek. 'Did I ever tell you about when Gary, my ex, came waltzing back into my life?'

'You mentioned that he had, and that he was surprised when you didn't take him back.'

She nodded. 'Yes, that's what I told you. What I didn't say is that I'd been seeing someone new. It was early days, but I really thought there could be something to it. But Gary was my husband, my children's father, the first man I'd ever made love with. He was my history, and when he came back with his apologies and his flowers and his promises, it was easy to remember the good times. When he found out I'd been seeing someone else, he was devastated. He whisked me away for a luxury weekend and told me over and over how much he needed me, what a mistake he'd made. I broke it off with Hugh – that was his name. I couldn't break Gary's heart, not when he'd made it clear that it was mine to break.'

'What happened?'

'Gary was back to his old tricks as soon as he thought he had me where he wanted me. The thing was, I was wiser now and I ended it. What I felt for him was guilt, not love – I'd moved past that.'

'And Hugh?'

'I'd been so busy considering the feelings of the man who'd trampled my heart before, that I hadn't considered the one who was offering me his heart. I thought it was too soon, that he'd be fine – but he wasn't. He couldn't be with me knowing that I'd chosen Gary over him, even if I had made that choice under a certain amount of duress.'

'Oh.'

'All I'm saying is, be very sure before you hop on that plane. The only heart that matters in this is yours – not Jamie's, and not Matt's. Yours. I can't tell you what to do – your experience could be very different to mine – but please don't stay with Jamie for any reason other than love. Your heart was singing last week – and that's how you deserve to feel.'

'Even if Matt and I don't have a future?'

'Oh, Callie, none of us can guarantee a future – but that's no reason to live in the past.'

When Alice called on Friday to arrange for the three of us to meet up that night, I attempted to make an excuse. 'No, Cal,' she said. 'We need to get together.' After her explosion last week, I wasn't brave enough to argue with her.

Tiff was flying out the next morning for work, so made us promise not to lead her astray. She seemed preoccupied. I had the feeling that Alice knew more, or suspected more, than she was letting on, but for whatever reason Tiff hadn't confided in me. I hoped it was because of Jamie and her disapproval of him, but feared she'd found out about what had happened between Matt and me.

'There's nothing worse than being stuck in the back of the plane with a hangover,' Tiff said. 'Bloody Ainsley.'

'As opposed to being in the front of the plane with a hangover?' asked Alice, smiling.

'If you're not happy there, why don't you leave?' I asked. 'It's obvious Ainsley's going to win, so I don't understand why you don't just cut your losses and get out.'

Tiff and Alice stared at me with wide mouths. I didn't blame them. I had no idea where the words were coming from, but once I'd opened my mouth they just kept spewing out.

'Cal,' Alice warned softly, casting a worried glance towards Tiff. 'Maybe that's not the most helpful thing you can say at the moment.'

'Why not? Tiff's never backward in telling us what she thinks about anything. Perhaps it's time she listened to some straight talking from one of us for a change.'

Tiff bristled. 'So says the woman who couldn't wait to run back into the arms of someone who cheated on her before and is probably cheating on her again now.'

'Oh, yes. You're very quick to dole out the advice and pass judgement when it suits you, but you can't handle it when it comes back your way.' My chin jutted out and I felt it quivering slightly. In all our years of friendship, this was the first time I'd ever stood up to Tiff.

Alice watched us glaring at each other and drained her wine. 'Oh, look, that's the end of the bottle – maybe I should get another. Cal? Tiff? Same again?'

Tiff took a deep breath. 'So why don't you tell me what you really think,' she said, her voice overly calm, almost flat.

'Oh, Christ,' muttered Alice to no one in particular. 'I really would like some more wine.' She looked wildly around for a convenient waiter – or a hole to disappear into.

'I just don't think you need to destroy Ainsley in order to prove you're top bitch in the kennel. I thought you were there already.'

Did I just say that? By the look on Alice's face, yes, I did.

'Oh man, she went there.' Alice reached over and drained Tiff's glass.

'Just look at the way you've been playing with Jake,' I went on. 'Pretending Matt's the perfect man for you when anyone can tell it's Jake you really want. Then there are the photos you've been taking. I've known you for a long time – we've known you for a long time.' I looked at Alice, who'd managed to catch the eye of a passing waiter and was mouthing, 'And hurry, please,' to him. 'We haven't seen you like this for years. When you showed me those photos you'd taken at Cockatoo Island, it was like you were coming alive from inside. You were the Tiff we knew and loved from school, before you decided to ditch photography for corporate warfare. It's like you've got your mojo back. Then when you're talking about work, or taking a call from Ainsley, the light goes out of you. You're tired, Tiff – and I don't just think it's physical. I think you're tired of pretending to be someone else. I think it's why you've been avoiding us. Or is it because you're still seeing Jake on the side? You never did tell us how that date went.

Are you still seeing him?'

Tiff blinked and swallowed. Her hand shook slightly as she reached for her glass, so she put it back into her lap. I should have stopped there, I knew, but something kept me going.

'You are, aren't you? That's why you haven't been around. So you're what – playing with him to amuse yourself while you chase the big prize, and then as soon as he gets too close you'll dump him and move on to someone else? Nothing gets between work and climbing that ladder of yours – didn't you say that? What about love? Oh, that's right – love doesn't belong in your world. What was it you said?'

'You tell me.' Her voice was dangerously soft.

'You said you don't believe in love.'

'Maybe that's a safer attitude than being such a total romantic that you don't think you're worth anything unless you've got a man. Think about your dating history, Cal – you've gone from the love of your life to the love of your life, and they've all been variations of Jamie. Think about how much he's held you back – from travelling, from progressing at work. You would have gone so much further if you hadn't let him convince you that you weren't ready. And now you're making the same mistake again. He's going to hurt you, Cal. I wouldn't be surprised if he's timed this trip to Phuket to make sure you can't go to the interview at Helium. Mark my words, Kylie was not an isolated incident. Men like Jamie don't have isolated flings.'

'Don't stop there, Tiff. Next thing you'll be telling me that he cheated on me with you.' When the silence became too long, my eyes began to well. 'Oh my god, you didn't!'

'No, I didn't,' she said, 'but he certainly tried it on. I'm sure he tried it with Alice too.'

'Don't involve me in this,' Alice said.

I turned on her. 'Well, did he?'

'Not so I noticed,' she replied. 'Sweetie, we love you, we'd never do that. Besides, that was a long time ago.'

'Why didn't she tell me then?' I demanded, gesturing towards Tiff. 'Is that why you've never liked him?'

'How could she tell you? She warned you at the time, but you were so in love with him that if she had told you, you'd have taken it out on her – and we both knew that at some stage you'd need us.' Alice rubbed my arm in a gesture of support.

I brushed it away. 'He has changed,' I insisted.

'Men like that don't change,' said Tiff. 'They just go into hibernation for a few months until they're sure of you again. They let you think they'd be lost without you and that you're the centre of their universe – until *they're* the centre of *your* universe. Then they back away. So you try harder and harder to make things right, and they withdraw more and more until your whole world is built around trying to keep them happy. Just a little more love, you think. You stop going out and you sit at home and wait. That's how it was last time, and that's how it'll be this time too. That's why I've never liked him – I've seen too many of his type before, and I knew how it would end.'

What she was saying sounded familiar, but I wasn't in the mood to listen. 'And what about men like Matt?'

'That's the second time you've mentioned Matt. We're not having a relationship. You don't have relationships with men like Matt Delaney – they don't do relationships until they're ready to do them. It's a commitment thing. Sorry, Alice.'

Alice cast a quick glance at me. 'No offence taken. I know exactly what my brother used to be like.'

'You act like Matt is some prize you want to win,' I told Tiff. 'I know you haven't said as much, but I think that when you decide to settle down, your intention is to do it with Matt. But you don't just get to decide that. You don't just get to say he's perfect and expect he'll be waiting for you when you're ready to take him back from whoever he's moved on to. That's not fair to her – or him.'

Tiff stared at me. 'What is with you tonight? Number one: Matt Delaney is not the type of guy you can decide to win – it's exactly the opposite. He's the type of guy who decides who he wants. He'll shag around until he finds her, and he'll stop shagging around once he does. But it won't be me – I've always known that. Yes, we've hooked up in the past, but it was just casual – there was no expectation of anything else from either of us. I'd say it ended months ago, except there was nothing to end. We just stopped having sex and started being friends instead. We're way too similar to be together, and I've never wanted us to be anything more than we were. I might joke about how he ticks all the boxes, but that's all it's been – a joke. Happy now?'

I looked at the floor. Was I happy? I didn't know.

'Why are you so interested in me and Matt?' Tiff's eyes narrowed as she looked at me. 'Hang on, didn't you used to have a thing about him way back in school? Please tell me that's not what this is about?'

'No,' I said. 'It's not about that. It doesn't matter. Look, I'm sorry – obviously I'm not great company tonight. I shouldn't have said what I did, and I don't know why I did. I'll see you later.'

I kissed each of them on the cheek, but couldn't meet Tiff's eyes. She couldn't meet mine either.

Alice gathered me in for a loose hug. 'Sweetie, don't overthink this. Just listen to your heart . . . and call me.'

I nodded miserably and left.

Thankfully Hen wasn't home when I unlocked the front door. She would have been the last straw. I looked at the pile of dishes in the sink. I was determined not to clean up after her again – even if it meant eating all my meals out, or from plastic. One month I'd given her, and I was standing by that.

I could do something about the mess though. Before I could change my mind, I retrieved the clothes basket from the top of the washing machine and filled it with Hen's dirty dishes, glasses, empty bottles and pizza boxes. Then I put it on her bed and shut the door behind me.

I opened a bottle of wine, rescued a glass from my bedroom – I'd taken to keeping a clean plate, glass, mug and set of cutlery in there – and took them both to the lounge.

I didn't know what had gotten into me. I'd had no right to talk to Tiff like that. It wasn't her fault I was in the mess I was in. Something was obviously going on with her as well – we'd both said things we probably shouldn't have. I knew Tiff would never apologise, but our friendship was too important to me to let it go indefinitely. I'd call her when she was home from Hong Kong.

Hong Kong led me to Matt. She'd made it clear she had no romantic interest in him, but would they see each other? Would he tell her about us?

My thoughts were interrupted by a text. If it was Jamie, I was going to tell him I was out with the girls. I still hadn't let him touch me and I knew he was wondering why. Last night when he'd dropped me home after dinner out, he'd kissed me and would have gone further except Hen interrupted us.

The message was from Clio.

I know you're probably out drinking and doing things I can't do now that I'm pregnant, but is there any chance you can come up soon? My boobs are the size of watermelons and I don't want to shop for maternity clothes with anyone other than you.

I drained my glass and poured another, then drained it too. I knew things were tough when I couldn't decide what I wanted to avoid the most – having sex with Jamie, or going shopping with my pregnant sister.

I replied before I could think about it any further: *How about I catch the first flight up tomorrow? Get your comfy shoes on, little sister – we're going shopping!*

CHAPTER TWENTY-TWO

I held my breath as I texted Jamie yet another lie. *Clio having a meltdown. I'm flying up tomorrow morning, will be back Sunday night. Have a nice weekend xxx*

Have a nice weekend? Seriously?

His call came through almost immediately. He didn't waste any time with greetings. 'Brisbane? That's pretty sudden, isn't it?'

'Yes and no. I told you the other day that I'd promised to go up in the next couple of weeks, but I had to change my plans because we're going to Phuket.'

'Forgive me for trying to surprise my girlfriend with a romantic escape. All you've done since I booked this trip is look for excuses.'

'I don't think wanting to see my pregnant sister qualifies as an excuse.'

'You could have seen her when you were in Queensland the other weekend.'

'So you've said.'

His tone softened. 'I'm sorry, babe. It's just that we haven't been alone together – not properly – for a couple of weeks and I was really hoping we could make up for that this weekend.' He paused. 'I miss you, Cal. And I think part of what's going on here is that you're frustrated too.'

I took a breath. This was my opportunity. 'Jamie, this isn't about sex, or the lack of it –'

'You don't need to apologise, babe. It's not just your fault. I know you've been sick, and I've been busy as well – with work and everything else. It's why I can't wait to get you alone. In fact, when we come back from Phuket I think we should talk about moving in together. I know it's what you always wanted, and perhaps if we'd taken that step before we wouldn't need to be starting again now.'

'We do need to talk, but not about –'

He didn't let me finish. 'I just want to make you happy, Cal. Go to Brisbane and see your sister. I'll be busy at work next week, but after that we'll have seven whole perfect days together. I might even let you out of my arms briefly to talk about our future together.'

'Jamie, I don't think –'

'Sorry, babe – there's another call coming through that I have to take. I love you and can't wait to get on that plane with you next weekend.'

And then he was gone. While I felt guilty about hurting Jamie, I couldn't go on allowing him to think that everything was going to be okay between us. It wasn't – and moving in together would be a disaster. As tough as I knew the conversation would be, somehow

I had to find a way to tell him that. I promised myself that I'd do it as soon as I was back from Brisbane. No more excuses.

Clio and Mum were both at the airport to meet me on Saturday. It was one of those perfect late winter days that Brisbane does so well – the sun was shining, and I began shedding my extra layers almost as soon as I got off the plane. I might not have lived in this city in many years, but it was good to be home.

After the usual reunion hugs and kisses, I stood back and looked closely at Clio. She was radiant – her skin glowing, her eyes sparkling, her hair thick and shiny. And Owen was right: there was definite growth in the breast department.

'Oh my, Mrs Morgan, that's quite some cleavage you're developing there,' I said.

'I know, right?' She shimmied proudly. 'I think I might spend the rest of my life pregnant if this is what happens.'

Mum shook her head and smiled. 'I'll bet your father's newest bike on the fact that you won't be saying that in another few months.'

'He's bought another one?' Dad had an array of road cycles already hanging on the garage wall.

'Yes, he's decided to train for an endurance ride in the Italian Alps.' Mum had never stood in the way of Dad's exercise goals – even when they took him away on holiday.

'At his age?' I said.

'Age is just a number, Calliope. He says it's something he wants to do before he's sixty.'

'Of course he does.'

'Why are we hanging about here?' Clio was getting impatient. 'I have a whole list of boutiques I want to get to.'

The list was exhausting. We stopped briefly for lunch in Paddington, but other than that went through until late afternoon, by which time Clio had purchased enough clothes and accessories to ensure she'd look fabulous all the way through her pregnancy.

I felt some pangs of envy at the start, but much fewer than I'd expected. Regardless of what happened with Jamie and Matt, I now knew that as much as I still wanted a baby, I wanted it with someone who would be completely involved in the entire process – not just the fun part of making it. Jamie was absolutely not that man.

When Clio dropped Mum and me off later, she took me aside. 'Thanks so much for doing this with me. I know it's been tough on you.'

'What do you mean?'

'The marriage and baby thing – that's always been your dream and it's accidentally happened to me. I can't imagine how much that must hurt.'

'Oh, that.' A lump of emotion rose up from my belly and lodged in my throat.

'I didn't want to upset you by saying anything, but you stood up with me at my wedding when your heart was breaking. And you're here now, even though part of you must be wishing it was you – and even though you should really be back in Melbourne getting ready for a romantic week away with Jamie. I just want you to know that I really appreciate it. That's all.'

She hugged me and I felt my eyes welling.

She stood back and studied me. 'You *are* looking forward to a romantic week away with Jamie, aren't you?'

For a brief moment I was tempted to confide in her, but as close as we were, we didn't really have that sort of relationship. Besides, I told myself, I didn't want to burst her happiness bubble with problems I'd created for myself. There'd be enough time for explanations once it was all sorted.

I forced a smile to my face. 'Of course I am. Now get yourself home so you can pick up Owen and come back here for dinner.'

Mum asked me about Jamie while we were preparing the dinner.

'You're still not cooking much then?' she said when she saw me struggling to peel and slice some onions for a salad. My lack of proficiency in the kitchen had always been a bit of a standing family joke.

'No,' I grinned. 'But it's on my bucket list to learn some day.'

'You'll need to learn if you intend settling down with Jamie.' She looked keenly at me. 'Are you intending on settling down with him this time?'

'I don't think so, Mum.'

She nodded. 'Well, it's best you work that out now before it's too late.' She rummaged through the vegetable crisper as she spoke. 'Where did I put that cucumber?'

I always knew Mum was there for me, but she was more comfortable providing practical rather than emotional support.

'How does next week's holiday fit into that?' she asked as she continued to chop and slice.

I shrugged. 'He didn't give me much choice in the matter. He wants it to be a new start – he seems quite serious about making it work this time.'

'And you're not?'

I shook my head.

'Oh well, at least you get a week away. You'll come home with a tan, and at best you two will decide to make a go of it.'

I smiled at her reference to my Melbourne-pale skin. 'True.'

'How are the Delaneys?' she went on. 'How many children has Laura got now?'

Mum had a weird, almost competitive attitude towards the Delaneys, especially Jane. I thought it was because I'd spent so much time at their house growing up and at their holiday house in the summer – almost as if I preferred spending time there than at home, which absolutely wasn't the case.

'They're good. You should go up and see them sometime. Tony's semi-retired, and I think Jane spends a lot of time with the grandkids. Laura has five boys now. She and Mick are still happy.'

'I know Alice is in Melbourne,' she said, 'but what about Matt? Where is he now?'

I felt my cheeks redden and lowered my gaze to the kitchen counter. I tried to make my tone neutral as I replied. 'He's been in Hong Kong for a while. Actually, he was home the other weekend for Mick's birthday. He's talking about coming back for Jane's sixtieth next month too.'

'Oh, really?' Mum didn't look at me as she added, 'Does he have anything to do with you not wanting to settle down with Jamie?'

'Why do you ask?'

'I just recall you having a thing for him at one time.'

I forced a laugh. 'Really? I'd forgotten all about that.'

Mum finally stopped chopping and looked up at me. 'You're a terrible liar, Calliope. You always have been.' She tipped the salad vegetables into a bowl. 'Be careful. It's rarely a good idea to mix romance and friendship, and Alice has been a good friend to you over the years. Of course, though, it's your life. Now,' she handed me some dinner plates, 'how about you get the table set?'

Neither Jamie nor Matt was mentioned for the remainder of my visit. Dinner on Saturday night was all about Clio and Owen and the baby, and Dad's upcoming marathon and the cycle tour he was contemplating. And by the time Mum had updated me on where she was up to with the family history, and what Angus was doing on Shetland, Sunday morning was virtually over and I had to leave for my flight home.

When Mum dropped me at the airport, she hugged me close. 'Just because you're away from us doesn't mean I don't like knowing what's happening, Calliope. You do what your heart tells you to do – and you know where we are if it all goes tits up.'

A laugh burst out of me. 'Tits up? Seriously, Mum?'

She shrugged one shoulder and grinned. 'I picked it up from Angus, and I think I'll use it a whole lot more. It certainly seems to apply to your situation.'

'It certainly does.' I reached out and hugged her again. 'I love you, Mum.'

'And we love you too.'

I phoned Jamie when I got home to let him know I'd arrived safely. He was out and about – with Josh Booth, he said – so we didn't talk long.

'I'm missing you so much, babe, but unless you

can move your dance class on Tuesday night, I won't be able to see you until the weekend,' he said.

'I really need to talk to you,' I protested.

'Well, I can't talk now, and I'm busy with work for the rest of the week – this project is finally going live. So it'll have to wait until the weekend.'

'But –'

'Sorry, babe, have to fly. Josh says hello.'

After lying awake all Monday night, I gave in and cancelled belly dancing on Tuesday night. Hen was going out so I arranged to have dinner with Jamie at my place. It would be the last chance I had to talk to him – and to pull out of this holiday.

'I'll bring some dinner in and we can talk,' I told him.

'That sounds great,' he said. 'I know how important your dance class is to you, so it means a lot that you're giving it up to see me. I'll be there about seven-ish?'

At 7 pm he texted to say he was running late, and at 8 pm I received another message to say they were having problems with a file transfer and he had to stay until it was fixed.

We can talk on the flight over. See you on the weekend. Love Jxxx

I'd heard nothing about my interview at Helium, then Marion finally phoned on Friday morning to book an appointment for the following Wednesday with Pip and Alex.

'I'm so sorry to do this,' I said, 'but is there any chance we could delay a week? Jamie's surprised me with a trip to Phuket leaving on Sunday, so I'll be away all of next week.'

I held my breath as I waited for her response. I knew what opinion I would have if a candidate wanted to pick and choose interview times and dates – and it wasn't a favourable one.

'Are you sure about this?' she asked. 'I thought you were really interested in the job.' I could hear her disappointment in me.

'I am. I'm more excited about this opportunity than I've been about anything in a long time.'

'Then why jeopardise it? You know as well as I do that if a candidate asked you the question you've just asked me, you'd wonder about their commitment.'

'Yes, I know. It's just that Jamie sprang this on me and I promised him I'd go.'

'Even if it costs you a job you really want? Are you really going to be that woman?'

Was I that woman? For the right man, I supposed I would be, but did I want to throw this opportunity away for a week with Jamie? A week I'd been guilted into accepting?

Marion must have taken my silence as answer enough. 'Don't do it, Cal – not for Jamie. Listen, Alex's schedule tends to be fluid and it wouldn't surprise me if he did change plans at the last minute, so how about I keep your appointment for Wednesday and if you do end up going with Jamie, you can call me. And if Alex's plans change in the meantime, I can call you. What do you say?'

'Thank you. I really appreciate this.' I paused. 'What did you mean when you said "not for Jamie"? Is this something about that job he applied for at DotPoint?'

She hesitated a few seconds. 'Look, I shouldn't have said anything. It's none of my business, and it was before you got back together.'

'What was before we got back together?'

'His fling with the director at GNA – it's why he left. Damien knows her husband. He said they're still together but they only just made it through. Apparently it had been going on for about six months.'

The breath left my body in a noisy sigh and I rested my forehead on my free hand. 'Is that why he didn't get the job at DotPoint?'

Marion paused, then said, 'Alex requires absolute integrity in his employees, especially his senior managers.'

'I see.'

'I'm sorry, Cal, I shouldn't have said anything. It was all before you two got back together.'

'It's fine. Don't worry about it. Whatever happens, I'll talk to you next week.'

'I'm hoping I'll see you next week,' she said.

After she'd hung up, I allowed myself to put two and two together. If what Marion said was true, Jamie had been having an affair with his boss at GNA while we were still together. Which meant he'd left me for her – not because he couldn't handle my mistrust. For months I'd been blaming myself for our break-up, but if this was true, it was all on him. Tiff had been right to be sceptical of his reasons for leaving, and spot-on in her dislike of Jamie.

I lowered my head to my desk. Christ, what was I thinking? Was I really going to throw away the possibility of a job I really wanted, and a love I really felt, for a man who had, it now appeared, spent most of our relationship lying to me? Were his tears part of that too? A tool to tie me to him until I needed him again like I used to need him – at which point he'd withdraw again like he did last time?

Andy chose that moment to come into my office. 'Hey, Jones . . . Oh, sorry, are you okay?'

I lifted my head. 'Yes, I'm fine. What's wrong?'

'I'm having a few concerns about Flick's performance.'

I let out a rueful laugh. 'You're surely not serious?'

'What do you mean?'

'Just that I'm tired of cleaning up after you. Either keep it zipped up, or save it for other teams. Don't shit in your own nest. And don't look at me like that – you know exactly what I'm talking about.'

'But –'

'Andy, I'm not in the mood. If you have a genuine performance concern with Felicity, bring me the data. If it's just that you want help getting rid of your latest conquest, you can take care of it yourself.'

He lingered for a few seconds without saying anything.

'Well, what's it to be? I don't have all day.' Even as I was speaking, I knew I was taking out my anger at my own stupidity on him.

A wide grin appeared on his face. 'Is this because I haven't asked you out again?'

I shook my head slowly. 'No, Andy, it's not.'

He continued to smile, perhaps convinced I'd laugh and turn it into a joke, but I didn't.

'Okay, you're obviously busy,' he said. 'I'll come back later.'

'You do that.'

If Tiff was right about Jamie, I owed her an apology – and there was no time like the present.

'I'm sorry, Cal,' she said as soon as she answered the phone. 'I'm glad you rang. I was going to call you tonight.'

I'd never heard her apologise before and was glad she wasn't there to see the surprise on my face.

'I'm the one that went off. I've got no idea what got into me,' I told her. 'I shouldn't have said what I did.'

'Actually, you should have. It was long overdue

and you were absolutely right – I have no idea how to mind my own business, but have no problem at all minding everyone else's. If Jamie makes you happy, who am I to deny you that. I'm your friend and I don't want to see you hurt, but that doesn't give me the right to stand in your way. It means I need to be here to pick you up. If the last few weeks have taught me anything, it's that I'm not right about everything after all. But we can talk about that later. What's happening with you? How's Jamie?'

Again I was thankful she couldn't see my eyebrows hit the ceiling. 'He's fine, but busy. I haven't seen much of him lately.'

'Aren't you flying out on Sunday? And Alice is leaving tomorrow too, right? I'd forgotten she's going to Bali until I spoke to her yesterday afternoon.'

Tiff also didn't do the forgetting thing, let alone admit she'd forgotten something.

'Yes, Alice leaves tomorrow morning and my flight's Sunday morning. And Alice said you're off to Fiji for Masters on Monday? You made it!'

'Yes.'

A few weeks ago she'd been full of the prospect of making it to Masters despite Ainsley's best efforts. Now she sounded almost despondent about going.

'Aren't you looking forward to it? After all, you won. You beat Ainsley.'

'I know. And yes, I'm sure it'll be fabulous.' She

didn't sound convincing at all. 'How's the packing going?'

'I haven't started yet.'

'Seriously? That's not like you. Last time you went to Phuket with Jamie, you were so excited it was all we heard about for days. You were packed and ready to go with all your outfits planned. Actually,' she paused, 'didn't we throw out your bathers in the great Jamie purge? Something about how the suspension had gone in them, you said. That means you have a beach to go to and a pool to lounge beside, but nothing to wear.'

'I hadn't thought about it.'

I'd been so focused on whether or not I should go that the actual logistics of packing hadn't occurred to me. Maybe having no bathers was the best excuse I had? I could just imagine myself saying to Jamie, 'I'm sorry, I can't come to Phuket – I've got nothing to wear.'

'Well,' said Tiff, 'it's lucky I have thought about it. I have absolutely no plans for this weekend, so we're going shopping for bathers tomorrow morning.'

Great.

'Are you sure?' I said. 'You've just got back from Hong Kong, and you must have heaps to catch up on before you fly out on Monday.'

'I'm absolutely sure. By tomorrow afternoon you'll be beach ready.'

Whether I wanted to be or not.

CHAPTER TWENTY-THREE

Kerry was positively fizzing at lunchtime. The reason became clear when she told me that Andy Campbell had finally asked her out.

'That's fabulous news!' I said. 'When did this happen?'

'About twenty minutes ago. He sat on the edge of my desk, focused his entire attention on me and said "So, Kerry, I think it's time we went out for a drink, don't you?"'

I was thrilled for her; she'd been wanting this for so long. 'When are you going out?'

'We're not.' My soup went down the wrong way, but a smile beamed across Kerry's face.

'What? Are you playing hard to get?'

'Absolutely not. I've decided that, like you said, Andy Campbell is one of those fantasies best left in my head. I suspect the reality could be a disappointment. Besides,' a pink hue spread across her cheeks, 'I think I've found someone – and she might be the one to make my heart sing.'

I reached over and squeezed her forearm. 'I'm so happy for you. Who is it, and how?'

'Louise – from belly dancing, the girl with the really curly hair and the purple coin belt.'

'Did you guys go for drinks again after class?'

She nodded. 'And then we ran into each other in a bar on Friday night and had a few more drinks and . . . I don't know how it happened, but I think this could be it. Is that too weird? It was just one weekend – how can I know after one weekend? I mean, I thought I was in love with Andy Campbell. How does something like this happen?'

I put my arm around her and hugged her. 'I don't know, but sometimes it just does. When you stop overthinking it, you find the one who makes your heart sing.'

'Like the shimmy-walk?'

'Yeah, like the shimmy-walk.'

I'd persuaded Tiff that there was no way I could go swimwear shopping without coffee, so we stopped at a place in Abbotsford that, by the looks of all the bikes chained up outside, was a favourite with the cycling crowd.

'Just what I need,' she muttered. 'Middle-aged men in lycra before I've had coffee.'

'Now, now,' I laughed. 'It's probably the perfect view before trying on bathers.'

'Perhaps.' She grinned and looked at her watch. 'Alice will be boarding that flight to Bali about now.'

'The things she'll do to get out of a shopping trip.'

'I know. Although she's less excited than I thought she'd be.' She looked across the table at me. 'You're also less excited than I thought you'd be.'

'You know Alice – she's not exactly the conference type, and going away with Tommy is a pretty big commitment for her these days.' I forced a smile. 'As for me, there's so much to organise.'

Tiff paused as a waiter set down our coffees. 'Still, it's nice that he's surprised you with a trip somewhere you both have good memories of.'

I sighed deeply and considered whether I should say anything more. Then I just blurted it out. 'I know I should be happy about it – it's just that there's the job at Helium. When I brought it up, Jamie just dismissed it like it didn't matter. And the interviews are happening while I'm away, so I guess that's that. Plus – and this is the biggie – I don't want to go away with him. There, I said it.'

Tiff looked as if she wanted to say something, but remained silent.

'I know,' I said. 'If this had happened even three months ago, I would have been beside myself with excitement. After all, not only is Jamie back – he says he loves me and he's doing everything he can to make up for what happened. I guess I'm just being ridiculous.

Hormonal maybe.' I smiled weakly. 'You know, I even –'

I stopped as I noticed two women sitting at a table near the door. One was small and pretty, with long dark hair; it was Emily, the woman I'd seen in the rain in Bourke Street that night. The woman with her was tall and slim, her medium-length blonde hair tied up in a ponytail. She was crying openly, and although Emily didn't take her eyes off her, she made no attempt to comfort her.

I couldn't stop staring at them. There was something courageous in the line of Emily's jaw, the set of her shoulders. She looked like a woman prepared to fight for something she believed in. Or someone – Jamie perhaps? An instinct told me that he had something to do with this, but I also didn't think he was who Emily was fighting for. Maybe she was fighting for herself?

Then I heard her call the other woman 'Suse'. That was the name on the text message Jamie had received the other night. *Call me*, it had said. From Suse. With three kisses.

A chill ran through me as I instantly knew that Jamie had been playing with both these women. They'd probably once been friends, but whatever had happened with him had ruined that. By the look on Emily's face, she was the innocent party, yet the other woman was wearing a wedding ring. Surely Jamie wouldn't have a fling with a married woman? My conversation with Marion about the director at GNA came back to me.

Yes, I decided, he probably would. How many other lies had he told me?

'Earth to Cal.' Tiff's voice brought me out of my pondering.

'Sorry,' I said.

'Do you know them?'

'No, but I suspect Jamie does,' I admitted ruefully.

'What makes you think that?'

'We met for dinner the other week, and Jamie told me he had to go to Sydney again, and kissed me – probably to distract me or keep me quiet.' How many times over the years had he done that? 'Anyway, it was raining and that woman was there, watching us – or rather, watching Jamie. I don't think she saw me at first. She seemed upset. When I asked about her, he told me her name was Emily and that he worked with her. He said she had a thing about him, but he hadn't reciprocated. I believed him at the time. Okay, I think I wanted to believe him. And the other woman – I think Jamie knows her too. I just heard Emily call her Suse, and I'm sure that was the name on a text he got the other night.'

'God, I'm so sorry, Cal.' Tiff reached over to hold my hand – a gesture more like Alice than herself.

'It's okay, you can say you told me so. You knew what he was like – everyone knew. I was the only one who didn't.'

'Even so, you love him. You can't help that.' She said the words in such a sad, yet matter-of-fact way that was completely without judgement – and completely not her.

'Are you okay?' I asked.

'Absolutely. Why wouldn't I be? I'm off to Fiji on Monday – sun, sea, cocktails, rubbing Ainsley's face in the fact that I've won. I can't wait.'

She was smiling, but it seemed forced. And there was an edge to her that hadn't been there a week ago – or perhaps I'd been so wound up in my own issues I hadn't noticed. Actually, it was the edge that was the problem. Tiff was normally prickly, but now she seemed . . . softer? It wasn't just that her clothes were more relaxed, or her hair hadn't been straightened, or she hadn't passed one disparaging comment about the grungy interior of the café. There was something else . . .

'Your nails,' I announced. 'This is the first time in years I've seen you without your nails done.'

Tiff curled her fingers into her palms, then placed her hands in her lap, out of sight. I couldn't hold back the grin.

'I just haven't had time to get a manicure done,' she said. 'I'll make sure I get one tomorrow morning so it's fresh for Fiji. I'm thinking bright pink, or coral?'

Across the room, the two women were parting. We watched them.

'Maybe it's not what you think,' said Tiff softly. 'Perhaps you need to give Jamie a chance to explain – you might have got the wrong end of this particular stick.'

I raised my eyebrows at her concession. 'Do you really believe that?'

She hesitated, then shook her head. 'No, I don't. But I do think you need to give him the chance to explain himself. After all,' she added a short laugh, 'you are supposed to be getting on a plane together tomorrow morning for a romantic holiday.' She covered my hand with hers again. 'You said you'd do anything to get him back; and that once you had him, you'd do anything to keep him.'

'Yes, I remember.' Was it really only a few months ago I'd felt that way? 'The truth is, it doesn't feel the same – being with him. It hasn't felt right almost from the start. There's something different – and I don't think it's him. Maybe I've changed.'

'Maybe he's not what you want any more?' She said it so quietly, I barely heard her. 'Maybe what you thought you wanted and what you really need are different? But don't listen to me. I'm the last person you should listen to right now.' Her smile was rueful.

'You're right – I don't want him any more,' I said. 'I deserve someone I can trust – and it's been made clear to me over the last few days that Jamie isn't that man.' I laughed. 'What do they say? Be careful what you wish for – you might just get it. Now I've got it, I don't want it.'

It surprised me that I didn't feel sadder, emptier. Matt's face floated into view, but I pushed it away. He needed his own space. I refused to share thoughts of him until my brain was cleared of Jamie.

'Ain't that the truth,' said Tiff.

'What do you mean?'

'I've worked so hard all year to prove Ainsley wrong and get onto Masters, and now the idea of spending a week pretending to be nice to that bitch and everyone else whose balls she keeps in a jar under her desk is the last thing I want to be doing.'

'What would you rather be doing?'

She started to say something, but stopped and looked over to where the blonde woman was watching Emily leave. 'You know what – it's a long story. You wouldn't want to know.'

'I do want to know,' I protested. 'Please talk to me, Tiff.'

Her eyes filled with tears and she fanned her face as if to force them back inside. 'No, sweetie, it's not the right time. You have bathers to buy, an excuse to listen to, and a holiday to pack for. I need to get my nails done, take a deep breath and harden back up. I will talk to you, I promise, just not yet.'

I hadn't seen Tiff cry since her parents separated. Her mother moved to Perth, where the head office of her company was based – and her father, an artist, stayed in Brisbane to look after Tiff. It was her final year at school, and her tears weren't due to anger at her mother for putting her career ahead of her marriage and family; they were directed at her father for what she saw as his lack of ambition. In Tiff's mind, her father had allowed her mother to dictate the terms of their relationship and, as a result, he was the one devastated by their break-up. Up until that year, Tiff was destined to be a photographer – we never saw her without a camera in her hand – but everything changed that summer. I'd often wondered whether her ambition and her refusal to allow any man to come between her and what she wanted were products of that time.

'You know, we all got what we wanted,' I said, 'but of the three of us, Alice is the only one who seems happy. Tommy fits the bill perfectly, and he adores the ground she walks on.'

'Hmmm,' Tiff mused, 'Tommy sounds nice, but Alice will be bored in no time. For all her talk of rules and structure, she needs someone who can let her be herself – and this controlled version isn't the real Alice. Matt said the same the other night – he didn't recognise this Alice.'

My heart fell into my belly at the mention of his name. 'You saw Matt?'

'Yes, we met up for a drink.' She saw the look on my face and misunderstood it. 'No, it wasn't like that. It was just two mates catching up.'

'I didn't think it was anything else.'

'Are you sure? Anyway, he was asking about you.'

Tiff watched me keenly and I felt the blush run up

my face. 'Really? Why?'

She kept her tone deliberately casual. 'He was just asking if you were still with Jamie. I told him you were going to Phuket with him, and he seemed . . . I don't know . . . disappointed?'

I felt my heart skip, but couldn't meet Tiff's eyes. What must Matt think of me?

'It's okay, Cal, we're not together – we never really were. It was only ever a sometimes thing. But he told me what happened between you two the other weekend. Why didn't you mention that?'

I looked up, horror on my face. 'Oh my god. He told you?'

'Is that why things are different with Jamie?'

'No, of course not.' I paused, 'Okay, maybe. I can't get that weekend out of my mind. I can't get Matt out of my mind. But he lives in Hong Kong, and he'll never settle with one girl. Even you said that.'

'No. I said he'll settle when he meets the right woman, and when he does she'll be the only one for him.'

'But he's like Jamie – he's as bad as Jamie.'

'Sweetie, you know better than that. Matt Delaney is nothing like Jamie. He's honest, and he's a good man –'

'But what about all the women?' I interrupted.

'Matt has never cheated on anyone in his life. He just hasn't committed to anyone, not properly.'

'Oh,' I said, my voice small.

'Until now.'

I was silent for a few seconds as I thought how best to say the next part. 'I didn't tell you about Matt and what happened because I thought he was yours, and I knew I should feel guilty about that – but I couldn't. I also didn't tell you because making love with Matt made me as bad as Jamie. I didn't believe Jamie when he told me that night with Kylie just happened. I couldn't believe he hadn't given me a thought. Yet that's exactly how it was with Matt.'

Tiff nodded slowly. 'I thought it might have been something like that.'

Then I said the words that had been keeping me awake for part of every night since Matt and I were together. 'What if it's always been Matt? What if all those years ago I was in love with him, and I never fell out of love with him?'

I didn't tell her the rest – that I was very much afraid I'd spent my entire dating life rebounding from Alice's brother and the possibility of what could have been.

'And what if he feels the same way about you?' Tiff suggested quietly.

I shook my head. 'I can't think about that. I have to decide whatever it is I need to do about Jamie without Matt Delaney and his fabulous kisses crowding my brain.'

'That you do.' She deliberately changed the subject. 'In the meantime, we need to buy you some bathers – and then you can decide whether you'll be wearing them on a beach in Thailand, or in the swimming pool in Matt's apartment complex in Hong Kong when you go to visit.' She grinned. 'And don't you dare throw that sugar at me.'

CHAPTER TWENTY-FOUR

I took my suitcase out from under my bed where I'd stored it. How long since I'd last used it? It had been the previous trip to Phuket with Jamie, the one we took after he'd confessed to the drunken indiscretion with Kylie. It was just the once, he'd said. A mistake. He'd sworn it had never happened before, and would never happen again. He realised how close he'd come to losing me, he'd said, and had begged for my forgiveness, said he couldn't be without me.

Tearing the tags off my new bathers and matching cover-up, I lay them on the bed. I sat back and contemplated the empty bag. What else?

Emily's face floated in front of me – her tears the other night, and the look on her face this morning. It was like seeing myself in a mirror not too many months ago. I was convinced that Jamie had caused Emily's tears, and the argument between her and Suse. Just like he'd been the reason for my tears in the past. I was certain that he'd lied to me the other night about Emily and Suse. And if I asked him about his boss at

GNA, I was sure he'd lie about that too – or at least not answer the question directly. I thought about the many times he hadn't answered my questions over the years, always finding a way to distract me or divert my attention – usually with kisses and sex.

I didn't know if Jamie had changed – and it no longer seemed to matter. The difference was that I had. I knew I wasn't prepared to tolerate his lies and infidelities any longer. Nor was I afraid to live my life without him, or anyone like him. I used to say that life without Jamie felt like being half-alive, but the truth was that life with him also felt like a half-life. I'd known things weren't right with us even before that magical weekend with Matt. Jamie didn't make my heart sing, and I deserved someone who did.

I'd had to get back with him, no matter how briefly, to really understand how much I'd changed – and how I no longer needed him. For the first time, I felt ready to end a relationship that wasn't doing me any good, and without having another to jump into.

A picture of Matt's face swam into view. No, I wasn't going there. Not yet. As I'd said to Alice, I suspected that whatever this was between Matt and me – or could be between us – was too important to rush into. And I couldn't risk it by going away for a week with a man who'd been lying to me.

As I slid the suitcase back under the bed, I heard the front door slam and Hen stomped into the house.

Squaring my shoulders I went out to face her.

'No lover boy today?' she said. 'Has he done another runner? That would be just like him – the day before you're due to go away.' There was a sneer in her voice.

I tipped my head to one side as I suddenly understood. 'You were with him, weren't you? Before?'

'What of it?'

She planted her heavy-booted feet squarely and faced me expecting . . . I didn't know what she was expecting.

I shrugged. 'Absolutely nothing. How are you going with finding somewhere to live?'

'Are you kicking me out because I shagged your boyfriend?' she said.

I shook my head. 'No. As I told you before, it's because I don't like you. Simple really.'

I turned my back and walked away. Tiff would say that I'd given the last of my fucks and had no more to give. She'd be right.

Jamie arrived soon after, letting himself in and coming to lean against my bedroom doorframe in the way he knew displayed his best angles.

'I just saw Hen – she said you'd kicked her out. I thought we agreed she was okay.'

'No, Jamie, you agreed she was okay. And now I know why. Besides, you don't live here. You have no say in the matter.'

He came across and tried to take me in his arms.

'No,' I said, 'you don't get to kiss me. We need to talk.'

'But you like me kissing you,' he said, grinning and pulling me closer. 'You like me doing lots of other things to you too. Is that the problem – is it frustration talking? I wouldn't blame you – I'm feeling it too. How about we talk later?'

I shook my head and pushed him away. 'You're not going to distract me this time.'

'Is this about me and Hen? That was years ago – way back when we were first together. It's got nothing to do with you and me now.'

He held his hands out as if pleading with me to understand, yet his look showed his confidence that not only would I believe him, I wanted him so much that I'd pretend it didn't matter.

'No, it's got nothing to do with Hen,' I said. 'It's about Emily and Suse.'

'Who?' He shook his head, as if he was puzzled and trying to place the names. 'Sorry, babe, I don't follow.'

'Emily, the girl we saw in Bourke Street that night, and her friend Suse.'

'That Emily? What does she have to do with us?'

Oh, he was good.

'You tell me, Jamie.'

'Babe,' he reached for me again, 'is this you being paranoid? I thought we were over that silliness.'

I looked at his lying face and knew I was done. I'd wasted enough of my time and emotion on Jamie.

'It seems we're not,' I said, moving away from him. 'You know what? I think we should just call it quits. Here and now. I know you're lying to me about Emily and Suse —' He opened his mouth to say something and I stopped him. 'No, I don't want explanations or stories or whatever you call them. I don't care about you and Emily, or you and Suse, or how I'm sure you've ruined their friendship. I also don't want to know if Suse is married, although I saw a wedding ring on her finger —'

'Where did you see Suse? Whatever she said to you was a lie.' His face had paled and a pulse beat in his jaw.

'I saw her and Emily having coffee this morning in Abbotsford. Both of them were upset. Don't worry, I didn't talk to either of them. I just put two and two together.'

He smiled then, as if confident of winning me over. 'We can talk this through, Cal. We have seven nights in Phuket and I can show you just how much you mean to me. It'll be just like last time.'

His words should have been seductive, his voice curling around me like it used to, but I just felt numb.

'Is she married — Suse?'

'Yes, but it was just some fun and she came onto me — she said she was bored. I wouldn't have gone there otherwise.'

I didn't know who I was angrier with in that moment – myself for allowing him to humiliate me again, or him for possibly ruining someone else's marriage without a care for their welfare. All Jamie cared about was himself.

'I'm not going to Phuket with you,' I said. 'I'm sorry, but I can't. I'm going to stay here and go to the interview at Helium.'

'But I've booked the tickets and the accommodation. You have to come.'

'No, Jamie, I don't. I didn't ask you to book the holiday. You go, have a good time. You'll forget about me quickly enough – we both know that.'

'But I love you, Cal.'

'Maybe you do, but I don't love you any more.'

'You'll regret this,' he said. 'When I walk out the door this time, I won't be back. Remember that when you're lonely and missing me.'

'Maybe I will be lonely, but I don't think I'll miss you. Not this time. I want to be with someone who's honest with me – I deserve that. And that person isn't you.'

'It's someone else, isn't it? You've met someone else. I fucking knew it. You've been weird since you got back from Queensland, not wanting me to touch you. Did you fuck someone else while you were away?'

His face was ugly with anger. I would have laughed at his hypocrisy if I wasn't so tired of it all.

'Yes, there was someone else. And no, I'm not with him.'

'Hah. I fucking knew it!'

'Are you really yelling at me because I had one night with someone else? We've just talked about you being with another three women while you were with me: Hen, Emily, Suse.' I counted them off on my fingers. 'Then there's Kylie and your boss from GNA – and they're just the ones I know about. And you're angry at me? I don't fucking believe you!' By now, I was yelling too.

'It's different for you,' he said. 'You can't separate sex and love. I can.'

If a grown man could sulk, that was what Jamie was doing. His bottom lip was pushed out and his expression was resentful.

'That's right, I can't separate the two,' I said, 'and I take both seriously. Which proves that obviously I can't love you if I was able to be seduced by someone else.'

He started to say something else but I stopped him. 'Please don't, Jamie. Don't make this harder than it already is. Surely you owe me that much.'

'Owe you? I owe you nothing. Yes, I was with Suse and Emily. Where do you think I was every Sunday morning when I told you I was running with Josh? And that four-poster bed in Daylesford? That was me and Suse. And that weekend you were off fucking someone else, so was I – there was no offsite. Suse was so hot for me she'd have left her husband and her miserable little life if I'd asked her to.' His face had twisted into an ugly sneer. 'Bree was the same – she would have left her husband for me too, but where's the fun in that? Afterwards, she made life so uncomfortable for me at GNA I had no choice but to leave. I liked that job.'

'And Emily?'

'She was just some fun. She's Suse's best friend, and I knew Josh had a thing for her, so . . .' He shrugged, uncaring of how he'd hurt his supposed friend, or how he'd destroyed Emily and Suse's friendship. And uncaring of how he'd treated me.

I felt sick when I thought of how desperately I'd wanted him, how I'd given up things I loved to sit at home and wait for him, how I'd blamed myself for our break-up, how I'd taken him back so easily, and believed his lies and his tears. Of course he wouldn't allow me to break up with him – that's not how it worked. He preferred to chip away at me until I was utterly dependent on him again, and then he'd throw me aside just as he had last time. I was worth so much more than that.

'Please go,' I said, my voice calmer than it should have been.

'If I do, I won't be coming back,' he warned.

'That's what I'm counting on.'

After he'd left, I sat down at the kitchen bench and allowed myself a few minutes of self-pity. It didn't last long though. Not only was there too much to look forward to, I also wanted to get to the bottom of whatever was going on with Tiff.

Matt rang me early on Sunday morning, just before I should have been leaving for the airport.

'Hey, you,' I said when I picked up. Hearing his voice for the first time since we'd been together sent a thrill through me, but I attempted to keep my tone light and breezy. 'What time is it over there?'

'I have no idea, but it's still dark out.'

'Okay.' There was silence. 'Matt . . . it's lovely to hear your voice, but what do you want?'

I heard him take a deep breath. 'I rang to ask you not to go with him – with Jamie – to Phuket. Tiff told me. Please don't go, Cal. I know I said I wouldn't pressure you, that I'd let you make your own mind up, but please don't go with him. I'm picturing the two of you together and it's doing my head in.'

My heart jumped into my throat.

'Calliope? Are you still there?'

I nodded. 'Yes, sorry, I'm nodding.'

'I'm too late, aren't I? You're probably on your way to the airport now. Is he there with you?'

'No.'

'He's not there?'

'No. And I'm not going with him. I told him yesterday that I don't love him and I wasn't going with him. I haven't been able to . . . you know . . . with him since you and me.'

'Really?'

'Yes, really.'

'I'm glad. Because I don't want to . . . you know . . . with anyone else but you.'

I could hear his smile across the miles and it wrapped around me and warmed me. It felt as though there was a promise of comfort and safety in his words.

'Cal, I —'

'Not yet, Matt. I need to take this slowly. Whatever this thing is with us, I think it's more than . . . I think . . .'

I couldn't tell him that I thought he was the person I'd been looking for, the person who made everything else fall into place. The words couldn't get past my heart in my throat.

'I know. I do too. All of that. I just need you to know that I think you're who I've always been looking for, Cal.' He paused, then said, 'With you everything makes sense, so take your time. We've got plenty of it — especially if he's out of the picture.'

CHAPTER TWENTY-FIVE

I spent the rest of the day removing every last trace of Jamie from the apartment. I even took the sheets off my bed and threw them out too. Then I cleaned everywhere except Hen's room, scrubbing and wiping until every surface gleamed.

It was midday before I realised I needed to get to the shops or I'd have nothing to sleep on that night. I also bought a Mexican-style striped mat for the front door, and a pair of plants in brightly coloured pots to put on either side.

Mrs Gianello came out to admire them. 'They really brighten your day,' she said.

'Thanks, Mrs G. I think so too.'

'Your young man gone again?'

'He has.'

'And the girl with the heavy boots?'

'Very soon, Mrs G.'

'You know, dear, I think this door would look very nice painted red.'

'I think you could be right, Mrs G.'

When I was done, I went back inside and surveyed the flat. I had a clean slate, all ready for me to start again, but this time completely on my terms.

I picked up the bottle of tequila I'd purchased and left to try to talk some sense into Tiff.

I buzzed her apartment and held the bottle up to the screen.

'Tequila?' she said as she let me in. 'This can't be good.'

Inside, I busied myself chopping up limes and pouring some salt into a saucer while Tiff found two shot glasses.

'Aren't you supposed to be in Phuket?' she said.

'I didn't go.'

'I can see that.'

'I changed my mind.'

She raised her eyebrows and poured the tequila. We clinked glasses and downed the shots in one go, grimacing as the raw alcohol hit the back of our throats.

'Just like that?' she said.

I nodded. 'Yep, just like that.'

I knew she was looking for signs of tears, but there weren't any. It was safe to say I'd never cry another tear over Jamie Aldridge.

'It's okay,' I assured her. 'I'm okay. The tequila isn't to drown my sorrows – it's to toast my decision.' I poured us another shot each, then looked hard at her.

'But you look like you need to drown some sorrows. Why the face? It's five degrees outside and you're off to Fiji tomorrow – you should be happy.'

'This isn't going to end well,' Tiff said, downing her shot and avoiding my question.

'Tequila rarely does. But it certainly helps with the telling of long stories – which is what you owe me.'

'Do you remember the three of us doing this when you broke up with Jamie the first time?' she said. 'We started with champagne and ended up on tequila.'

'I sure do. Alice talked me into doing that banishing ritual – where I wrote his name over and over on a piece of paper then cut it up into tiny little pieces.' I popped my finger into the salt and sucked on it reflectively. 'I should have left him in the freezer. Alice warned me I had to be careful.'

'You took him out again? You should have just burned the bastard. That's what I would have done.'

We looked at each other and giggled.

'That calls for another shot,' Tiff said, and did the honours.

'I wish Alice was here.'

'Yeah, me too.' Tiff took a photo of the shot glasses and the bottle and texted it to Alice.

'We did this when Alice first arrived in Melbourne too,' I said. 'Remember that? We smuggled Stella into the apartment and sat around on the floor and did shots.'

'And Alice made the declaration that from then on she was going to follow the rules and be responsible.'

'That's right – no more shagging other people's almost husbands, no more speaking and acting without thinking.'

'I miss that Alice,' Tiff said.

'You can blame Luke for that.'

'I'll drink to that.'

Her phone pinged with a new message: *Tequila? Without me? That isn't going to end well. These days I'm the responsible one, so who's going to tell you when to stop? What's the occasion?*

Tiff looked at me. 'You didn't tell her?'

'I didn't want to, not before she went to the conference. You know she was looking for an excuse not to go.'

Tiff typed: *Callie didn't go to Phuket.*

Wow, that's big. I'm on free wifi so let's Zoom?

'Why didn't I think of that?' Tiff said, and then Alice was there.

'Sorry, girls, there was no tequila in the minibar, but Tommy found me some Bintang. I'll do beer shots instead.'

'Isn't that against the rules?' I said.

'We'll make an exception.'

In the background we could hear Tommy moving about the room.

'Hi, Tommy,' called Tiff.

'Hi, girls.' He leaned in and kissed Alice on the forehead. 'You could be a while, so I'll go do some work in the bar.'

After we'd heard the door shut, I said, 'He's such a good man, Ally.'

'Yeah, I know. He's lovely. So, Cal, what happened? Why aren't you in Phuket with Jamie? Not that I'm sorry you didn't go.'

I shrugged. 'It's a long and boring story. I caught him out in a few lies, but essentially it's because I don't think he's changed, and because I don't want him any more.'

'Of course he hasn't changed – he was never going to,' said Tiff.

'And that's why he should never have come out of the freezer,' said Alice. 'I warned you about what happens when you stick the pieces together again.'

'We should drink to that,' said Tiff.

So we did.

'What did he say when you told him?' Alice asked.

'He tried to turn it back on me like he did last time, saying I was just being paranoid. Of course, he then assumed there was someone else. According to him, that would be the only reason any woman would dump him.' I sucked thoughtfully on a wedge of lime. 'I told him there was, but the truth was that I didn't love him any more. He got really mean, so I know I made the right decision, but part of me feels a little bit sorry for him. Perhaps he really did love me and now I've broken his heart.'

'You're hopeless,' laughed Tiff.

'On the upside, now I'm completely over him, there's room for someone great in my life,' I added. 'You girls were right – you never end up with Mr Big. That's not how it works.'

'Oh, I'm not so sure any more,' said Alice. 'I'm beginning to think that sometimes it can work – that Mr Big can also be Aiden. The wrong man can also be the right one. It would be an exception to the rule, but I'm thinking that rule possibly needs re-thinking. Like Matt – he was your Mr Big, but he could also be your Aiden.'

'Why is it that all your rules suddenly become flexible when alcohol makes an appearance?' I asked.

'I know, right? That's what got me into trouble in the first place!'

'Let's drink to that!' Tiff said.

So we did.

'How's Bali?' I asked. 'Are you and Tommy having a lovely time together?'

'Yeah, it's great. Tommy's very considerate. It's like he's read the handbook on How To Be A Perfect Boyfriend. He follows all the rules, so in two days we haven't got on each other's nerves once. We have another week here, and then I'm heading to the conference and he's going diving over in Java somewhere. Anyway, enough about me. Are you really okay, Cal?'

'I'm fine. Better than fine. I've still got the time off work, so I'll go to the interview at Helium and spend some time looking for my own apartment. I think it's time I took responsibility for my own life. That's the other thing I've forgotten to tell you – I told Hen to find somewhere else to live.'

'Oh, sweetie,' said Tiff, 'you're making me go all misty. I need another shot to deal with that. Cheers.'

'Now, on to more important matters,' began Alice. 'Why are you looking so glum, Tiff? What gives? You're off to Fiji tomorrow – five degrees versus twenty-five. Need I say more?'

'Yes, Tiff, time for that long story of yours,' I said.

She poured another shot and downed it, then took a deep breath. 'I've been seeing Jake. Past tense – we're not any more – it's over. It all got a little too serious for me.'

'What happened?' I asked softly.

'You're not going to ask why I didn't tell you more about him?'

I shook my head. 'I'm sure you have your reasons, and I suspect the main one is that he knocked you off your feet and you didn't know how to handle it.'

There was a pause as Tiff made a production of pouring more tequila. Every shot was requiring more concentration.

'Something like that,' she said. 'He asked me to go to Taiwan with him. He reckons we can make a go of travelling the world – him writing the words and me responsible for the images. He already has the contacts and the reputation, and says he can help me sell my photos.'

'What do you think of that idea?' Alice asked.

'Well, it's ridiculous of course.'

'Is it?' I said. 'You haven't been happy at work since Ainsley took over – and you used to want to be a photographer.'

'Of course it's ridiculous. As if I'm going to throw my job in to take up freelance photography and follow Jake Stewart around the globe just because I don't like my boss. Besides, Jake's not my type. You know that . . . right?'

'I haven't met him, but from the little you've told us and the fact that he ticks none of your boxes, I think he's exactly your type,' ventured Alice. 'You're in love with him – we know that, he knows that. The only person who hasn't seemed to work it out is you.'

'I can't be in love with him.'

'Next you'll be saying that it's just some silly phase – like in the song.' I sang a few lines from 10cc's 'I'm Not In Love'.

'Oh, ha ha. He's a freelance writer, for god's sake, no different to an artist – and I always said there was no way I'd end up with an artist. Look at what happened to my parents.'

'Are you trying to persuade us or yourself?' I asked.

'I can't be in love with him.' This time she didn't sound quite as convinced.

'If you say so,' Alice said.

'Do you think I'm in love with him?' she asked me. I'd never seen Tiff so unsure of herself.

'Ummmm, yeah. As Alice said – he's exactly your type. You've always wanted to be in charge of your own destiny. And deny it as much as you want, but we knew you when your dream was to do something creative. This is your opportunity to give that a go. What have you got to lose?'

'Only my future!'

Neither of us agreed, but it was Alice who voiced it.

'You're the one who said we shouldn't be holding out for a hero to provide for us, Tiff. Take the bull by the horns, you said. Look after yourself. Surely that means being responsible for your own income? Besides, do you really need all the brand names if you don't have anyone in the office to impress? Maybe the only person you should be impressing is yourself.'

'Maybe Jake will save you from yourself,' I offered. 'Maybe he really is your hero.'

Tiff drained her glass again. This wasn't going to end well.

'I don't need a hero,' she said. 'And the only saving I'm interested in is the sort that can buy me a new bag and shoes.' She shook her head. 'How can we even joke that I'd be happy to pass over Prada for a Nikon, a broad smile and regular multiple orgasms? The idea is ridiculous and I'm not going to think about it any more.' She shook her head. 'No, I like Jake, but he's not from my world and I'm not going to think about his offer ever again.' She reached for my glass and drained that too, as if to punctuate her words.

'Okay, but say you did think about it, and you did decide to go with him,' Alice asked. 'When would you have to make your mind up?'

'In a few days. Jake's back in Hong Kong on Monday, and he'll be flying out to Taiwan on Wednesday.' She plastered a stern look on her face. 'Not that it matters – I told him there's no way I can go with him. I said it wasn't happening, and that we couldn't work together – that it had always just been sex and I didn't love him. Besides, I have to be in Fiji for Masters on Monday.'

'Oh, Tiff.'

'What about Project Yes?' asked Alice, trying to inject some humour into the situation. 'Doesn't that mean you have to say yes?'

'Not for something as big as this,' Tiff argued. 'You don't have to say yes to stupid decisions. The whole point of yes month was to force us into situations we're not normally comfortable with, like me with that bus tour that gave me the idea in the first place, and you with conferences, dating and bikini waxes, Alice. And Callie with . . . well, pretty much anything.' She smiled weakly at me. 'It wasn't meant to cause this much upheaval – not in my life anyway.'

'You know,' said Alice, 'it's okay to change your mind about the things you want. Maybe we shouldn't be trying to control the outcomes. Maybe we're not the best judge of what it is we really need.'

'Now you're talking like an astrologer,' muttered Tiff. 'Next you'll be prattling on about journeys.'

'Perhaps. But maybe it's okay to let go of what we think we want and follow our heart instead, and just see what happens?'

'Why did he have to ruin everything?' Tiff wailed. 'Our deal in the beginning was sex. Great sex. Then he had to go and make it all complicated and turn it into something more than that. I told him he didn't need to ask me to go with him – things could continue as they were – but he says that's not enough for him. He wants the whole forever thing. God, I don't even know if he's got adequate superannuation.'

Alice sprayed beer out of her nose onto the screen. 'Really? That's the story you're telling yourself? For fuck's sake, Tiffany, forget your ridiculous checklist for once. You love him, he loves you. He's even taken all the guesswork out of it by telling you how he feels. Just fucking do it.'

We could tell Alice was serious – she'd broken her no swearing rule again.

'It's easy for you to say – you got a redundancy to fall back on when you left the corporate world,' Tiff said. 'I don't have that luxury.'

'Yes, but I've also had to work to build the structures I've got now. You can do the same. Throw the rule book away.'

'Really? Is that the old Alice speaking?' Tiff said.

'Maybe. I still need the rules, but you, my dear, do not.'

'What if none of it works? What if we don't get on? What if his editors hate my photos? What if it is just sex after all and when it finally does burn out I'm left without a job?'

'You can keep asking the what-if questions for ever and a day – can't you, Cal?'

I nodded. 'I've spent the last two weeks asking myself why I wanted to walk away from someone I'd spent so many tears getting back. Then I wondered whether I'd always be alone. Then I realised that the answer to my "what ifs" was "so what".' I put my arm around Tiff. 'Maybe that's the answer you need to give yourself.'

'I can't. It's all too late. I have the Masters conference – and I've worked too hard to get there to miss that. It's too late.'

'It's never too late,' argued Alice.

'It is this time.'

I topped our glasses up again – this really was not going to end well. Miles away, in a resort by the beach, Alice ripped the top off another beer.

'What about you, Cal?' she said. 'Where does my brother fit into your plans?'

'I'm not sure.' I frowned as the acidity of the lime hit the roof of my mouth. 'He rang me this morning and asked me not to go with Jamie. He also said he understands that I need to be alone for a little while before I start something new. I've always rushed into new relationships because I haven't wanted to be alone. And Matt . . .' I took a deep breath, 'he's the real thing and worth taking my time to be with. We were too young before, but we're not now.'

'So what's the problem then?' Tiff asked. She'd slid off the lounge and onto the floor.

'He's in Hong Kong. I don't think I can do the long distance thing – even though when I'm with him everything else makes sense.'

'Well, at least we've moved on from the other excuses.' Tiff counted them off on her fingers. 'You thought he was my perfect man and were worried I'd decide I wanted him; I'd slept with him so you were worried I'd have ownership issues; you were worried he'd shag around on you; he's not the committing kind –'

'He doesn't want children,' Alice added. 'As Tiff said, at least you've moved on from the bullshit worry excuses. Besides, he's my brother and no one's asked me what I think about the idea of him and you hooking up forever.'

I looked up from the images that had begun to

appear in my tequila. Images of Matt and me doing the together-forever, happily-ever-after thing. 'What do you think of it?'

'I think you two are perfect for each other.'

'So do I,' added Tiff. 'In fact, I don't think I could think of anyone more perfect for you.'

'Do you love him?' Alice asked.

I didn't hesitate. 'Yes. Madly, deeply, completely. I think I've always loved him.'

'He loves you too,' said Tiff. 'He told me so last week. He said he knew it as soon as he saw you. He could even describe your dress. He also said some rubbish about how it was like you were standing in the middle of a million dancing lights and jumped out of a mural to make him fall in love with you.' When Alice giggled, Tiff added, 'We might have had a few too many by that stage and I could have got that wrong.'

Alice laughed even harder. 'No, you heard it right – it's from *Xanadu*. We were talking about it that night at the surf club. My brother must have it bad if he's quoting Olivia Newton-John.'

I reached for the tequila to hide the emotion that had hit the back of my throat and the mist that was clouding my vision.

'He lives in Hong Kong,' I said stubbornly. 'Anyway, Tiff, I think you were right when you said that no man should come before my career. I'm going to that interview at Helium, and if I get the job, I'm going to throw myself into it. Then I'll allow myself to think about Matt.'

'That's the problem though, Callie, I'm not sure I was right about that.' Tiff again looked more miserable than a woman who was heading to Fiji in triumph should look.

Alice opened another beer. 'Perhaps none of us were right. I'm beginning to think that we have no idea what we really need until we get what we think we want and realise it's not what we thought it would be.'

'Be careful what you wish for,' I said.

'Because you might just get it,' added Tiff.

CHAPTER TWENTY-SIX

Jane's sixtieth birthday invitation was brief but explicit: *Wear denim – double if you like, triple if you dare.*

As I dressed for the party, I had Matt in mind. It was all for him. My hand shook as I attempted to draw a line across my eyelid. It smudged and I rubbed at it in exasperation.

Alice laughed, poured me another glass of wine and picked up the eyeliner to do it for me. 'Doesn't this take you back? Getting ready to go out for the night and doing our make-up together? Me having to do your eyeliner because you're so nervous about meeting a boy you can't draw a straight line.'

'I so am not nervous about meeting a boy.'

'You so are. What's really awkward is that you're thinking about sex with my brother.'

'I so am not.'

'You so are.'

She finished my eyeliner and stood back to admire her handiwork.

'You're right – I so am.' I took a sip of my wine to

hide the grin that thinking about sex with Matt brought to my face.

'Eeeew, enough with the dirty smiles. That's my brother you're thinking those thoughts about!'

I rummaged in my make-up bag for mascara and bronzer. I'd fluffed my hair into an approximation of a wind-machined Farrah, so was keeping the rest of my face simple, except for shiny lipgloss I was hoping Matt would kiss off.

'What if it's different?' I said. 'What if he's changed his mind? You said it yourself – Matt's quick to decide what he wants. Doesn't that mean he's also quick to decide what he doesn't want?'

Alice pressed her face closer to the mirror as she drew a heart on her cheek and coloured it in with lipliner. 'Usually his boredom threshold is quite low, but he's decided you're the one that he wants. I don't think you have anything to worry about. What do you think – one heart, or maybe a few little ones as well?'

'We haven't spoken in ages though. What if I've changed my mind? What if I see him and feel nothing?'

She raised her eyebrows at the suggestion.

'Yeah, I know,' I said. 'Unlikely. As for the hearts, with everything else you've got going on there, maybe just stick to one.'

She was wearing loose denim overalls, with the bottoms rolled up to her ankles, over a tight white T-shirt. Her red mane had been teased to stick up wildly all around her face and she was now picking up a black bowler hat to stick on top of it all.

'The only reason you haven't spoken is because you enforced that ridiculous give-me-space thing,' she said.

'You know why I did that. I didn't want Matt to think I was rebounding to him. Also, I had other things I needed to sort out – the job, my apartment. I didn't want to rush into any decisions – it all felt too important.'

'And not even a tiny part of you was testing him, or at least giving him the opportunity to change his mind before anyone got hurt?' She fiddled around with the hat, making various strange poses in front of the mirror.

'Maybe,' I conceded. 'Although maybe I was giving myself the same opportunity.'

'Nah, you didn't need it. You've been in love with him since you were eighteen – probably even before that.'

I laughed ruefully. She was right.

'How on earth did they keep these on their heads?' she complained as the hat fell off for the third time. 'There's way too much hair.'

I giggled. 'What look did you say you were going for?'

'Kiki Dee, of course.' It was my turn to look sceptical. She was definitely channelling more Bananarama than seventies' girl next door. 'Tommy's going to be Elton. Did I tell you Mum and Dad have ordered a karaoke machine? We're going to do a double act. I bet you can't guess what we're going to sing?'

' "You're The One That I Want?" '

'Oh, ha ha. That can be you and Matt much later in the night, leading us all on a conga dance around the club.'

'Too funny, but there's no way you're getting me near a microphone – you've heard my singing!'

'Not even to serenade Matt?'

'Especially not to serenade Matt. I don't want to turn him off me just yet.'

She stood back from the mirror and looked me up and down. 'Trust me, sweetie, you won't be turning him off you in that outfit. You look amazing – just like a Charlie's Angel. All you need is a skateboard. Can you even move in those jeans?'

I'd chosen seventies-style tight bell-bottomed denim jeans and a midriff-baring boob-hugging T-shirt. The break-up diet had been working beautifully – except this time I was pining for Matt rather than Jamie.

I squatted to demonstrate the range of movement I had in the jeans. 'Thankfully they're stretch denim. I probably could ride a skateboard in these babies – if I knew how to ride a skateboard.'

'Let's drink to that!'

There was a loud knock on the door and Jane yelled through it, 'If you girls want a lift to the club with us, this is your five-minute warning!'

As it had been when we were much younger, that was our cue to fall back on the bed with squeals and giggles.

When we finally made it out of Alice's old bedroom, Tommy, in an outfit that matched Alice's but without the teased hair and floating bowler hat, whistled and looked me up and down in appreciation. 'Look. At. You.'

Alice thumped his arm. 'What about me?'

'You're my Kiki – of course you look cute.'

She raised her eyes to the ceiling and dramatically clutched at her heart. 'Cute? You're breaking my heart.'

'I couldn't if I tried,' he sang back to her.

We all laughed, but I couldn't help feeling that if anyone's heart was likely to be broken in this relationship, it would be Tommy's.

The surf club was heaving with people when I walked in with Alice and Tommy.

'Wow, your mother sure knows a lot of people,' I shouted over the music.

'I know – and how fabulous is it they all came dressed to theme.'

Virtually everyone had made an effort, with outfits ranging from sixties' hippy style, to tiny denim festival shorts and floating kimono tops, to rugged straight-off-the-farm jeans with riding boots and flannelette checked shirts. The balloons and streamers we'd hung in full daylight this afternoon had seemed overdone, but now looked perfect. The DJ was blasting dance music – mostly from the seventies and eighties – and everyone seemed to be having a fabulous time.

'Is Matt here yet?' I asked Alice, trying to insert a don't-really-care attitude into my voice.

'No, not yet. Mum said she heard his flight was delayed – and don't forget, he'll still have to drive up from Brisbane. I hope for his sake he makes it – Mum will be so upset if he doesn't.' I swallowed my disappointment and she looked at me with concern. 'He'll get here, Cal.'

Get a grip, I told myself and plastered a wide smile on my face. 'What does a girl need to do to get a drink and a dance around here?'

Sometime much later, I dragged myself off the dance floor and gulped at a glass of water. My voice was hoarse from singing along to the retro pop music and my platform shoes had long ago been tossed into a corner. I eyed Alice's white trainers with envy.

'I can't remember when I last danced so much,' she panted, linking her arm through mine.

'Me neither. Your parents sure know how to throw a great party. Where's Tommy?'

'Over in that corner, talking tech with some of my cousins.'

'And now we have a very special request,' announced the DJ.

Alice looked at me and smiled. 'This'll be something from Dad to Mum.'

We heard the opening chords to 'Xanadu' and Alice's grin grew wider. 'Somehow, I think this one is for you.'

The tingle started in my belly and rose up to my breasts and to the lump in my throat. It cleared that in a single bound and settled at the back of my eyes. I blinked a couple of times to clear the moisture. Happy tears.

I looked around and there he was, striding through the crowd like a dream come true. It was as if everyone else faded into the background like an old photograph, and he was blinding colour. He was dressed in tight denim jeans, a white T-shirt with a peace logo on it, a denim jacket tossed over his shoulder and thongs on his feet. If I'd feared my attraction to him had faded over the last few weeks, the chaos of butterflies that went flying through my body told me otherwise. I couldn't look away from him. My eyes didn't leave his, and his didn't leave me, as he approached.

'I think this is my dance,' he said when he finally reached me. It seemed to have taken an age even though the first verse of the song had only just started.

'I think it could be.'

We stared at each other, the butterflies within me fluttering madly, my heart banging so hard against the wall of my chest I was absolutely sure he'd be able to see it through the thin fabric of my top.

'It's good to see you, Calliope.'

'Yeah, you too. I was beginning to think you weren't going to make it.' I felt the colour flooding my cheeks.

'Can you imagine Mum if I didn't?'

'She would have been disappointed, but she'd have forgiven you – you've always been the golden child.'

He shrugged. 'True. But what about you? Would you have been disappointed?' I felt his eyes burning into mine.

'Yes,' I said quietly. 'I would have been disappointed.'

He exhaled then, as if he'd been holding his breath waiting for my answer. 'I'm glad – because I haven't thought about anything but this night since we said goodbye.'

'Me neither.'

We stood there with the music and guests swirling around us, unable to look away from each other in case one of us disappeared. He smiled, his grin wrapping around me and drawing me towards him. He tossed his denim jacket to Alice, and finally I was in his arms and he was kissing me. I clung onto his shoulders to stop myself from falling.

His head lifted, and he rested his forehead against mine as we swayed to the music. 'I've been thinking about that too.'

'Anything else?' I rested my chest on his chest, his arms still tightly wrapped around me.

'Oh yes, but this isn't that sort of party so it will have to keep until later.'

I pulled back slightly to look up into his eyes and saw them darken as I said, 'I look forward to it. And after an entrance as cheesy as that one, I think the tone is quite low enough for now.'

A grin spread across his face, his eyes twinkling. 'You think that's cheesy? I thought it was the least I could do for a muse who's been sent on a shooting star to Earth to inspire mortal men like me to fall in love with her.'

The butterflies all banded together to cushion my heart. 'And the cheese-o-meter just bounced into dangerous territory.' I tried to lighten my tone, even though there suddenly wasn't any air in the room.

'Too much?' he asked.

I shook my head. 'No. Not nearly enough.'

'Good, because there's plenty more where that came from.'

As he lowered his head to kiss me again, we were interrupted by Alice. 'Okay, I let you have your grand hero entrance, Matt, but this is Mum's party and she's going to start to wonder why you haven't said hello to her yet.'

'Fair call,' I said and pulled away, but Matt held on to my hand.

'No, you're not getting away from me that easily.' He took a closer look at Alice's outfit. 'Who are you supposed to be?'

'Kiki Dee, of course.'

'Right you are. I don't recall Kiki Dee having teased hair – or a bowler.' He took the hat off her head and spun it around on a finger out of her reach. 'And Tommy – is he a Dexys Midnight Runner?'

'Really? You don't recognise Elton John when you see him?'

'Of course.'

She gave up trying to reach for the hat. 'Actually, you can keep it. It keeps falling off my hair anyway.'

He placed the hat on my head and tilted the front up so he could kiss me. When he drew back he handed the hat back to Alice. 'On second thoughts you can it back. I don't want to have to deal with it every time I need to kiss Cal.'

Close to midnight, the karaoke machine was blessedly switched off and people began to drift away. The music was turned down and changed to something a lot mellower. I'd found a seat and was watching the goodbyes. Alice and Tommy were still swaying to the music.

Matt came and sat beside me and handed me a wine glass. Although he'd stayed close to my side all night, we hadn't had even half a second to ourselves.

'Is it completely over?' he asked. 'You and Jamie?'

'Yes. Finally.' I hadn't heard anything from Jamie

since that Saturday four weeks ago.

'And the flatmate from hell?'

'Gone. Thankfully.'

After asking me for an extension of the deadline I'd issued, Hen had reluctantly packed her things and left the weekend after Jamie and I split for the last time. It took me several attempts to vacuum up all the dust and fluff from where her bed used to be. I didn't think she'd done any cleaning at all since moving in.

He nodded. 'That's good. And Alice said you got the job at Helium?'

'I did. I start Monday next week. The process took longer than it should have because Alex McInnes, the founder of the project, wanted to interview me too and it took a couple of weeks to set that up. But the offer came through immediately afterwards. My old boss, Roger, tried to make me work the maximum notice period, but I had so much leave accrued that the CEO insisted he release me. I finished there yesterday, and Pip, my new boss, said she'd like me to take a week in-between jobs, so I'm fresh to start with them.'

Matt covered my hand with his. 'I'm glad. This job sounds exactly like you.' He idly traced circles on the back of my hand with one finger, sending ripples of sensation hurtling along my veins.

'How long are you here for?' I tried to make the words sound casual.

'I have the next two weeks off work.'

The finger that had been making circles on my hand began stroking along my arm. Back and forth. Back and forth. I swallowed hard as the warmth within me spiralled lower.

'Do you have plans?'

He smiled slowly. 'I do.'

'And they are?' I held my breath as I waited for his answer.

'I thought I might spend a week visiting my family here, and then a week visiting Alice in Melbourne.' The twinkle was back in his eye. 'Or you and I could spend a few days together somewhere, and then I could visit you in Melbourne. What do you say?'

He ran his finger lightly down my cheek, across my jaw and along my lower lip until my lips parted. I nodded.

As he leaned in to kiss me, I put a finger to his lips before they could meet mine. 'I have other news too.'

'That sounds momentous.'

He took my hand and kissed my open palm, looking up at me. I let out a breath as the erotic charge sliced through me.

'It is. I nailed the shimmy-walk.'

'And I can't wait to see it. Now shut up and let me kiss you.'

Alice chose that moment to interrupt. 'Come on, you two, I need some help cleaning this place up. Mick and Laura have gone home to rescue the babysitter, and I think Mum and Dad have just about had it, so I'm relying on you.'

'Oh man, what is it with you and the interruptions?' Matt said. 'You really know how to pick your time, don't you, little sister?'

'What can I say?' She shrugged and one of the braces on her overalls slipped off her shoulder. 'It's a talent. You've got plenty of time to make eyes at each other when we're finished. I've snaffled another couple of bottles and some more snacks, so I reckon when we're done we head to the beach. What do you say?'

'At this time?' I looked out the window to where the white caps of the waves were visible as they rolled into shore.

'Why not? It's a lovely night. Hey, I know, let's stay out and watch the sun rise.'

'The day might have been warm, but the nights are still cool. It's only September still,' I reminded her.

'Good point. I'll bring blankets.' As always, she had an answer for anything.

'How about we just get this place cleaned up first and then see what happens,' Matt said. He put his arm around me and pulled me closer. 'Besides, I could have other plans.'

Alice rolled her eyes. 'You've waited six weeks, you can wait another couple of hours.'

'But can I really?' he murmured in my ear.

'I don't think I can,' I whispered back.

Sometime later, the four of us walked onto the beach with bottles, blankets and shoes in hand. Alice was in charge of the snacks. She handed me a blanket. 'Go make eyes at each other – or whatever it is you intend to do,' she said, and grabbed Tommy's hand to drag him further along the sand.

'It's just like old times,' I joked to Matt, holding the bottle out so he could drink from it. 'You and me and stolen wine.'

'It sure is, but we're all grown up now and I won't be stopping at kisses tonight – as delightful as yours are.'

He pushed me back onto the blanket and kissed me, the hardness of his body pressing mine into the sand. His lips strayed down my neck, my head tilting to give him better access, my soft moans urging him lower.

'This tight little T-shirt has been torturing me all night,' he said, pushing it up and reaching behind me to unclip my bra. 'Oh yes,' he murmured as my breasts were released. 'The memory of these has been torturing me for weeks.'

His tongue circled one nipple, then took it into his mouth to nip and suck, before repeating the process.

'Oh, Matt,' I breathed.

I reached between us to undo the button and zip on my jeans before doing the same to his, my hand sneaking inside to hold his hardness. He groaned into my breast and lifted his head briefly, his eyes half-closed, as I squeezed and released.

'Christ, Callie. That feels so good.' He took a deep breath. 'It feels too good.' He kissed me again, then rolled onto his side next to me, breathing hard. 'But I don't intend making love to you out here – and certainly not before we've talked.' He gazed at my breasts and reluctantly pulled my top down to cover them, tracing a long delicious line along my bare midriff. 'No matter how much I'm tempted.'

I screwed my face up in disappointment.

'I know, I'm mad for you too, but we have too much to talk about,' he said.

'We do.' I looked longingly at his lips. 'But do we need to do it now?'

I reached out to run my finger along his length, feeling him harden even more under my touch. He groaned and took hold of both my hands and held them above my head on the sand. My back arched under his gaze, pushing my breasts up towards him. He squeezed his eyes shut, as if searching for the strength to resist me.

'Matt?' I murmured.

He opened his eyes and looked down at me, my arms restrained above my head, my hair wild around my face, my lips parted, my breasts half out of the skimpy T-shirt, my jeans wide open.

'Oh fuck it,' he said. 'You're right, we can talk later.'

We made love as if we were starving for each other – perhaps we were. My cries as we came together were muffled by his kiss. Afterwards, he snuggled me into his chest.

'Cal,' he said, 'I love you. I know it's been quick, but I really do love you. I loved you back then too, but we were so young, and I was going away – as were you – and you were my sister's best friend. That night we had was perfect, but it could never be more than that. But then at Mick's party, when I saw you twirling around in that dress under the lights, you took my breath away. I knew immediately that the love hadn't gone away, and this time it was never going to go away.'

I reached up to stroke his cheek. 'I love you too. I don't think I ever stopped. When I'm with you everything makes sense.'

'It does, doesn't it?'

'Matt, how are we going to do the distance thing?'

'We won't have to for too long – this past six weeks has been unbearable. I've already applied for a transfer back to Australia. There are plenty of people younger and hungrier than me who want an expat gig, so I'm hopeful of getting a transfer. If not, I'll resign and look for a job in Melbourne. Now that I've found you, I'm not losing sight of you.'

We drank some more, kissed some more, and talked a lot more, making plans for the future together that we both believed in. At some point we must have slept, wrapped in the blanket and in each other's arms.

When I woke, Matt was sitting up and watching

the sky change colour in the east – just the palest light. He turned to face me and I could see the same light in his eyes – the light of a new day dawning just for us.

'Where's Alice?' I asked.

'I don't know. I think they must have gone home sometime during the night.'

'Maybe we should go back too.' I indicated the early morning walkers who were already making their way along the beach. 'We can sneak in like last time.'

He smiled at me, and bent to kiss me lightly. 'Except this time you won't be sneaking back into my sister's room. And this time, we've got all the time in the world.'

BEFORE YOU GO

If you enjoyed *I Want You Back* I'd love it if you left a review in the usual places. If you'd like to stay up to date with my next happy ending, you can sign up for my newsletter at my website: https://joannetracey.com

You can also drop by and see me – virtually speaking, of course – at any of these places:

Facebook: https://facebook.com/joannetraceywriter
Instagram: https://instagram.com/jotracey

ACKNOWLEDGEMENTS

When I first began writing this novel back at the end of 2016 I was living in Sydney. It had been, not to put it lightly, a terrible couple of years and Mooloolaba, where part of this novel is set, was a happy place that we escaped to for our annual holidays. I think that as I wrote I was doing some escaping of my own.

Fast forward a few years and we now live on the Sunshine Coast and walk on Mooloolaba Beach each morning. Art imitating life or life imitating art? Whichever it is, while I hadn't set out to write a love letter to Mooloolaba, in a way that's exactly what I've done. I have, however, taken some artistic licence here and there — for example, there isn't a balcony off the function room in the Surf Club — but maybe one day there might be. I suspect this won't be the last story that I set in this beautiful part of the world. Watch this space.

As always, my thanks and appreciation to my editor, Nicola O'Shea. I am so very grateful for your ideas and suggestions — your instincts are always spot on and you truly inspire me to continue to work on my craft.

My gratitude also to my sister-in-law Pieta for not only putting up with my brother, but more importantly for being my beta reader every single time.

While I've been wanting to write Callie's story ever since I wrote Baby, It's You, it really wasn't until I took some belly dancing classes here on the Sunshine Coast that it all fell into place. Just don't ask me to do a shimmy walk!

As always, though, I couldn't juggle all the moving parts without the love and support of my family – Grant, Sarah and Kali aka Adventure Spaniel.

ABOUT THE AUTHOR

Joanne Tracey lives on the Sunshine Coast in Queensland Australia with her husband, daughter and a cocker spaniel who takes her role as resident flop-dog and guardian of Jo's office very seriously. She has, however, been known to sleep a tad too much on the job – the dog, that is, not Jo.

An unapologetic daydreamer, eternal optimist, and confirmed morning person, Jo writes contemporary romance, romantic comedy, women's fiction and what she likes to call foodie-lit – which is the perfect excuse to indulge her baking habit in the name of research. Her characters cook whatever it is she wants to be cooking – or learning to cook. Then there's their occupations; through her characters Jo can try out occupations she'd never conceivably do or the business ideas that her husband says, "maybe that needs a little more thought darling." It's the daydreaming thing again.

Even though she lives in paradise, it's Jo's travels that inspire her stories. From Melbourne to Queenstown, Bali, Hong Kong and The Cotswolds, you never quite know where you'll end up, but it will be somewhere that takes you away from your every day.

When she isn't writing or day jobbing, Jo loves baking, reading, long walks along the beach, posting way too many photos of sunrises on Instagram and dreaming of the next destination and the next story.

Jo's life goals (apart from being a world-famous author) are to be an extra on *Midsomer Murders* (perhaps a dog walker in Badger's Drift), to appear on *Desert Island Discs*, and to cook her way through Nigella's books – yes, all of them.